OMNIVM LVX CIVIVM

BOSTON
PUBLIC
LIBRARY

THE MEN THAT GOD FORGOT

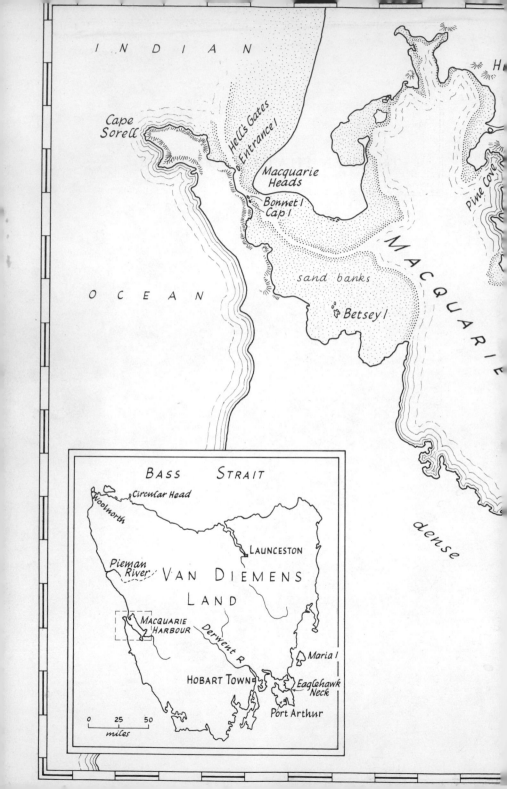

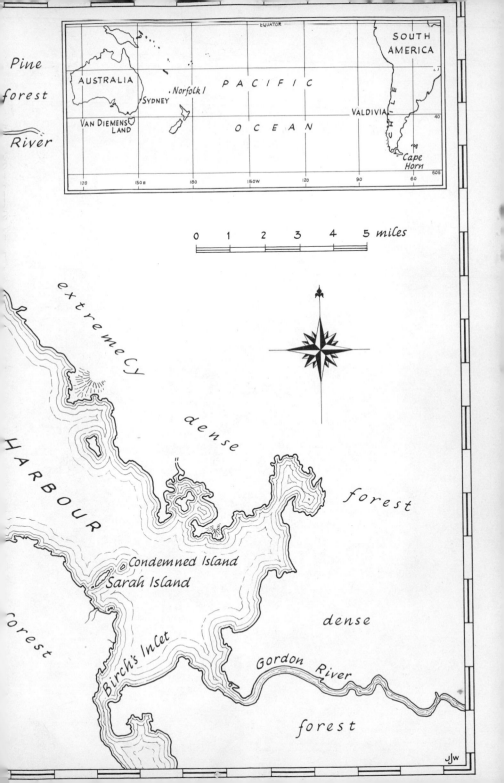

Richard Butler

THE
MEN THAT
GOD
FORGOT

ST. MARTIN'S PRESS   NEW YORK

Copyright © 1976 by Richard Butler
All rights reserved. For information, write:
St. Martin's Press, Inc., 175 Fifth Ave., New York, N.Y. 10010.
Manufactured in the United States of America
Library of Congress Catalog Card Number: 76-29857

Library of Congress Cataloging in Publication Data

Butler, Richard, 1925—
    The men that God forgot.

    I. Title.
PZ4.B9868Me3   [PR6052.U85]   823'.9'14   76-29857
ISBN 0-312-52955-4

To the one who was with me on Settlement Island

Author's Note

On the eighteenth of January 1973 — one hundred and thirty-nine years, almost to the day, after the chief incident upon which this book is based — I spent a day on what used to be called Sarah Island, the site of the infamous penal settlement in Macquarie Harbour on the south-west coast of Tasmania. It had not been easy to reach that lonely little island. A helicopter cannot land there and no vessel of any size can approach it because of its surrounding reefs. In the town of Strahan at the head of the Harbour, a fisherman had told me frankly that the island 'had a bad name' and he didn't care to go near it. Finally, I met the skipper of the *Denison Star,* the 107-foot twin-diesel vessel that takes tourists down the Harbour, and to him I express my gratitude for the loan of the ship's boat in which he dropped me to row ashore to the island and be picked up on the *Star*'s return run.

Even on that sunlit midsummer day it was an eerie, desolate place. Tree-ferns, rustling with snakes, spread their fronds over the brick ruins of what had once been a gaol; trees grew thickly in all that remained of a shipyard; the roofless stone shell of a hospital loomed like a medieval fortress over the water. There was a brooding silence, a sense of profound sadness, a feeling that the human misery that had been endured here had been absorbed in sweat and blood into the very soil. For this was the place of which John West, in his *History of Tasmania,* wrote: 'The name of Macquarie Harbour is associated exclusively with remembrance of inexpressible depravity, degradation and woe. Sacred to the genius of torture, Nature concurred with the objects of its separation from the rest of the world to exhibit some notion of a perfect misery. There, man lost the aspect and the heart of man . . .'

This book is a reconstruction of the events that took place on and near that island when, after the closing down of the settlement in 1833, ten convicts who had been left behind to complete the building of a brig overpowered their guards, seized the vessel and escaped in her. It is the story of ten men's search for freedom, of mankind's endless rejection of the cage and the chain. It is the story of the Liberty Men.

It is, in fact, a story that has been touched on before by such eminent writers as Marcus Clarke and John West. But they, working on a broad canvas, could not be expected to provide the minute brushwork involved in the portrayal of a single incident in the brawling, boisterous history of Van Diemen's Land. In consequence, my version differs in many respects from theirs — and, indeed, from many other accounts of the seizure of the *Frederick.*

The facts are history, and can be verified. The documents quoted — apart from the log of the brig — actually exist. I have drawn extensively on the narrative of James Porter, convict; on the sworn testimony of Captain Charles Taw, David Hoy and others concerned in the affair; on the newspaper reports of the period; on the Dispatches of Lieutenant-Governors Arthur and Franklin, and on the correspondence files of the Colonial Secretary. The characters, emotions and inter-relationships of the men themselves, however, are the product of my imagination — but even here I have, in the case of the Liberty Men, been able to use their convict records, which are meticulous down to the smallest physical detail and from which it has been possible to form my own impression of these ten men as they were in life.

For all this wealth of material I am indebted to Mrs Mary McRae, Principal Archivist of the Archives Department of the State of Tasmania, without whose enthusiastic assistance this book would not have been possible. I wish to thank also Captain Ian MacRobert; Mr and Mrs Willing, of Monash University, Melbourne; the National Army Museum, London; the National Maritime Museum, Greenwich; the Marine Board of Hobart; the State Library of Tasmania; the State Library of Victoria; the Tasmanian Library Board; the Tasmanian Government Tourist and Immigration Department; the Tasmanian Museum and Art Gallery; and countless other people, in Tasmania and elsewhere, who have given me assistance and encouragement with this project.

In conclusion, I would add that Sarah Island is now called Settlement Island; the name of Hobart Town was officially shortened to Hobart in 1881; and, following the cessation of the transportation of convicts to Van Diemen's Land in 1853, the name of that colony was, on 26 November 1855, changed to Tasmania.

Melbourne
January 1975

9

Extracts from the convict records

JOHN BARKER . . . born 1797 at Warrington, Cheshire. A former gunsmith and watchmaker. Tried at Lancaster on 18 May 1829 for felony (stealing silver plates) and sentenced to transportation for life. Arrived Van Diemen's Land December 1829 on the transport *Surrey*. Had been previously transported to Bermuda for seven years, of which he served four. Married with two children — wife at Stokeneath, Cheshire.

WILLIAM CHESHIRE . . . born 1810 in Birmingham. Formerly a butcher. Tried at Warwick on 20 March 1827 for house-breaking (robbing a cottage) and sentenced to be transported for life. Arrived Van Diemen's Land November 1827 on transport *Asia*.

JOHN DADY . . . born at Cowcross in 1801. Formerly a brick-layer. Tried in London on 27 October 1825 and sentenced to life transportation for felony (stealing a handkerchief). Arrived Van Diemen's Land August 1826 on the transport *Earl St Vincent*.

JOHN FARE . . . born 1807 at Leith, Scotland. A seaman by trade. Tried at Southampton on 25 February 1833 for house-breaking and sentenced to be transported for life. Arrived Van Diemen's Land July 1833 on the transport *Enchantress*.

JOHN JONES . . . born 1792 at Liverpool. A seaman. Tried at Middlesex on 6 September 1832 for larceny (street robbery) and sentenced to be transported for fourteen years. Had previously been transported to Bermuda for seven years, of which he served five years and three months. Arrived Van Diemen's Land July 1833 on the transport *Enchantress*.

JAMES LESLEY . . . born 1805 at Bristol. A shipwright by trade. Tried at Bristol on 18 October 1824 and sentenced to life transportation for stealing a reticule containing a silver scent box and other articles by force from a lady in the park. Had been previously convicted at Monmouth. A bad character. Married with one child — wife Mary at Lawford's Gate. Arrived Van Diemen's Land September 1825 on the transport *Medina*.

CHARLES LYON . . . born in Dundee, Scotland, in 1806. A seaman. Tried at Perth on 4 April 1823 for housebreaking and sentenced to fourteen years' transportation. Arrived Van Diemen's Land January 1824 on the transport *Asia*.

JAMES PORTER . . . born 1805 at Bermondsey, London. A former beer-machine maker. Tried at Kingston on 30 March 1823 and sentenced to life transportation for burglary. Blind in the left eye. Arrived Van Diemen's Land January 1824 on the transport *Asia*.

BENJAMIN RUSSEN . . . born 1804 at Norwich. Formerly a weaver. Tried at Norfolk on 23 March 1822 and sentenced to be transported for life for burglary. Bad character and connexions. Arrived Van Diemen's Land November 1822 on the transport *Arab*.

WILLIAM SHIERS . . . born 1795 at Thornhill, Yorkshire. Tried at York on 4 March 1820 for highway robbery and sentenced to be transported for life. Behaved very badly in gaol. Arrived Van Diemen's Land December 1820 on the transport *Maria*.

1

For the first time in three years, Brevet-Major Percy Baylee stood and admired the view from his office window.

Below him, as he watched, feet correctly spaced apart, hands correctly linked behind his back, a stretch of grass sloped down to his personal wharf on the eastern and sheltered side of the island, where, a cable's length offshore, the two barques *Larkspur* and *Atlas* swung at anchor, their holystoned decks white in the morning sunlight. A flock of Pacific gulls hung screaming and swooping round their sterns, fighting for the after-breakfast scrapings from the mess-tubs. Beyond them and five miles across the inland sea called Macquarie Harbour the grey-green shoreline was backed by mountain ranges that merged, hazed with distance, into the cornflower blue of the sky. Had the major known anything about painting, it might have crossed his mind that, on this summer morning of 1833, the view had the Mediterranean limpidity of a landscape by Claude Lorrain.

But Major Baylee's appreciation of the view began and ended with the two transports that lay offshore and the third, *Maria,* that was moored at the main wharf below him and to his right. He watched them with the love of an admiral for his fleet, with the gratitude of a shipwrecked mariner saved at sea. At intervals during the morning he had left his desk and walked across to his window, as if to reassure himself that they were still there. For these were the ships that were to take him and his detachment of the 63rd Regiment of Foot back to Hobart Town, where they would embark for India and active service; the ships that would put an end to his three years as Commandant of His Britannic Majesty's Penal Settlement at Macquarie Harbour in Van Diemen's Land.

It would be three years next February. To be precise — Major Baylee valued precision highly — he'd been in command here two years, ten months and ten days. How in God's name had he survived it? The climate alone was bad enough, with the water-laden westerlies striking the mountains, to shed their millions of tons of moisture in a rainfall of a hundred inches a year. And the howling fury of the Roaring Forties in winter! It was only the high palisades erected as windbreaks by Captain James Butler, a previous commandant, that made any kind of existence possible here on Sarah Island at the southern end of the Harbour. Two years, ten months, ten days. He'd spent them compiling inventories, accounts and reports for the government clerks in Hobart Town. He'd spent them doing duty as a combined workhouse master and prison warder, counting bags of flour and handing out punishment of appalling savagery to men whom the transportation system had reduced to devils incarnate. Two years, ten months and ten days he'd spent, in this hell on earth called Macquarie Harbour.

That was what the convicts called it. Simply, and with hideous sincerity: Hell. In the chain-gangs, in the pick-and-shovel squads on the roads, even aboard the convict transports coming out from England, men lowered their voices when they spoke of Macquarie Harbour where the rain, draining from the mountains, carried with it a red dye from the tree-bark so that the water of the inland sea looked as if it were

14

forever stained with blood. Macquarie Harbour, on the desolate, mountainously inaccessible south-west coast of Van Diemen's Land, was a maximum-security hard-labour camp for men who had committed felonies as convicts or who had made repeated attempts to escape elsewhere. It was at the very bottom of the inferno-like system of convict classification devised by George Arthur, Lieutenant-Governor of Van Diemen's Land; it was a hell where men deprived of the means of suicide had been known to commit murder solely for the privilege of being taken in chains to Hobart Town to be hanged, and thus escape.

There was no other way out. The penal settlement on Sarah Island was the end of the line, a prison for incorrigibles, a place to rot in until you died. For even if you could steal a boat or if you were one of the very few who could swim, where could you escape to? If you absconded to Hobart Town or Launceston, you'd be picked up sooner or later and sent back and given your hundred lashes. Then you'd be put to work rafting Huon pine for shipbuilding, working up to your neck in the ice-filled Gordon River from dawn to dusk on a breakfast of flour and water, with the logs ready to crush your arm to a bloody pulp if you made just one error of judgement. You could escape from a working-party, sure — and enjoy a few days of liberty in the bush until you starved to death. Or you could be like Alexander Pearce, the man-eater, who'd got away with seven other prisoners. He'd had a half-eaten human arm in his pocket when he gave himself up to be hanged because he was the sole survivor, and they didn't call him the man-eater for nothing. You could escape like the tall, handsome Robin Hood of bushrangers, Matthew Brady, and live the life of an outlaw. But only for a time, because they hunted him down and caught him, and his quixotic chivalry didn't help him much when they hanged him publicly in Hobart Town.

Nobody had ever escaped from the Harbour and lived to boast about it.

But now Macquarie Harbour was being closed down — had been closed down, officially, two weeks ago. After eleven years of misery and degradation, the settlement had been found to be too remote, the cost of its upkeep too great, the climate too inclement for the gaolers themselves. A new prison had been built at Port Arthur, sixty miles from Hobart Town on the end of a peninsula where, at Eaglehawk Neck, a line of half-starved dogs backed by armed patrols kept the convicts where they belonged. So now the lawn in front of Major Baylee's office window was reverting to rough grass. It would never be cut again.

Baylee went back to his desk and glanced through the Return of Buildings that the adjutant's clerk had left for him. He sat down, picked up his pen, examined the nib carefully and dipped it in the inkwell. At the foot of the document he wrote in his small precise hand:

All the Articles belonging to the above Buildings worth Removing, as enumerated in the Board of Survey already forwarded, I left Orders to be brought away by the new Brig 'Frederick'.

12th. Decem^r. 1833.

P. Baylee
B^t. Major 63rd. Reg^t.

Not, he thought, that there were many articles left worth removing. But Lieutenant-Governor Arthur valued precision even more than Baylee did, and everything would have to be accounted for, down to the last nail. Well, the *Frederick,* due to be launched any day now, could have the honour of being the last ship out of the settlement and taking the odds and ends with her. It would mean Captain Taw and David Hoy, the shipwright, staying on for a few weeks more, but that couldn't be helped. The 63rd was required in India, thank God, as it had been required in the West Indies twenty-four years ago. He'd been just a lad then, but he could remember over the years the clean, sharp call of the Charge . . . Martinique in '09; Guadeloupe, 1815.

16

There was a loud knock at the door. It flew open and Colour-Sergeant Mayhew, boots thundering on the wooden floor, crashed to attention. As befitted the senior non-commissioned officer at the settlement, his cross-belts were pipe-clayed to the whiteness of snow and, at their junction on his chest, the square shoulder-belt plate bearing the regimental insignia flashed golden fire from its eight-pointed star that contained the numeral 63 and the scrolled battle-honours. His face was like sun-dried leather and his voice would have been more than adequate if Baylee had been on the other side of the island as he announced, 'Parade ready to witness punishment, sah!'

Baylee nodded. How many last things there were! The last ship — the *Frederick*. This, the last day, on which the last convict was to be flogged. A hundred lashes for stealing a cheese from the Officers' Mess. The fool. He stood up, picked up his plumed shako and sword-belt and went out into the sunshine. 'Have you,' he asked as Mayhew fell into step beside him, 'selected the military guard that is to remain behind with the *Frederick?*'

'Yessah!' They crunched rhythmically past the chaplain's house and took the downhill path that crossed in front of the military barracks, whose state of repair Baylee's report had described as 'ruinous'. Mayhew stared ahead so as not to see the unmilitary condition of its peeling paintwork and sagging roof. 'Dearman will be in charge — he'll need to be made up to corporal, with your permission. He'll have Privates Kent, Gillespie and Gathersole. All reliable men, sir.'

'Reliable enough to take charge of a crew of twelve convicts, no doubt. And they'll be assisted by Captain Taw, Mr Hoy and the mate.'

Baylee knew perfectly well that Mayhew had selected four amiable sheep, men the regiment wouldn't miss if they failed to turn up later in India. He swung right as the path turned towards the open space between the gaol and the commissariat stores, where the blood-red coats glowed in the sun as the detachment of the 63rd stood to sweating attention. Facing them in equally stiff ranks with their backs to the gaol stood a hundred convicts, their faded yellow uniforms drab and ugly against the glittering brass and cross-belted pageantry of the infantrymen. A group set apart from the others wore trousers buttoned down the sides so that they could be removed without taking off the leg-irons that clamped their ankles a rigid eighteen inches apart.

It was hard to believe that the prisoners came from the same race as their guards. They were much smaller, their growth having been so stunted by childhood privation and a lifetime of poor food that few of them stood over five feet three inches in height. They were pock-marked, bushy-haired, some with scars or a finger missing. And their faces were the faces of the damned — lined, despairing faces, secretive and inhuman, faces that were as old as crime itself. They stared like caged beasts into the wooden, well-fed faces of the soldiers. Every now and then their eyes shifted to take in two things — the brown, bony back of the man who was to be flogged, and the three-foot-long cat-o'-nine-tails that dangled from the flagellator's wrist.

The weather-bleached timbers of the whipping triangle stood in the middle of the space between the troops and the convicts, the man undergoing punishment chained to it by the wrists and facing it. The flagellator, a fifteen-stone private who did the job without emotion for a five-shilling bounty and a tot of rum, stood at ease on the left. Like the man he was to work on, he was stripped to the waist. Behind the triangle were the surgeon and his assistant, who carried a pail of water. Behind them again were the free men, time-expired convicts who had elected to work in the shipyards. David Hoy, the master shipwright, and Captain Taw, the pilot, stood near them. Baylee's standing orders for a whipping were that every person at the settlement must be present. The chaplain stood as far from the triangle as he could without actually being off parade

Colour-Sergeant Mayhew saluted the commandant violently, marched across to the adjutant, saluted him and shouted into his face, 'Commanding Officer on parade, sah!'

The adjutant acknowledged, stood the parade at ease, brought it to attention again and marched across to Baylee. His half-basket-hilted sword flashed in the sun as he lifted it in salute. 'All present and correct, sir,' he said crisply. 'The prisoner has been prepared for punishment.'

Baylee nodded. 'Carry on.'

The adjutant saluted, whirled about and snapped, 'Commence punishment!'

Unhurriedly, the flagellator turned and settled his feet in the beaten earth, moving backwards and forwards slightly as he measured the distance with his eye, the cat-o'-nine-tails gripped in his right hand and lying across his left palm. Rising on his toes, he swung the whip back and up. Simultaneously, the kettle-drums of the Regiment began their roll.

The lash whistled as it came down, a thin sound that was drowned in the thwack of leather striking human skin and the gasp from the man on the triangle. The bare back arched convulsively and a red weal appeared between the shoulder blades. Above the roll of the drums Colour-Sergeant Mayhew bawled, 'One!' The man with the whip moved back, balanced and struck again. 'Two!' A convict, secure in the knowledge that his whisper could not be heard, said out of the corner of his mouth, 'Plug o' nigger-head that he cries out on the fifth touch?'

His mate thought for a moment. Negro-head tobacco was not to be wagered lightly. 'Aye. A proper shriek, though.'

'Three!' roared Mayhew. The weals lay neatly spaced down the man's back. So far, the only sound he'd made had been an agonized hiss at each blow. The first convict chuckled. 'He'll shriek, right enough. Flogger's doing the five-barred gate, see? Four in a row, then the fifth to lie across the others. That's when the bastard'll chirp. They always do.'

'Four!' The flagellator shifted his right foot forward a fraction. Grunting with effort, he brought the cat down with all his fifteen stone behind it. 'Five!'

There was a bubbling scream of agony. The prisoner jerked like a gaffed salmon, blood welling from the four points where the last stroke had intersected the four parallel weals. 'Plug o' nigger you owes me,' said the convict softly.

'Two plugs,' said the loser to recoup his loss, 'that he swoons afore the twentieth?'

'Nah!' said the other contemptuously. 'He'll go under long afore then. Besides, you ain't got two plugs. I know that.'

'Eight!' The whip went up, gleaming wetly in the sunshine. The flogger, his back moist with sweat, was working a little lower and the prisoner was screaming continuously now, screams that were punctuated with harsh grunts every time the whip struck. By the eighteenth stroke his back had been torn open and the flagellator was being spattered with blood. 'Twenty-two!' Baylee, his face impassive, shut off his mind from the scene that had revolted him so often before and tried to calculate the date of the regiment's disembarkation at Madras. 'Twenty-three!'

By the thirtieth, the screams had subsided into whimpers of air forced out of the prisoner's lungs by the impact of each stroke. The man was hanging limply by his wrists. 'Thirty-seven!' The convicts watched with interest, pitching their whispers to reach only the next man in the ranks, speaking without moving their lips. For them, it was a break in the routine. Far better to stand here in the sun and watch a man being tickled than to work your guts out.

'Forty-one!' The flagellator, sweat pouring down his back, swung the whip upwards.

The surgeon said abruptly, 'Hold. I wish to examine the prisoner.' He walked forward to the triangle, lifted the man's head, then put a hand on the skinny chest. He beckoned to the adjutant. The man with the whip stood back and picked up a rag that came away sodden and blood-stained when he wiped his face and chest with it. The drums stopped.

20

The adjutant came to attention. 'Sir,' he said to Baylee. 'The prisoner has died under punishment.'

In the silence, a convict hissed, 'So it's back to work, blast his eyes. And I thought we was good for another ten minutes stand-easy 'ere.'

Baylee said curtly, 'Sergeant Mayhew. Have the body unchained. Then detail four prisoners and a guard to remove it for burial. The chaplain will accompany the party and perform the last rites.' He raised his voice. 'Captain Taw. Mr Hoy. A word with you both in my office, if you please.' He returned the salute as the regiment presented arms. Then he walked briskly uphill to his quarters. For some reason that the chaplain would have understood very well, he had a profound desire to wash his hands.

He found Captain Taw, red-faced and smelling strongly of rum, waiting outside his office with David Hoy. Baylee sat down behind his desk and gave them chairs, which set the tone of the interview as far as Taw was concerned. Last time he hadn't had a chair — he'd had a blistering reprimand after he'd run a brig aground on the narrow, sandbar-streaked entrance called Hell's Gates at the northern end of the Harbour. Baylee studied Hoy's white face. 'If I had known,' he said, 'that your illness was troubling you, you could have absented yourself from parade.'

Hoy smiled painfully. 'My back is, indeed, giving me some trouble, sir. But there is much to be done, with the new brig about to be launched, and I find that, if I apply the ointment the surgeon has given me and poultice the area each night on retiring, I can obtain some relief. I find also that . . .'

'It is, in fact, the new brig that I wish to discuss with you.' Baylee knew that once he allowed Hoy to start on his rheumatoid reminiscences there'd be no stopping him short of physical violence. 'Captain Taw, you are to take the *Frederick* to the new settlement at Port Arthur, together with the items of equipment that remain here after I have left with the regiment.'

21

Taw shifted his heavy body in the chair. 'Aye,' he said in his flat Yorkshire voice. 'I thowt that's how it'd be. Suits me well enough. I've some bits and pieces of my own up at the Pilot's Establishment. Happen I can taken them wi' me.'

The bits and pieces would be mainly jars of rum, Baylee thought. Aloud he said, 'As you please. You are to be in sole command here after tomorrow, accountable only to His Excellency.'

'Aye.' Taw nodded thoughtfully. He had, Baylee knew, applied for the job of Port Pilot at Hobart Town. Lieutenant-Governor Arthur's approval was essential and the successful accomplishment of this clearing-up operation might be the means of earning it. 'I'll have a military guard to keep the damned canaries in check?'

Baylee disliked the term 'canary', given to the convicts because of their yellow uniform, but he made no comment. He said, 'You will have a corporal and three men. They will be on marine rations and will keep watch two and two. They will be entirely under your command on the voyage.'

'I'd like a free man to act as mate. Not a canary. Tait would do.'

'The obvious choice. Mr Hoy, you will, of course, take passage on the *Frederick* with your personal servant, William Nicholls. The convicts who will form the crew are' — he reached for a sheet of paper — 'William Shiers and William Cheshire, who have worked with you, Mr Hoy, in the ship-yard. James Porter and Charles Lyon, who have been part of your pilot boat's crew, Captain . . .'

'That Lyon's a bad 'un.' Taw shook his head doubtfully. 'Devil for the women. Sent here for rape, he was. And that one-eyed blackguard Porter, he was sentenced to be hanged afore the Supreme Court commuted it to life. He's had three hundred lashes already.'

'I am conversant,' said Baylee icily, 'with the records of these men, Captain Taw. Take whatever means you choose to control them. I must emphasize that you and you alone as ship's captain will be in charge of the final arrangements at this settlement.' And, for my part, he thought, after I've left, Charles Lyon can rape everybody on board the *Frederick* from the captain to the ship's cat. His eyes went to the paper again. 'Joseph MacFarlane, John Dady, John Fare and John Jones. All quiet, well-behaved men. Fare and Jones are former seamen. Then you'll have James Lesley and Benjamin Russen. Both violent, hardened criminals, but Lesley is a shipwright and Russen is a handy man who will be useful during the fitting-out of the brig. As will John Barker.' He paused. 'I should watch Barker carefully, Captain, if I were you. He is a highly intelligent man, with some knowledge of physics and mathematics. He is a former gunsmith and watchmaker and very clever with his hands. If you can persuade him to work with you, he can be of some influence with the others, and . . .'

'Persuade him?' Taw snorted. 'I'd as soon try to persuade a fiend from the pit. The only persuasion that kind of scum understands is what we've just seen being administered. The cat. So John Barker will work with me whether he likes it or not.'

'Very well, Captain.' Baylee wished his choice of command could have been better. Hoy, for example. The convicts had worked well under him in the shipyard. But Hoy's state of health would never permit him to take the *Frederick* round the south-west Cape to Port Arthur, nor was he qualified to do so. Taw was the only choice. 'The fitting-out should take a month, so you should be in Port Arthur by the end of January. You will be given water and provisions for three months, more than sufficient. The weather at this time of year is mild, so —'

'Pray leave it to me, sir.' Taw levered himself to his feet. 'I've handled bigger vessels than the *Frederick* in my time. Aye, and worse crews, too. We'll have a merry Christmas here in the settlement, with a merry voyage to follow. After all, sir,' he chuckled confidently, 'what can go wrong?'

2

There is something of childbirth in the launching of a sailing vessel. An embryo, conceived in the mind of the designer, passes through a period of gestation on the stocks until the moment arrives for it to be eased gently out into the world. Like most children, it is given its name while still in the womb. Then the checking-hawser, like an umbilical cord, is removed and the ship — always a girl-child, even if she bears a man's name — is fitted out with her christening gifts and dressed in her finery of fresh new paint. And the *Frederick* was a special ship, the last of fifteen born at Macquarie Harbour, a child of the settlement's old age, as was Joseph, the son of Jacob. David Hoy, like Jacob, loved her more than all his children.

She was a late arrival, the culmination of eleven months' pregnancy on the slips at the south-east end of Sarah Island. Hoy and his men had worked on her since the eighteenth of January, creating her out of timbers brought with sweat and blood from the banks of the Gordon River, five miles down the Harbour. In the last few months it had been a race against time to put her into the water before the settlement closed down. Hoy had lost, but honourably. It was only three

24

days since *Larkspur, Atlas* and *Maria* had sailed, and now the brig was ready for launching.

John Barker stood in the soft summer rain, looking at her from the top of the slope where the administration block ended and the shipyard began. Not being a shipbuilder, he'd been given the job of taking window-frames out of the new penitentiary on the other side of the island. That suited him, since it kept him out of the rain. It had meant, too, that he'd been able to spend some time, unsupervised, in the blacksmith's shop, after which he'd hidden in the penitentiary a certain article, the discovery of which in his possession would have had him treading air on the end of a rope.

The buildings, empty under the gun-metal sky, were eerily silent. For the first time in eleven years Hell was quiet, with no demented shrieks from the gaol, no groans from the hospital, no raucous laughter from the barracks. Only a door slamming in the light wind, the cry of a sea-bird, the tap of Barker's footsteps along the stone-flagged passageway of the penitentiary. *Stand to for the officer, damn you! . . . the sentence of the Court is that you be given one hundred lashes . . . Bring out your buckets, you scum! . . . to work in irons for six months . . . Sir, the prisoner has died under punishment . . .* It was all over at the Harbour. 'All the pain and sorrow done,' said Barker aloud as he stood watching the rain-dimpled water and the grey mist that hid the far shoreline and the mountains.

Below him, there was feverish activity round the brig, but he was in no hurry to join in. He could see Hoy, wrapped in a soaking-wet boat-cloak, directing operations from the slip-head. Convicts with sledgehammers, their hair plastered to their skulls, were spaced along the hull ready to knock away the oak timbers that had cradled the one-hundred-and-forty-ton vessel ever since her keel had been laid. Privates Kent and Gillespie, miserable in the wet, stood in the lee of the ship-wright's workshop doing the pointless guard duty that soldiers have done, and will do, throughout history. Nobody was likely to take it into his head to swim five miles away from food and shelter to die in the bush. Nobody was likely to attack Taw or Hoy, the only two who could get the party off the island. But Kent and Gillespie had to stand with the damp creeping up through their boots while they kept their flintlocks dry and thought morosely of the hot sun and the brown-skinned girls their mates would soon be enjoying in India. Taw and Corporal Dearman were nowhere to be seen. Barker hoisted up his window-frame and started down the slope.

Before he'd gone halfway there was a ragged cheer and he saw the brig sliding slowly and smoothly down her greased slipway to the water. She entered stern first with hardly a splash, the men on the guide-ropes running to the capstans to secure her and warp her alongside. Hoy, his back temporarily forgotten, stood grinning in the rain with William Shiers, William Cheshire and James Lesley, joined with them for a brief moment in the comradeship of craftsmen admiring their work.

And the *Frederick,* even though mastless and unfinished, was worth admiring. Hoy's artistry showed itself in the eager rake of her bow, in the line of the billet head that raised the fo'c'sle above the flush deck to give her more height for'ard in a heavy sea. Square-rigged on fore and main masts, with fore-and-aft staysails, jibs and spanker, she would be a lovely sight under full sail. Even Kent and Gillespie, bored and wet, had taken their shakos off and were waving them. 'Gawd bless 'er!' shouted Kent loyally. 'And Gawd bless 'is Majesty King William!'

God bless her indeed, thought Barker. He smiled to himself and rubbed his long nose. God bless those who will sail in her, too.

'And God bless Lieutenant-Governor Arthur!' Captain Taw, a mug in his hand, had appeared at the door of the boatswain's hut next to the workshop. 'Three cheers for His Exshellence — Excellenshy!'

He was drunk. His nose shone like a larboard light as he raised his mug and bawled, 'Hip! Hip! — '

Kent and Gillespie yelled, "Hurrah!" but they were on their own. The convicts stood grinning. Hoy had suddenly found it necessary to check one of the mooring lines. Taw shouted again, but his voice tailed off as he realized he wasn't holding his audience. He stared round at the convicts, then he pointed erratically at Charles Lyon with his mug.

'There's a man there,' he said thickly, 'as isn't cheering.' He pushed off from the doorpost and tacked across to the slipway. 'Why,' he said to Lyon, 'don't you cheer, you dog?'

Lyon, at five foot seven the tallest of the prisoners, looked past him at the rain drifting across the water, the grin still on his face.

'Insolence!' Taw raised his voice. 'Insolence as well as disloyalty. But you've always been an insolent, disloyal bugger, Lyon, haven't you? I know you. Why didn't you cheer, you bastard? Answer me, or by God I'll — '

Lyon said in his soft Lowland voice, 'Ma feelings was chokin' me, Captain. Ah couldna utter a squeak.'

'I'll make tha squeak,' said Taw furiously. He flourished his mug, rum spilling down his coat. 'Cheer now, damn you, or I'll leave you here to rot after we've sailed. Go on. Cheer, you insolent — '

'Captain.' Hoy had seen the cornered, dangerous set of Lyon's face. He took Taw's arm. 'Sir, let it be.'

Taw shook him off, glaring at the convict. 'I want to hear him cheer!' he shouted. 'They'll all cheer when I tell 'em, or I'll leave 'em all behind.'

'Sir.' Hoy grabbed his arm again. 'Let's go in out of the rain.' He beckoned to Corporal Dearman who, his face flushed with rum and his uniform jacket unbuttoned, was staring from the door of the hut. 'A toast between gentlemen to His Excellency would be far more fitting to the occasion.'

'A toast, you say?' Taw stood swaying and looking into his empty mug. 'Aye, you may well be right, David. But, none the less . . .' Reluctantly, he allowed himself to be led away by Hoy and Dearman. Over his shoulder he shouted, 'But, next time, it won't be your bloody feelings that'll choke you, Charles Lyon. I'll remember this. And, when we reach Port Arthur . . .' The three men disappeared into the hut.

With the grins and sniggers that followed, Barker propped his window-frame against the weatherboard wall of the ship-wright's workshop and said to the soldiers, 'A devil of a thing, gentlemen, is drink. It's fortunate indeed that we have up-standing, temperate men like yourselves to guard us.'

Gillespie frowned importantly and straightened his back a little.

Barker said, 'But, to be sure, they've chosen the best men from the regiment for the task, eh?'

Kent smirked. ''Tis a responsible task, to be sure. Colour-Sergeant told us not every man could be trusted so.'

'And to find your own way to India!' Barker shook his head admiringly. 'You'll be colour-sergeants yourselves soon, I shouldn't wonder.' He looked at the brig. 'A fine ship she is, for the service of the King. Would I be permitted to go on board her, do you think?'

'Why not?' Gillespie looked at Kent, who shrugged indiffer-ently. 'You ain't a-going to steal her, though?' He grinned.

Barker smiled back, knuckled his sloping forehead gratefully and sauntered down to the wharf. As he passed Lyon he said, 'Follow me, Charlie, but not too eager, like. 'Tis time we had a bit of a talk.'

William Shiers was rigging a gangplank. Barker said, 'Want a hand, Will?'

'Aye, lad.' Shiers wiped his wet black hair out of his eyes. He'd been a farm labourer at Thornhill in Yorkshire before the Enclosure Acts had given him the choice between starva-tion and highway robbery. He'd done six years at the settle-ment and thirteen years altogether in Van Diemen's Land; longer than any of the others. At thirty-nine, he was the second oldest of the convicts left at the Harbour. He said, as he and

28

Barker lifted the gangplank into position, 'That Taw! He'll end up in the Harbour wi' a knife in his back if he don't mend his ways.'

'And not only Taw.' Barker let the pause stretch out while the rain hissed softly on the oily sea. 'Mr David Hoy, the four redcoats and maybe the mate as well.'

'Oh, Mr Hoy's a reasonable man. And the four soldiers . . .' Shiers straightened up from the rope he was securing. He stared at Barker, then at Lyon, who had strolled down to the wharf. 'What,' he said slowly, 'art tha planning, John?'

'Then,' Barker went on as if Shiers hadn't spoken, 'there'd be nobody to stop us taking the *Frederick* wheresoever we chose, eh?' He went up the gangplank. 'Come on board out of this bloody rain. I've obtained permission.'

They went aft to the Captain's cabin. Barker squatted down among the wood-shavings. Shiers, at the foot of the ladder, said, 'Now hearken, John, afore you speaks. Whatever you've got in mind, I want no part of it if it means murder. I've worked wi' Mr Hoy these three and a half years . . .'

'And Captain Taw's from your own county and you bloody Yorkshire puddens stick together.' Barker, a Lancastrian from Warrington, chuckled. 'Sit you down, Will, and hear me out first.'

Shiers remained standing by the ladder, frowning. Lyon coiled himself up on the deck opposite Barker. 'Aye,' he said. 'We'll give ye a hearing, John. But, if you're planning to take the *Frederick*, you might also give a thought to what happened to the men who seized the *Cyprus*.'

'Those bunglers?' said Barker contemptuously. 'They deserved to be lagged.' (Four years previously, in August 1829, the brig *Cyprus* had taken shelter in Recherche Bay on the south-west coast of Van Diemen's Land while on her way to Macquarie Harbour. Her consignment of lifers, led by a convict named Swallow, had overpowered the military guard and put forty-five people ashore. They sailed to Japan, scuttled the brig and scattered across the world to enjoy a brief

29

period of liberty before they were hunted down.) 'They should never have left anybody alive to tell the tale. We won't make that mistake.'

Lyon said uneasily, 'I've never killed a man in my life. To be hanged for murder . . .'

'If there's no corpse, there's no murder,' said Barker authoritatively. 'Any fool knows that. So we ain't a-going to leave nobody, dead or alive, to give evidence against us.' He leaned forward. 'There was a man, see, at the time of the American Revolution, who said, "Give me liberty or give me death". Now, 'tis that self-same situation we're in, lads. Liberty for those of us who'll seize the *Frederick* and sail her to foreign parts. Death for all the others.'

Shiers couldn't comment on the way Barker had twisted Patrick Henry's words to include a massacre. He shook his head stubbornly. 'I'm taking part in no murder.'

Barker's hazel-brown eyes went as empty as those of a lizard's. You bloody fool, he thought. It'll be justice, not murder. Justice for the men who've died here on the triangle, like that poor bastard the other day. Justice for the leg-irons, the starvation diet, the warders' boots. Aloud he said, nodding, 'Very well, mate. So be it. But what if it can be done without bloodshed?' There were more ways of killing a cat than one, and Taw and the others were going to be silenced whether Shiers liked it or not. They'd have to be, if the break-out was to conform with Barker's no-risks, no-chances standards of perfection.

'Without bloodshed? Wi' seven of them armed and us twelve wi' only our bare fists?' Shiers grunted. 'Tha'rt daft, lad.'

'It'd be nine of them against ten of us.' Lyon shifted his buttocks on the deck. 'Will Nicholls is Hoy's shadow, and Joe MacFarlane's been over-friendly wi' yon Private Gathersole, I've noticed. For a few wee plugs o' baccy.' He spat on Captain Taw's deck. 'So there's the two of them, and the four soldiers, and Taw and Hoy, and the mate. Almost equal odds, and us unarmed. We'd never do it. And where would we go, after? There's no country as would shelter the likes of us.'

'I know one as would.' Barker grinned. 'One where folk have struggled like us for their liberty against cruel oppression — aye, and who've gained it, too. They'd be sympathetic to us. A place wi' a climate to dream on — sunshine and warmth and mild winters. A place filled wi' good food an' wine an',' he paused, watching Lyon, 'beautiful dark-eyed passionate women. A place — '

Lyon sat up. 'Where?'

Barker shook his head. He'd no intention of telling them where they were bound — not yet. He daren't. The dangers were so great, their objective so remote that they'd rebel, lose heart, as much as if he'd told them they were to make for the moon. 'I'm not saying where until we're under way as free men. But, take my oath on it, mates, it's a place where we'll be safe from the bloody Navy.'

'I havena had a woman for three whole years,' said Lyon slowly. 'Not since that bitch Abigail shouted rape. when her husband found us in the hayloft.'

'And how,' asked Shiers, with blunt Yorkshire common sense, 'do we sail the brig to this land of milk and honey? How do we get her across t'Bar and out to sea? Who's to navigate us? Only Taw can do that.'

'I can navigate,' said Barker. 'And we've four seamen in our number, including two of the pilot's crew, James Porter and Charlie here, who know the Bar as well as the backs of their hands. Then there's John Jones from Liverpool, and John Fare, practised mariners both. It's summer, so the weather's on our side.'

'Aye, we'd manage the brig right enough.' Lyon scrambled to his feet. As if already tasting freedom, he prowled round the tiny cabin in the half-light. 'Anyway, I'd rather take my chance of drowning than rot in Port Arthur. Liberty! By God, I'd . . .'

'Very well,' Shiers said. 'So we could handle the brig. But, John lad, there's four redcoats wi' muskets to overcome first.

And Mr Hoy has a brace of pistols, don't forget.'

'So have I. One, leastways,' said Barker quietly.

There was a little silence while the others gaped at him. Lyon said, 'Have ye, now? And where did you get it?'

'You've never taken one of Mr Hoy's?' Shiers stared at Barker incredulously. ''Tis a hanging matter, that. Where is it?'

'You think I'd tell you?' Barker was grinning triumphantly. 'It's safe enough, that's all you need know, and it'll be brought out at the proper time. And it ain't Hoy's, neither. I'm a gunsmith, aren't I? They put me to repairing guns for the military. I made it.' He leaned forward, savouring his moment. 'I been planning this for months, mates. Ever since word came that the settlement was to be closed down. Y'see, I know these places — I did my four years in Bermuda besides the four I've done in Demon's Land. They're like machines — and I know machines, too. When all's well, they tick along hissing and powerful. Try to interfere with 'em, and they'll crush you. But, when they slows down, they loses power, see? They rattle and wheeze. Put a strain on 'em and they'll stop altogether.'

He stood up, his eyes gleaming in the light from the hatchway. 'Well, this machine called Macquarie Harbour's run down and now's our chance to be free of it.' He looked at Shiers. 'You talk of Taw and Hoy and the bloody redcoats as if they was Baylee and Mayhew and the whole regiment. What are they? Eh? A rum puncheon, a sick man and four ninnies. Overpower them, and we're men of liberty, wi' a new life in a new country afore us.' He paused. Then, suddenly brisk, he said, 'Now, mates, there's no time to lose. Speak up. Are you to be Liberty Men or gaolbirds for the rest of your lives?'

Lyon said instantly, 'I'm with you, John.' Somewhere, there'd be a girl, different from any he'd ever known. Soft yet hard, swooning in his arms yet wild with passion, with a body like a goddess and hair like a raven's wing. He'd spent his life searching for a girl like that. A girl to bear his children, a girl to dance with, live with, lie with. A man can't live without a woman, and it had been three long empty years . . . .

'Good lad. On the voyage, I'll be needing you as boatswain.' He was easy, Barker thought. Promise Charles Lyon a woman's naked belly and he'd do anything, go anywhere. He'd desert you for one, too. But Shiers was the key. Once he came in, he'd never let up. Nothing could deflect that bull-like onslaught of determination. On the other hand, if he stayed out, the plot was over before it had begun. His seniority, added to his native shrewdness, gave him as much influence with the others as did Barker's book-learning. If the camp split into two factions, they were all as good as locked up in Port Arthur. Casually, not rushing it, Barker said, 'And you, Will?'

Shiers stood by the companion, rubbing a horny hand up and down the timber, weighing the odds. He'd had a clean record for six years, ever since he'd come to the Harbour. He'd worked well, and Hoy had promised to make things easy for him when they reached Port Arthur. On the other hand — liberty. Warm sunshine and a mild climate. That'd mean good farmland, better even than Thornhill. A place, maybe, where a man could have a bit of land of his own. Suddenly, with heart-wrenching clarity, Shiers saw the rich earth break like a bow-wave under the plough-share. He could smell it, feel it, damp and crumbling, between his fingers. God, he hadn't walked over ploughland for thirteen bitter years.

Matter-of-factly, he said, 'Tha can count me in, John. But, mind, no blood to be spilt.'

Barker nodded. Shiers could make what conditions he liked as long as he came in.

Lyon said, 'You're to be captain, o' course, John?'

'On the voyage. No more.' Barker trod warily round that one. If anything went awry, he certainly wasn't going to be the ringleader they'd single out for hanging. 'In other matters, decisions 'll be taken by us all, casting our votes as equals. But, in the meantime, not a word to anyone. I'll sound the others out one by one.'

'I can vouch for Jamie Porter,' Lyon said. 'We've been together, on and off, ever since we came out from England on the *Asia*. He's got away seven times afore.'

'And been brought back seven times,' snapped Barker.

Porter, a former beer-machine maker from Bermondsey, had tried everything from stowing away on the Sydney packet to stealing a boat. In addition, his colourful career in Van Diemen's Land had included butter-stealing, robbing sailors, fighting with the military and using a government vessel to take his friends for pleasure trips up and down the River Derwent. As a kind of afterthought, as if he'd been casting about for new crimes to commit, his record showed that he'd been charged with 'failing to take care of some tobacco', for which offence he'd received twenty-five of his three hundred lashes. He'd had every punishment they could give him from flogging and six months' chain-gang down to the treadwheel and twelve days on bread and water. Yet still, like the pugilist he had tattooed on his left forearm, he came back fighting for more.

Barker said shortly, 'Vouched for or not, you'll tell him nowt — not till I'm ready. What a man don't know, he can't blab.' With a foot on the companion, he added, 'Near dinner-time, so we'd best be off. Keep away from me and from each other lest anyone should suspect our design.' He liked that last phrase; he'd heard it in a play once in Manchester.

Lyon said, 'A question, John, before ye go.'

Barker looked at him.

Lyon said, 'When?'

3

The boards of the brand-new leather-bound book were stiff. They cracked as Captain Taw, in a pair of old canvas trousers and a shirt open to the waist, turned to the fly-leaf and rubbed a hairy paw up and down the spine of the book to hold it open. He reached for his pen, wrinkling his nose at the smell of fresh paint and newly-trimmed timber in the hot, stuffy cabin, and wrote in a large jagged hand: 'Log of the Brig Frederick, Charles Taw, Master.'

His quarters, the size of a small garden shed, had been fitted with a double-tiered bunk along the starboard side. The table at which he sat faced aft to the ladder and the cabin door and, to his right on the port bulkhead, hung an oil lamp, a pea-jacket on a hook and a set of shelves that held rolled-up charts, a quadrant and two pewter mugs, with two bottles of wine and a stone jar of rum placed handily on the deck. Two sea-chests stood against this bulkhead. One, brassbound and battered, was Taw's; the other, made of varnished oak, was the property of David Hoy, who was to share the cabin on the voyage to Port Arthur. Ventilation and light were provided by a hinged skylight and by a sliding panel in the door at the top of the ladder. A plank partition separated the cabin from the half-deck where the four soldiers were to be quartered.

The fitting-out, under David Hoy's exacting but benign supervision, had been completed and the brig, her name emblazoned across her stern and her decorative ports picked out in black and yellow, seven a side, was moored at the main wharf. The convicts had worked hard, the nine recruited by Barker spurred on by the thought of their break-out and all of them enjoying the picnic atmosphere that prevailed as long as Commandant Taw was kept in a good humour. There'd been good victuals and plenty of them, especially at Christmas. There'd been rum, too, to drink the King's health — in fact, the captain had shown so much loyalty that he'd had to be locked up on one occasion in the boatswain's hut for the night. One or two discords, it was true, had occurred in all this harmony. Charles Lyon had spent the last few days in gaol for insubordination. And Captain Taw had taken it upon himself to cut out the brig's main course — the lowest of the four square sails she would carry on her main-mast — and had made a complete botch of the job, so that an old cutter's mainsail had had to be adapted for the purpose. But, none the less, the Captain was satisfied with the success of his clearing-up operation. He hoped Governor Arthur would be equally pleased.

He muttered under his breath as his pen dropped a blot of ink. Well, no matter. With luck, he'd enter but the one voyage in this log. The position of Pilot at Hobart Town carried with it a fine house and several assigned convict servants, male and female, to run it. There'd be no more dossing down in cramped hen-coops like this cabin if he could secure such a plummy post. No more damned voyages up and down the west coast, with the westerlies screaming like demons as they fought to smash your ship to splinters on rocks that weren't even on the charts. And, by God, there'd be no more eating humble pie to little jacks-in-office like bloody Major Baylee who, if there was any justice in the world, would soon be sliced into pork chops by the heathen in India.

No, as Pilot, he'd be a man of mark in Hobart Town. This was a new ship and a voyage into a new life. He turned to the first page and, with a flourish that sprayed ink freely over the table, wrote: '11th January 1834. At Sarah Island in Macquarie Harbour. This Day I informed the Prisoners assembled at Morning Muster that we sail for Port Arthur on the morrow. I instructed the Military . . .' No, dammit, he thought. I forgot. Best do it now. He threw down his pen, clambered, puffing, up the ladder, and climbed out on deck.

He felt as if he'd stepped into a furnace. Ashore, the buildings of the settlement seemed to quiver as the heated air boiled up from the ground. The Harbour was a sheet of purple-tinted glass that mirrored every detail of the shoreline and reflected the afternoon sun with a dazzle that made Taw screw up his eyes.

And, in full marching order with knapsacks, Privates Kent and Gillespie tramped up and down the wharf, meeting and turning about and stamping off again, their fixed bayonets and brass shako-plates flashing like heliographs. They must, Taw thought wonderingly, be bloody mad.

Midships, the deck looked like the result of a collision between a marine store and Noah's Ark. Two pigs gazed fraternally at Taw through the slats of their pen, while a goat suckling her kid munched a pair of trousers that somebody had left out to dry. Ducks, geese and hens waddled noisily among a confusion of chests, pots and pans, bags of nails, tools, lengths of timber, a balance with its weights from the Commissariat stores and kegs of beef, bags of flour and wooden boxes of tea. Benjamin Russen, his naked, muscular chest running with sweat, appeared at the head of the gangplank, a side of bacon over his shoulder. A former weaver from Norwich, he had a record of violence equalled only by that of his bosom friend James Lesley.

'You there, blast you,' said Taw. 'Tell Corporal Dearman to report to my cabin directly.'

He went below, took two mugs off the shelf and sat down on the kitchen chair behind his table.

A few minutes later Corporal Dearman's glossily-polished half-boots appeared on the ladder followed by his white trousers, scarlet high-necked coatee with its corporal's chevrons of regimental lace on the right sleeve, and his freshly-pipeclayed cross-belt, bayonet frog and pouch. Then followed his face, shaved to the bone and almost the same colour as his coat. As he ducked through the hatchway his leather-bound shako with its white worsted plume fell off and thumped to the deck. He picked it up, jammed it on his bullet head and threw a salute that was a fair imitation of Colour-Sergeant Mayhew's. 'Corporal Dearman!' he said. He'd been a ploughboy before he took the King's shilling, and his voice carried undertones of Devonshire cider, haymaking and the lush farmland of the West Country. 'Reporting as requested, sir!'

'For God's sake! I know who you bloody well are,' said Taw irritably. 'Sit you down, take off your hat and coat and be easy, will you? It fair makes me sweat to look at you. Sit down, man, and take a tot o' rum.'

The corporal hesitated. Then he removed his shako. 'Thankee, sir,' he said sheepishly. ''Tis a hot day, to be sure.' He took off his cross-belt and coatee and became Henry Dearman, civilian, as he sat down on Hoy's sea-chest.

'Now, lad.' Taw picked up the stone jar and sloshed rum into the mugs. 'Concerning the voyage to Port Arthur. Do you know your duty?'

'Aye, that I do, sir.' Dearman loosened his shirt at the neck and repeated mechanically, 'We stands watch, two and two. We draws marine rations. We'm to ensure that not more'n six prisoners be on deck at a time, and none at night. We . . .'

'Lad,' said Taw patiently. He pushed a mug across the table. 'I'm not asking you what Mayhew told you. The prisoners are the crew, d'ye see? How the devil am I to work the ship if they're not to be allowed on deck?' He drank some rum. 'Your duty, according to the orders left by Major Baylee, is to obey me as captain in all things. "They will be entirely under your command on the voyage." That's what he said to me concerning your duty. His very words.'

'Yes, sir.' Dearman sipped his rum and coughed. 'Your pardon, sir. Under your command it is, to be sure. There'll be two sentries with loaded muskets . . .'

'And what manner of use will sentries be once we're at sea? To prevent the gaolbirds from jumping overboard?' Taw shook his shaggy head. God save us from the military mind in peacetime, he thought. Hadn't His Grace the Duke of Wellington's Peninsular campaign, in which spit and polish had been abandoned in favour of marching ability and marksmanship, taught them anything? 'No, Corporal. If you stand about wi' loaded muskets in your hands, 'twill be the easiest thing in the world should one of the scum have a mind to knock you on the head one dark night and relieve you of your weapons. The muskets must be kept loaded and ready for instant use, but locked away in the arms rack in the half deck. I'll have one in here, and Mr Hoy has a brace of pistols in his chest. Keep your watches, always two of you together on deck, night and day. Be alert, eh?'

'Yes, sir.' Dearman wrinkled his forhead fiercely and looked as alert as he'd ever be.

'Good lad.' Taw swigged his rum. 'But there'll be no trouble wi' the canaries, never fear. Apart from Charles Lyon, they've been quiet and well-behaved these four weeks. The dogs know their master, I think. And they know what they'll get if they cross me.'

Dearman nodded respectfully. If these were the captain's orders, it was his duty to obey them — and it suited him to do so, too. It would make the care of the Pattern 1802 muskets easier if their rust-prone flintlock mechanisms and their socket bayonets weren't exposed to the damp and spray of the open deck. In fact, it would make things easier all round if he followed Taw's free-and-easy régime. Already Dearman's command, however minuscule, was bringing its burden of loneliness. Gathersole, Kent and Gillespie, his friends and drinking companions when he had been a private, were now reserved, wary and even resentful of his promotion and the duties he allotted to them.

'Since you mention Charles Lyon, sir,' he said hesitantly. 'Is he to be released? There's talk among the prisoners that you intend to leave him behind.'

Taw guffawed. 'Eh, lad, that was merely my manner of speaking. Leave him to starve? I'd never do that, although 'tis no more than he merits, the impudent blackguard. Come now, drink up your rum and be off with you to the gaol wi' one of your men. I'll come and release the rascal myself.'

When Dearman had gone, his coatee and belt in one hand and his shako in the other, Taw picked up his pen and completed the sentence he'd begun: 'I instructed the Military Guard that they were to act in accordance with the Orders left by the former Commandant, Major Baylee; that their Muskets were to be always ready to Hand and that they should keep a close Watch on the Prisoners by Day and Night.' That should take care of the damned canaries and, he thought cannily, at the same time it would keep his yardarm clear — just in case a convict or two should happen to get away. He'd issued his orders. Now it was up to Corporal Dearman to carry them out.

And Dearman would. But, if the Captain had been a little more perceptive, he would have realized that Wellington's Peninsular veterans, their minds sharpened by hunger and by the necessity for killing Frenchmen before they were killed themselves, were a different kettle of fish from a well-fed ex-ploughboy who had very little in his mind at all. Dearman needed a Colour-Sergeant Mayhew to tell him when to get up, when to clean himself and his equipment, when to march — when to die, if necessary. And he'd do all that. Give him an order and he'd obey it. But it would take more than Captain

40

Taw to make him think for himself. At that very moment he was saying to his astonished but delighted subordinates on the wharf, 'Take off your coats and packs, my boys, and be easy. 'Tis the captain's order. You, Private Kent, sit down in a patch of shade, and mind you be alert. You, Private Gillespie, are to come with me to the gaol and await the captain.'

Taw finished his entry: 'We embarked as Cargo everything left at the Settlement that could be of Use and we took on our Provisions, which consisted of . . .' Here followed a catalogue of livestock, food and drink in which Taw carefully separated those articles that were his own property from those owned by the government. He concluded: 'Having released Charles Lyon from Gaol, where he was detained for Insubordination, and the Vessel being in every way ready to put to Sea, we shall sail, given fair Weather, on the Morrow.'

Tired by his literary labours, he tossed off the rest of his rum, belched sonorously, wiped the back of his hand across his mouth and stumped up on deck, where James Tait, the mate, was supervising the stowage of the cargo in the hold and the rigging of an awning to protect the animals' pens from the sun.

Tait said, touching his forehead, 'D'ye think the weather will hold, Cap'n? A day like this could mean a thunderstorm, I'd say.'

Taw grunted. 'There's no telling in this part of the world.' He didn't dislike the mate, but he could never feel comfortable with him. After all, it was only a year or two since the fellow had been walking about in convict dress. Tait had a weak bladder, too, and his habit of relieving himself frequently over the side could be a confounded nuisance in a varying wind. 'Tis blistering hot and airless. A thunderstorm would break the calm.'

'True, sir. A breeze would be welcome. Even more welcome tomorrow, then we'll see how she handles, eh? A fine ship, Cap'n, to be sure.' The mate touched his forehead again and turned back to his sweating work-party. 'Russen! Stir your stumps and bear a hand with that cask!'

Aye, thought Taw with grudging satisfaction, the *Frederick* should do well enough. He ran a professional eye over the two masts that still had the scent of Huon pinewood on them, the rigging hairy and rough with newness, the yellow deck-planking that had yet to be stained with salt-water. All was shipshape. The launch and whaleboat amidships had their gear tidily stowed; the smaller jollyboat hung over the stern on its davits, to which John Barker was busily applying yet another coat of paint. Eighty feet long and twenty in the beam, the brig lay sleeping on the calm water, ready now to awake and fulfil the purpose for which David Hoy had designed her.

Aye, she'll do. Taw clumped down the gangplank and made his way uphill to the gaol, swiping at the flies that swarmed round his head. Lyon, he reflected as he eyed its thick red-brick walls, will be a damn sight cooler in there than I am. High time he came out to sweat like the rest of us.

Barker, a dry paintbrush in his hand and no paintpot, scowled as he watched him go. A plug of nigger-head to Tait had bought him a thinly-disguised stand-easy in the stern where, through the open skylight, he'd been able to overhear every word of the conversation between Dearman and the Captain. Blast Taw to hell, he thought savagely. The kind of incident that the Captain had mentioned — a silent, murderous attack on the sentries in the dark and the seizure of their muskets — had been exactly what Barker had intended. The *Cyprus* had been taken in that very way, but in broad daylight, when nine prisoners brought on deck for exercise had rushed their two guards. Now he'd have to think again. There was no point in killing the redcoats on deck if all the weapons were in the hands of the off-duty soldiers below. He had his pistol, true; he'd smuggled it aboard without any trouble at all. But what he hadn't told Shiers and the others was that he'd been unable to steal powder and ball for it. Even if he had, he knew it would be useless against the combined fire-power

42

of the soldiers' four flintlocks, plus Taw's musket and Hoy's pistols.

Whoever held those weapons held the ship. Taw knew that, damn him for a cunning old bastard. So now the guns were to be locked inaccessibly away and there'd be locks and padlocks to be forced and chains to be broken and seven men, maybe nine, to be overcome. Not only that. The weapons were in two different places, so that while you were struggling to take the guns out of the arms rack in the half-deck you could be fired upon from the cabin next door through the thin partition, and vice versa. Therefore the cabin and the half-deck would have to be rushed simultaneously, with clockwork precision. But only one man at a time could pass through the narrow hatchways.

With an obscenity, Barker slung his paintbrush over the side. It couldn't be done — not without considerable risk. He, John Barker, a self-educated, intelligent man, had been outsmarted by that oafish, rum-swilling old fool, Taw. For a wild moment of red rage he thought of shouting to the others to smash Tait's head in and cast off while Taw, Hoy and the military were all ashore. But, in the flat calm, the *Frederick* was as good as part of the island for all the way they'd get on her before the others came running. It would be madness to break weeks of good behaviour for an abortive attempt that could only end in them all working the ship to Port Arthur in handcuffs. No, there must be no chances taken. Better no attempt at all than one where there was a possibility of failure.

And it had been daft to throw that paintbrush away in a fit of temper. As Barker's mind came back to its normal cold methodical state, he looked round. Nobody, luckily, had observed him. There was but the one sentry ashore and he, surprisingly enough, was in his shirt-sleeves, sitting in the shade with his musket across his knees, idly watching the men who were battening down the hatch-covers on the hold. Barker moved into the line of men.

Shiers, next to him, used the convict ventriloquial trick of

43

speaking without moving his lips. 'Redcoats seem to be slackening the reins, John. When's the time? Tonight?'

'No. We need a wind.' Barker busied himself with a wedge.

'But we sail tomorrow, man.' Shiers paused, wiping his chest with his shirt as he watched Barker. James Lesley and the one-eyed convict Porter unobtrusively closed in. Shiers said as he began work again, 'If we take the ship at sea we must either murder the others or take 'em wi' us. So it must be tonight.'

'Tonight, did you say?' whispered the soft West Country voice of James Lesley. 'Well, I'm game, for one. I'll pass the word.'

'No.' Barker could feel the thing getting out of hand. 'The arms are to be locked away, out of our reach. I heard Taw telling Dearman.'

'Couldn't be better.' Lesley grinned ferociously. 'If they're unarmed, we'll have no trouble. We have a pistol and our bare hands. We can get knives. What more do we need?'

'The fact is, mates,' said Barker, 'we may have to think again.'

'Think again?' Lesley looked round. Tait had his back to them as he watched Charles Lyon and his escort coming down from the gaol. 'What kind of talk's that?'

'While you're using your knives and bare hands on the men on deck the others will have you at their mercy. Besides,' said Barker craftily, 'Will here made me promise there'd be no murder done.'

'But I made no such promise.' Lesley's mouth was twisted with disappointed rage. 'You snivelling little bastard, Barker, you're backing down.'

'John's right,' said Shiers. 'We must take t' muskets from 'em and do 'em no injury.'

'But that's bloody impossible,' said Porter quietly. All over, he thought bitterly, before it had even begun.

'Of course it's impossible.' Lesley raised his voice. 'By God, Barker, you'll pay for this. Raising our hopes with all that talk of Liberty Men, and now . . .'

44

'That'll do!' Tait swung round sharply. 'Enough of that whispering there. You men'll have to learn to hold your tongues when you get to Port Arthur. Swab down the deck and clean up this farmyard. Look lively, now!'

'I'll tell you this.' Lesley's voice was so quiet that Barker could only just hear the venom in it. 'If you back down now, you'll never live to see Port Arthur. So you'd better think of a way of escape, and quickly, too, because for you, mate, it's liberty or death right enough.'

4

They sailed at eleven in the morning on the following day. There was, as Taw had said, no telling what the weather would do in that part of the world, and the heat of the previous day had changed to a light, cool sou'-westerly, with flotillas of small clouds spreading their white sails to it. As the lines came in, David Hoy stood on the quarter-deck, the pain in his back temporarily forgotten as he looked at the settlement for the last time. A cloud-shadow that had darkened the central range of buildings from the commandant's quarters to the guard-house slid away to the north-east, leaving them sparkling white in the sun. That profligate poet fellow, Hoy thought, who died in Greece — Byron, that was the one — would have made much of a thing like that. The age of darkness giving way to the light of reason, and similar romantic nonsense.

Taw's laconic orders were relayed in a brick staccato by Tait. The helm click-click-clicked as the helmsman spun it starboard and a swiftly-widening strip of eddying water appeared between the *Frederick*'s hull and the wharf.

None the less, Hoy reflected, it was slightly eerie to think that the island was once again as devoid of human life as it had been before Captain James Kelly had discovered it nine-teen years previously and named it after Sarah Birch, the wife of his employer. It was strange to see no flag flying from the staff at the northern end of the island; to look for men walking among the buildings and to see none. After all these years of labour during which no beast of burden other than man had been allowed on the island — years of erecting buildings, laying out roads, setting out garden plots — this was once again a desert island. Now nature would slowly but surely obliterate the work of man so that one day a visitor — a historian, perhaps — might come searching among the trees and ferns and bushes that would swallow up those white-painted build-ings and he would find far less than had been found at Pompeii.

It had all been for nothing.

No. Not entirely for nothing. Hoy searched for the ship-wright's workshop and the master-shipwright's house, dwindl-ing and indistinct already, where he had spent the last ten years of his life. There were fifteen vessels afloat in the waters of Van Diemen's Land and New South Wales to prove it had not all been in vain. Cutters and brigs and schooners with sweet, mellifluous names — *Charlotte, Isabella, Adelaide* — and the 225-ton barque *William IV*, the biggest he'd built. And this one, the *Frederick* — Hoy turned his back on the settlement and stared up at the bellying canvas — was the best work he'd ever done. Taw, seizing the chance to try out his ship and his crew, was crowding on every sail he had from jibs to spanker in the light breeze and the brig, leaning to star-board, was slicing through the purple water like a dolphin. Hoy caught the eye of the seaman-convict John Jones at the helm.

'She runs well, eh?' he said, smiling.

In the catarrhal accent of his native Liverpool, Jones said, 'Aye, sir. She does that.' He grinned back. A small, swarthy man, branded with the badge of his profession, a mermaid and compass rose tattooed on the inside of his left arm and a sailor embracing a woman on his right, he was, at forty-two, the oldest of the convicts. He and his fellow-mariner John Fare had arrived in Van Diemen's Land together aboard the *Enchantress* transport the previous July and had done less time in the Colony than any of the others. They had been sent to Macquarie Harbour as seamen, not as hard-case convicts. Fare had only one entry in his convict record, for drunkenness. Jones had a completely clean sheet, the only one in the settlement, although, like Barker, he'd served five years in Bermuda.

Hoy said, 'She'll run still better when she tastes the Southern Ocean under her keel, mark my words. You could sail her to China without a care in the world.'

Jones's face closed up. 'Aye, sir,' he said flatly.

He stared woodenly ahead. It was the same sullen, empty look, Hoy remembered, that most of the prisoners had worn since — when? Last evening, to be sure. During the last few weeks they'd worked cheerfully and well, with James Porter singing his endless repertoire of Cockney ballads; even the hard cases, Lesley and Russen, dancing an impromptu jig one evening while the others had sat round clapping out the rhythm and bawling a bawdy ditty about a parson in Hobart Town. Now, all of a sudden, they'd closed in on themselves, performing their duty but no more. He'd even caught a glance of open hostility from one or two of them. Only his servant, William Nicholls, and Joseph MacFarlane had remained talkative and in good spirits.

It was, Hoy reasoned, because the picnic days of the fitting-out were over and they were filled with fears of the unknown. Foolishness, of course, since Port Arthur, as all the world knew, was to be a model prison where His Excellency the Lieutenant-Governor, acting through Captain O'Hara Booth, desired only to give the convicts a chance to earn good treatment — to train them, in fact, to take a useful place in society when released. There had, certainly, been a stringent régime at Macquarie Harbour. In a camp for incorrigibles, what else was to be expected? But those days were over. There was a new attitude abroad in England; a reformed House of Commons, with Althorp's Factory Act and the Act for the Abolition of Slavery passed only last August. As for Port Arthur, there was even talk that Captain Booth planned to abolish flogging and that, in one of the best-built churches in the Colony, the convicts would be taught the precepts of a godly way of life. No, Jones and the others would be far better off where they were going than was the average farm labourer back in England.

Bastard, Jones thought, as Hoy went below to have his back rubbed with liniment. We could sail the brig to China, depend on it, if that long-nosed little Warrington swab had come up to the mark. In the fo'c'sle the night before, while Nicholls was serving Hoy's supper and MacFarlane was on deck with his crony Gathersole, there'd been a move afoot to rush the sentries and damn the consequences. But then there'd been a hastily-suppressed brawl between Shiers and Lesley concerning the cutting of throats, and a general argument about who should be leader. It had all come to nought. They needed Barker, that was the devil of it, needed his clever, scheming brain. Nobody else, not even the seamen, understood enough of the art of navigation to take them clear of the fast frigates of the Royal Navy that controlled the oceans of the world.

Jones stared gloomily at the sun striking sparks off the water, at the grey-green of the bush three miles to port and four to starboard, at the silver gulls planing lazily across the *Frederick*'s jutting bowsprit. Well, he wouldn't be in John Barker's shoes, that was for certain. Lesley and Russen had sworn to stun him and slip him over the side the night before they berthed at Port Arthur, and they'd do it, too.

'What are you about, Jones?' snapped Taw, appearing with a suddenness that almost made the seaman let go the helm. 'Watch your blasted course, damn you.'

The shoreline came in to meet them as the shadows of the masts shortened and lengthened again, and they passed through Hell's Gates to drop anchor outside the Harbour at three in the afternoon. North and south, the sea creamed gently on the rocky beaches of a shallow bay where navy-blue-and-white oyster-catchers whistled mournfully and dug their scarlet bills into the sand for worms and molluscs. Taw's weatherboard house, the Pilot's Establishment, overlooked the bay in a patch of ground wrested from the bush and cultivated by convict labour.

Taw said, as the *Frederick* swung placidly at her anchor, 'Mr Hoy, we'll go ashore, if you please, wi' four men. There's potatoes in my garden that we could well do wi' on the voyage. If you will oversee the digging of them, I'll fetch my belongings from the house. Mr Tait, lower the jollyboat.'

There was no great competition among the convicts to spend the afternoon forking potatoes while everybody else stood easy. Tait picked four non-seamen; Russen, Shiers, Barker and John Dady, a former bricklayer from Middlesex who had been transported for stealing a handkerchief and whose convict record in the Colony included the odd offence of 'having in his possession a frock and a pair of stockings belonging to Mrs Cecil and being unable to give a satisfactory account of the same'. Later, he'd graduated to stealing trousers and received fifty lashes and three months' chain-gang. He had absconded four times previously.

As the four prisoners waited in the jollyboat for Taw and Hoy to descend the ladder, Tait said quietly to the captain, 'A word with you, sir?'

'Aye.' Taw stood with a hand on the rail. 'What is it?'

'I think it my duty to tell you that the prisoners are behaving somewhat strange, sir.'

'Strange?' Taw stared at him. 'In what way? If they're shirking their duty, by God, report the first culprit to me and —'

'No, sir. They work well enough, but —' Tait hesitated. 'They're aye whispering together. And there was some disturbance in the fo'c'sle last night that stopped almost as soon as it had begun. Nobody'll go near John Barker — it's as if he has the pest. And —'

'Barker's got no friends. A queer fellow — thinks too much. And these degenerate bastards are always fighting and whispering together.' Taw almost added, 'As you yourself should know, having been one yourself,' but he managed to hold his tongue. These bloody free men, he thought. Always trying to curry favour. Aloud he said shortly, 'Nothing strange about that.' He went over the side.

Hoy, preparing to follow him, said reassuringly, 'Tis the thought of Port Arthur, Mr Tait, that oppresses their spirits somewhat. I know some of these men well; Shiers and Cheshire have worked with me for years. They mean no harm.'

'Aye, aye, sir.' Tait, joined by Joseph MacFarlane who, equipped with fishing tackle, was going to try his luck over the stern, watched as the four prisoners splashed the jollyboat unhandily to the beach. They dragged the boat up a little way, then the six men went up to the house. Taw and Hoy disappeared inside; the four convicts went round the back and reappeared a moment later carrying forks and sacks. As they began to dig, the sun went in. Tait glanced up. The blue sky was giving way to an overcast spreading in from the sea.

The jollyboat returned at four-thirty, laden with sacks, a wooden box and some stone jars that Taw had brought from his house. The oarsmen, tired and buffeted by the strong breeze that had sprung up, crabbed and wallowed alongside the brig.

Tait said anxiously as Taw came aboard, 'Wind's veered nor'-west, sir. Going to blow hard.'

The captain grunted, staring at the sea, green now under the overcast, that was beginning to pile up in booming surf on the beach. He knew what Tait was thinking — that the chart bore an express warning against attempting to cross the Bar in a nor'-wester and that Taw had already run aground here once before.

'There's no call for alarm,' he said curtly. 'We'll not be crossing the Bar tonight. Get the boat unloaded and we'll run back into the Harbour.' He looked down at the tangle of oars as Shiers and Russen fended off from the brig while Dady, staggering, tried to lift the wooden box. Barker, his face pea-green, was sitting in the sternsheets. 'And mind how you go wi' those things of mine. Drop 'em int' water and I'll drop you after 'em.'

By the time the boat was unloaded, the *Frederick* was kicking at her anchor and the nor'-wester was whistling shrilly in the rigging. Taw, scowling hideously, clawed the brig round gingerly while the jollyboat was still being hauled up in its davits. For a moment the ship hung with the wind in her teeth and the rock-fringed beach dangerously close. Then she came round and fled like a stag into the choppy, eddying waters of the Gates.

They sailed two miles down the Harbour to Wellington Heads on the western side of the channel and dropped anchor three hundred yards from the shore. The grey expanse of water was flecked with white caps and the scudding clouds seemed no higher than the ship's mainmast. But, protected by the two-hundred-and-fifty-foot headland, the brig lay snug and secure in the rain-squalls that flattened the small waves as they ran before the wind.

Taw, looking like a man who had been reprieved from the gallows, wrote in his log: '12th January 1834. Sailed from the Settlement this Day with a light SW Wind which, on our attempting the Bar, shifted NW with a heavy Surf. I therefore gave Orders that we should run for Wellington Heads, where we secured the Ship and set an Anchor Watch at 6:30 p.m.'

In the grey half-light, Barker cowered miserably in the lee of the whaleboat, his mess-tin in his hand. The rain had dripped into his stew, turning it into a greasy, waterlogged slop that revolted a stomach already queasy from his afternoon's sea-sickness. He was cold, his clothes were soaked and, worst of all, Tait, hoping for more plugs of nigger-head, had given him the anchor watch with Lesley and Russen. But Barker had no more tobacco. And now Lesley and Russen were in the fo'c'sle with the others, eating the fresh schnapper and gurnet that Joseph MacFarlane had caught that afternoon. Barker prayed they'd stay there.

He was desperately afraid. The hideous problem that confronted him coupled with the nausea in his stomach had paralyzed his mind and body almost to the point of catalepsy. All he wanted to do was hide, keep absolutely still, pretend he didn't exist. For, above all things, Barker was terrified of physical violence to his own person. A year after arriving in Van Diemen's Land, he'd been committed for trial on the charge of receiving a gold watch, knowing it to be stolen. He'd spent three sleepless weeks before the trial, expecting to be flogged, and he'd almost swooned with relief when they'd sentenced him to fourteen years at Macquarie Harbour. If his plan to take the *Frederick* had gone forward, he would have provided the brain only; the mere thought of taking a musket ball in the chest — the bone splintering under the impact of the ounce of lead, the ruptured arteries pumping out his life — was enough to bring him out in a cold sweat. No, if there had been any fighting to be done, Shiers and the others would have had to take the risks.

But now, with a nightmare logic that he of all people could follow only too well, there were no risks — only certainties. On the one side, a futile scuffle with men whose weapons were ready to hand and who, for their own survival, would use them unhesitatingly. On the other, a blow on the head and the black waters of the Southern Ocean in his lungs and the long slide down to . . . He shuddered. Lesley and Russen would do it, he knew. They'd sworn so to the others. An appeal to the captain would be useless; Taw was under the delusion that no dog dared bark while he was in command and, in any case, any such appeal would result in Barker's being charged with conspiring to form a mutiny. Besides, in his two years at the Harbour, Barker had seen some of the things that happened to convicts who peached on their mates. If he stole a boat — assuming he could get it into the water alone — he'd die in the bush. He was trapped. Whichever way he looked, death stared him in the face.

'Well, damn me if it isn't Admiral Sir Johnny Barker!' The voice he least wanted to hear cut across his misery like a lash. Lesley, hands on hips, stood grinning wickedly at him. He said, his Somerset drawl deceptively soft and friendly, 'What be you doing out 'ere all on your lonesome?'

'He'll be having a bit of a think, I'd say.' Benjamin Russen eyed Barker malevolently. 'About how sorely he's disappointed his true comrades and how he plans to make amends.'

'To be sure.' Lesley nodded sagely. 'And he always thinks best with a plate of cold stew in his hand, don't he?' He flipped the mess-tin, jerking a gobbet of soggy meat and gravy down the front of Barker's shirt. 'Well, and have you thought of anything yet, my bucko?'

'Nah,' said Russen contemptuously. 'And he won't, neither. So let's put him over the side now, Jim, and have done.'

'No!' Barker shrank back against the butt of the mainmast, wiping the mess off his clothes with his fingers and looking round desperately for the sentries he'd planned to murder. But all four soldiers were obeying to the letter Taw's order to be easy and were sitting snugly in the half-deck, playing cards. 'I'll think of something, I swear it. On the voyage, maybe. After all,' he improvised hurriedly, 'we need Taw to take us across the Bar.'

'You're lying.' Lesley leaned a hand on the mainmast so that his face was inches away from Barker's. 'You know as well as I do that Lyon and Porter were the pilot's crew and could take us out better'n Taw himself. So, either here in the Harbour or out on the open sea, you'll have to come up with some scheme, my flash spark, or — '

'John Barker?' Joseph MacFarlane appeared out of the gathering gloom carrying a tin plate. 'I've brought you — ' He broke off, his wizened face frowning as Lesley and Russen brushed past him and made for the fo'c'sle. 'Is anything amiss?'

54

'No.' Barker checked an impulse to laugh hysterically. 'No, all's well. Never better.'

'Well, I don't know for why the others should treat you so bad, and 'tis no affair of mine. So I've brought you some fried schnapper I kept back. It seemed a fair shame you should be denied it. 'Tis hot and fresh-cooked.' He offered the tin.

'I haven't the stomach for it, Joe, and that's a fact.' Barker eyed the golden-brown, still-sizzling piece of fish with revulsion. 'But thankee none the less.' Anxious for company in case the other two returned he added, 'Caught it this afternoon outside the Gates, didn't you?'

'Aye, over the stern.' The little Scot nodded, grinning proudly. 'I just dropped ma line in, and there 'twas. The seas abound wi' fish hereabouts.'

'And in the Harbour?' At the back of Barker's fear-driven brain the merest flicker of an idea began to form. A light in the darkness that could never burst into flame, but when everything else was hopeless . . . 'You've fished here, too?'

'That I have — an' been well rewarded for ma pains. I'll have ma line out again the morn, you'll see.'

'But we sail tomorrow. As soon as the gale abates.'

'It won't abate in a hurry. A nor'-wester's the terror of this coast and Taw willna sail until it's quite blown away. So I'll be hanging over the stern again first thing tomorrow, mark my words.'

The small spark caught in Barker's mind.

'A pity,' he said, his fear and queasy stomach forgotten, 'you couldn't borrow a boat.'

'A boat?' MacFarlane twisted his skinny neck to stare up at Barker. 'Are you crazed, mon? I'd never be allowed a boat. Taw'd think I was planning to abscond.'

'You're right there.' Barker shrugged. 'To take a boat would mean taking a redcoat along with you, of course. 'Twas merely an idle thought, Joe.'

'Aye,' said MacFarlane absently. 'Aye, just a thought.'

55

Barker could have laughed aloud at the images that were flitting through the Scotsman's mind. A boating trip . . . some food and drink, maybe . . . a few hours' fishing, like a free man, away from the ship . . . with a friend — who also happened to be a redcoat . . . 'Well, now, I'm truly sorry you canna eat the schnapper. Maybe Private Gathersole might like a second helping. I'll awa' and see.' He hurried aft to the half-deck.

The spark had blossomed into flame, clear and bright. Barker smiled his twisted smile and rubbed his nose for the first time in two days. A very pleasant sport, fishing.

All you needed was the right bait.

5

Detached, unruffled and caring nothing for the two-legged insects that brawled and swam on its surface, the Harbour slept under the quiet stars. The moon was down and, to the north, the constellation Crux flew like a jewelled kite against the mazarine velvet of space. To the east, where the mountain ranges were outlined against a pearl-grey luminescence, the five visible stars of Ophiucus were already beginning to fade. The shoreline ringed the Harbour like a wall; solid, impenetrable and forbidding. From somewhere, a brown owl, a boo-book, called plaintively to its mate, and a wallaby that was drinking at the freshwater stream south of Wellington Heads lifted its nose, rotated its ears, sniffed, then turned and lolloped uphill, crashing noisily through the dense scrub.

Private Gathersole jumped and peered at the shore.

'Corporal!' he whispered. 'There's somebody there. Blackfellows!'

Corporal Dearman snorted.

'Blackfellows my arse. That'll be a kangaroo, depend on it. Or one of those creatures like badgers — wombats, I think they calls 'em. Natives wouldn't behave so. Don't you recall the campaign the regiment conducted against 'em in the spring of '30? They're silent, Private Gathersole. Silent, that's what they are. And black. So you don't neither hear nor see 'em when they creeps up on yer, all black and silent, and rams one o' their barbed spears into your belly.'

'Gawd!' Gathersole shuddered, staring out across the dark water where the stars were reflected palely like flecks of dying phosphorescence. 'I hate this place. No human soul except those black devils between us and Hobart Town an' nothing but miles of forests and rivers and lakes. I hear tell there's wolves in those forests, too, wi' stripes like tigers. An' deadly snakes an' — '

'Never you worry about them,' said Dearman. 'We're a-going to sail to Hobart Town, ain't we? Not march. So just give me a fill of baccy, Private Gathersole, and I'll have a pipe afore we wakes Kent and Gillespie.'

The greyness in the east was tinged with saffron now, and the first sleepy bird calls came across the water. It was the dawn of a new day — Monday. Monday the thirteenth of January 1834.

Gathersole watched Dearman stuffing tobacco into his pipe.

'I wish we'd gone to India with the regiment,' he said wistfully. 'Instead o' being put to serve here with a lot of cut-throat convicts.'

Dearman shook his head, puffing as his pipe caught.

''Tis our duty to form a reliable rear-guard. Colour-Sergeant said as much. Besides,' he added consolingly, ''tis pleasant enough under Captain Taw. No drills. No marches. No parades. A prime and plummy life, Private Gathersole, compared wi' garrison duty in India.'

'Aye, Corporal. You're right, no doubt.' Gathersole paused, wondering if it was a good time to advance a project he had in mind. 'Corporal,' he said hesitantly. 'Joseph MacFarlane says there's good fishing to be had hereabouts. Would we be permitted the use of a boat, d'you think?'

'Fishing?' Dearman grunted derisively. 'No hope of that,

58

Private Gathersole. This is no pleasure cruise, you know. Besides, we sail today.' He jerked his pipe at the Harbour. 'See. Water's as unruffled as a nun's bedsheet.'

'Joseph MacFarlane says that the surf persists long after a nor'-wester. He says we'll be here all day and most likely sail in the evening.' He paused again. When Dearman said nothing he went on slyly, 'But 'twas foolish of me to hint at it. Your standing with Captain Taw would not be sufficient for the request of a boat, so — '

'Captain Taw and me,' said Dearman coldly, 'are on excellent terms. He commands the ship; I command the military. Damn me, if I wished to ask for the use of a boat, I'd ask. I don't fear him, you know.'

'Of course you don't, Corporal,' said Gathersole humbly. 'But 'twould take a power of persuasion, I don't doubt, to — '

'Persuasion? A man-to-man request, nothing more. Why, I've a mind to do it — and to spend a day angling myself. I'll say to him, "Sir, I'd be obliged for the loan of a ship's boat for an hour or two," and he'd say to me — '

'Damnation seize us all, who's on watch?' Taw's head, his bushy grey hair on end, popped up like that of an elderly Punchinello above the roof of his cabin deck-housing. 'Corporal Dearman, is that you? Be so good as to rouse Mr Tait.'

'Yessir.' Dearman, thrown into confusion, snapped to attention out of force of habit, hiding his pipe behind his back. 'Private Gathersole, I hands over the guard to you while I — '

'The day's half gone already, blast it,' snarled Taw. 'Never mind your toy-soldier tom-foolery. Just fetch me the bloody — Ah, Mr Tait, there you are.' The mate, aroused by the stamping and shouting, had appeared at the fo'c'sle hatchway. 'I want the whaleboat lowered and a boat's crew wi' a lead-line to sound the Bar.'

'Now, sir?' Tait glanced at the pink-flushed sky and the shoreline that was rapidly taking on definition.

'Let the men have their breakfast first. I'll be ready in half an hour.'

Tait stuck his head into the fo'c'sle. 'All hands on deck! Come on, look sharp! Jones, Porter, Lyon and Fare — you are to be boat's crew to sound the Bar. Cheshire, get below and give us breakfast. The rest of you, bear a hand to lower the whaleboat. Lively, now!'

Grumbling and yawning, they swung out the heavy, fourteen-foot whaleboat and rigged a ladder on the port side while Tait prepared the lead sinker with its line, marked in fathoms, that would find the depth of water in the treacherous channel outside the Gates. Taw was obviously not going to risk another grounding. Wearing a coat and hat against the morning chill, he went over the side and the whaleboat, expertly handled, set off on its two-mile trip to the Bar.

By the time it returned at ten o'clock, the sun had dried the deck and the woodwork of the rail was already warm to the touch. Taw, perspiring vigorously, came aboard carrying his hat and coat. He said, as Tait hurried forward, 'We'll not sail this day. Summon all hands, if you please, and secure the whaleboat alongside.'

He went below to put on a dry shirt. The prisoners lined up loosely, facing aft, with the four soldiers behind them. Tait stood by the starboard rail with Hoy, who was warming his back in the hot sunlight.

Taw, unshaven but with a clean shirt and his hair brushed, came on deck and stood beside Hoy so that the sun was behind him and shining into the faces of his audience. He put his hands behind his back and cleared his throat. 'Now, attend, you men. As some of you may know, a nor'-wester is no light matter on this coast, bringing as it does a heavy surf which is slow to abate. Therefore, 'tis far too dangerous to attempt the Bar at present and we must delay our departure until this evening; happen, even until tomorrow.'

'What did I tell you?' whispered MacFarlane to Barker.

'Stop that damned shouting there!' roared Taw. He glared, outraged, then lowered his voice again. 'In the meantime, those prisoners who have dirty clothing may go ashore to

60

wash it in yon stream after you've had your dinners. How many wish to do so?'

Barker said loudly, 'All of us, Captain. And thankee for the privilege.'

Heads turned to stare at him. It was the first time he'd spoken up since they'd left the settlement.

Taw said, surprised, 'All of you? Hands up those who have clothes to wash.'

There was a brief pause, then James Lesley said, 'We all have.' His hand went up. 'Don't we, lads?'

'Aye, that we do!'

Every prisoner except Joseph MacFarlane raised his hand. The sullen faces relaxed into grins. Johnny Barker had come up to the mark in prime style after all. He had something in that brain-box of his, depend on it. Aye, they'd go, even though washing clothes was extra work and a waste of time at that, since they'd only get dirty again sooner or later.

'Very well.' Taw gazed at his crew benignly. By God, it just showed what could be done wi' a gang of evil, perverted wharf-rats if you handled them properly. They knew he didn't want his ship cluttered up wi' their bugs, lice and filth. They wanted to be clean to please him. Eh, they were good lads. He might even permit one of them to give his own washing a bit of a rub. 'Corporal Dearman! Send two of your men ashore with the prisoners. I want them back on board by four o'clock. Carry on, Mr Tait.'

The convicts dispersed, laughing and talking excitedly. An object lesson, thought Hoy, in the state of mind brought about by a cleanly life. The men were obviously delighted at the prospect of having clean clothes to wear. Yes, cleanliness is indeed next to godliness. None the less —

'Nicholls,' he called. 'I fear I cannot spare you this afternoon. I require you to make up some more unguent for my back.'

Nicholls nodded obsequiously. 'Certainly, Mr Hoy.' He could see a good life opening up ahead if he played his cards right. Hoy might be a damned old woman in everything but shipbuilding, but there'd be rich pickings and easy days for the man who was his servant at Port Arthur. 'I'll stay aboard and prepare something special for your dinner.'

Corporal Dearman, sweating with apprehension, approached Taw as the Captain made for his cabin. 'Captain, sir. If I might be favoured — I wanted to ask — Indeed, sir, 'tis a fine day, and — '

'I know it's a fine day,' snapped Taw impatiently. 'What the devil do you tell me that for?'

'Sir, I'd be much in your debt if — ' Dearman gulped and took the plunge. 'I want to ask the use of a boat. To go a-fishing.'

'Fishing?' Taw's bristly eyebrows shot up. So did his voice as he said, 'You want one of my boats to — ?' He paused, about to tell Dearman he'd see him in hell first. It was, indeed, a fine day and he could see his crew smiling and slapping one another on the back and there'd be no harm in — 'Well, damme, why not? Eh?'

'The prisoners'll all be ashore,' said Dearman rapidly, 'with Privates Kent and Gillespie. I'll take Private Gathersole and Joseph MacFarlane if you — '

'Why not?' said Taw again. 'Take the jollyboat, Corporal, and good angling to you. On condition that I have my pick of your catch, of course. You'll not go beyond the point there, and you'll return by four.'

'Why, thankee kindly, sir.' Dearman gasped with gratification. This would show Private Gathersole the kind of standing he had with the captain. 'Indeed, sir, back by four and not beyond the point.' He saluted and rushed off, anxious to give Kent and Gillespie the boring task of supervising the laundry before Taw changed his mind.

In the atmosphere of a Sunday school outing, the ten convicts shinned down the ladder and into the boat with the two soldiers. On the brig's afterdeck, Tait was assisting Dearman, MacFarlane and Gathersole to lower the jollyboat. Barker said softly to Shiers as they pulled for the shore, 'Mark that, Will. It'll be the salvation of us.'

'What? This afternoon? Tha'rt mad, John. We'd — '

'Not this afternoon.' Barker pulled at his oar. 'This afternoon we'll do our washing and be as good as gold.' He grinned. 'For the last time, Will.'

They pulled the boat ashore under a low bluff and wandered, laughing and skylarking, to the stream. Barker watched the sentries. Kent stood on one side of the group of kneeling convicts, Gillespie on the other.

Barker said loudly, 'Tis a good thing the old days are over, eh, lads?'

'Old days?' James Porter looked up from the shirt he was dunking. 'How so, John?'

'Why, merely that this puts me in mind of the murder of a constable that took place at the settlement in '23. When a gang of ten prisoners took him and held his head under water until he drowned.' He looked up at Kent and smiled amicably. 'A good thing, I say, that times has changed, eh, Private Kent, and all the old hatreds is dead and gone?'

'Tis so indeed.' Kent looked him straight in the eye. But, all the same, a few minutes later he strolled casually across to Gillespie and the two soldiers walked off to sit on the gunwale of the whaleboat and light their pipes in the sun.

'Well done, John.' Lesley chuckled. 'You've cleared the decks a treat. Now, what's the plan?'

'Continue working,' said Barker sharply as the men further along the stream stood up and began to crowd him. 'Stay close enough to hear, but look busy. And the plan's simple enough and should satisfy even you, Will Shiers, but it depends on one thing — that MacFarlane should take the redcoats fishing again this evening, after supper.'

Benjamin Russen said menacingly, 'And suppose he won't? Or is not allowed?'

'Then it's all off — for the time being,' Barker added hurriedly as Lesley's grin changed to a scowl. 'Any plan I put forward has to work. Otherwise I'll none of it.'

'That makes sense,' said Jones quietly. 'Stop bullying him, you two, and let him speak.' To Barker he said, 'So it's to be tonight, then?'

'Aye.' Barker nodded. 'And another thing — once we go back on board, I'll want you all to obey me without hesitation. My way can't fail if you'll all do exactly as you're bid. Will you do that?'

'They will.' Jones looked at his friends Fare and Dady. 'We'll see to that.'

'James Porter, I'll want you to chirp a ballad or two, so be ready. Summat lively, summat as we haven't heard afore.'

'You can take your pick,' said Porter. 'There's "Fanny my Queen from Top to Toe" — I been saving that one. Or there's — '

' "Fanny" should serve our purpose.'

'She'd serve mine,' said Charles Lyon. There was a roar of laughter.

Barker frowned. 'But, listen, lads. When Porter's well into — '

'Fanny or the ballad?' asked Lyon innocently. The others shrieked and somebody pushed Lyon into the stream.

'Will you listen?' hissed Barker. 'Or do you want the bloody redcoats back?' When the sniggers had subsided he said coldly, 'Now just get one thing straight. Once we start this, we go right on to the finish with no skylarking, understand?' He looked at Lyon. 'There'll be no more jests until we hold the *Frederick*. No more back answers to Captain Taw or me or anybody. Understand?'

Lyon, dripping wet, nodded. 'I was only having a wee bit o' fun, John. There's no need — '

'There's every bloody need. Get it into your thick skull that this is a hanging matter we're about, not a bit o' fun.' Barker looked round. 'Who can handle a musket?'

Several hands went up. Barker rubbed his nose, considering.

He needed at least two executioners — men who would kill without question. 'James Lesley and Benjamin Russen are to have muskets.' They'd shoot each other if he made it worth their while. Jones, Dady, Fare, Lyon and Porter would be needed to handle the ship. 'And Will Cheshire.' A weak lad, the youngest of the convicts, and one who'd do as he was told without thought of the consequences. Shiers would threaten but never fire. 'Will, you can have my pistol.' Barker himself would have the fourth musket for his own protection.

Shiers wrung out a pair of trousers thoughtfully. 'What happens to the nine when we've overcome them?'

Barker was expecting that. 'We've talked long enough. Now let's act for our liberty. Eh, lads?'

There was a growl of approval; but not, Barker noted, from Shiers, nor from John Jones and his pals Dady and Fare.

It could be that they might have to be got rid of, too, in the long run.

The jollyboat was being swung up into its davits as the convicts, quieter now, returned on board. Barker nudged Porter and Lesley and said to Dearman, 'A good catch, Corporal?'

Dearman looked depressed. 'A bloody poor one. And the captain'll take the best of it.'

'Maybe you went at the wrong time of day?'

'That's what I told 'em.' MacFarlane looked triumphantly at the soldiers. 'But they wouldna listen. They put the blame on me and said I wanted only the boat trip. And me,' he said bitterly, 'as had to do all the rowing!'

'When is the best time for fishing in these waters?' asked Barker off-handedly.

'Evening.' MacFarlane's face turned from disappointment to piscatorial lust. He eyed the sunlit water, mentally stocking it with wriggling silver shapes that fought madly for his bait. 'A summer eve like this is going to be, ye'll have clouds of gnats and the like low on the water and bloody fish coming up so thick you could walk on 'em.'

'Maybe,' said Barker, 'you could go again?'

'We canna.' MacFarlane looked at the soldiers wistfully. 'Yon Taw would never permit it.'

'Why not?' asked Barker. 'He let you go once, didn't he?'

Lesley came in. 'He won't care, as long as the soldiers go too.'

'He's not such a bad old devil,' said Porter, 'if you treats him right.'

'Corporal can have him eating out of his hand,' said Gathersole admiringly.

Dearman coughed. 'Well, I don't deny Cap'n and me has an understanding. But to ask again, and so soon — '

'I don't see,' said Barker judicially, 'as you need to ask again. After all, you're provisioning the vessel, aren't you, and he won't want you to be running to him every five minutes wi' requests for boats. As a commanding officer, Corporal, you'll know that some decisions are left to responsible men.'

Dearman nodded doubtfully.

MacFarlane said, 'Aye, Barker's right, I'd say. Maybe he expects us to go. Maybe he'll be angry if we don't have a good catch for his breakfast.'

'Anyway,' said Barker gently, 'he'd never even miss you. The whaleboat's alongside. Why not borrow it for half an hour? After supper's over and the ship snugged down — '

'Could we, Corporal?' asked Gathersole. 'Afore we relieve Kent and Gillespie?'

Dearman hesitated. And was lost. 'Well, I don't see the harm in it.' After all, hadn't Taw himself told them to be easy? 'Not if we just goes as far as the point.'

MacFarlane danced a little jig. 'I'll go,' he said, 'and prepare some bait.'

At half-past six on that Monday evening, when the crew sat down to supper, the Harbour was like liquid gold. The sun struck straight through Hell's Gates from above the two small islands called Cap and Bonnet that lay in the channel, so that the trees and scrub on Wellington Heads on the brig's port side were already in twilight. The long, slowly-swinging shadows of the masts pointed across the water to the sand-flats where gulls stood watchfully with folded wings. In the fo'c'sle, nobody spoke. MacFarlane had started a story about salmon poaching in Scotland but had given up when nobody listened. Tait sat eating his stew, looking up at the others every now and then, a slight frown on his face as his eyes met ten other pairs that quickly switched away. Spoons scraped metal plates loudly in the silence and, on deck, the boots of Kent and Gillespie thumped like the slow beat of muffled drums as they strolled up and down. They heard Kent say, 'So I says to the old harlot, "If that's your best beer, may God save us from your worst," and she says to me . . .' His voice faded as the two soldiers moved aft.

Tait gave a belch that sounded like a pistol shot. He stood up, washed his plate and spoon in the bucket and took out a ship model he was working on. Everybody watched him. Barker said to himself, 'We should be talking. Skylarking. He'll suspect.' Aloud, he said to the mate, ''Tis taking shape well. What ship is it?' Not, he thought, that it matters a fig. You'll never finish it.

'A barque I sailed with once when I was a lad. She's — '

Gathersole stuck his head down the fo'c'sle hatch. 'Come, Joe, we're off. Do you have the bait?'

'Aye, that I do.' MacFarlane picked up a small sack and headed for the ladder.

Tait said, 'Where are you going?'

'Fishing. Wi' Corporal Dearman and Private Gathersole.'

'With the cap'n's permission?'

MacFarlane said evasively, 'Corporal's in charge.' He went out.

Tait worked on for a few more minutes. Then he put down his model and stood up. 'Phew, 'tis bloody airless in here. I'm going on deck.' He paused on the ladder, looking at them. 'You're a lively lot this evening, and no mistake. There'd be more cheer in the condemned cell at Newgate.'

When he'd gone Barker said softly, 'Where's Nicholls?'

'In the galley,' said Cheshire. He'd been biting his nails, Barker noticed. 'Preparing Taw and Hoy's suppers and eating one of his own.'

'Are Taw and Hoy drinking?'

Porter shook his head. 'Taw never does on board; not to excess. You'll not catch him befuddled, if that's what's in your mind.'

Barker went up the ladder and put his head out. Private Gillespie was standing with his back to him ten yards away. Kent was aft, talking to Tait. Barker turned back to the questioning faces.

'Now, lads, this is the time. When I go out, I want Lesley, Russen, Cheshire and Fare to come wi' me. Fare, you're to engage the mate in some seaman's matter. Russen and Lesley, you seize Private Kent. Will Cheshire stays wi' me. Now, Jamie Porter, strike up your song.'

Porter's stomach was in knots and he'd never felt less like singing. He cleared his throat and croaked:

> O Fanny my queen from top to toe,
> I loves to touch your hair-O,
> To stroke your brow so pale and white
> And to kiss your eyes so fair-O.

'For the love of God,' said Barker edgily, 'is that the loudest you can warble? It sounds like a frog in a fit. Louder, man, louder.'

Porter said, 'Chorus. All join in when you knows the words.' He bawled:

> O Fanny my queen from top to toe,
> There's nought I have denied you.
> And the only time I'd ever lie
> Would be in bed beside you.

Private Gillespie appeared in the hatchway, looking down. Porter sang, getting into his stride:

68

I'll kiss your pretty dimpled cheeks
And next your rosebud mouth.
My hand rests on your shoulder, love,
But 'tis headed further south.

Gillespic clumped down the ladder, grinning. He sat next to Shiers and joined in the chorus.

Porter went on, the song becoming bawdier as it methodically traversed the fascinating Fanny's anatomy. As it approached the promised land, Barker stood up and, still singing, he nodded matily to Gillespie and went up on deck. Kent was still aft on the port side, watching the receding whaleboat.

Fare came on deck and looked round. 'Where's the mate?'

Barker grinned, jerking a thumb over his shoulder. 'His bladder needs easing. He's in the forechains. Go and talk to him.'

Lesley and Russen came up in a bedlam of laughter and singing. Kent, attracted by the noise, turned and began to walk for'ard.

Barker said, 'Grab him and take him below. Then do the same with Tait. No killing, mind — not yet. Will Cheshire, as cook you're freer about the ship than most. Go into the half-deck and try your hand at the lock on the muskets.'

Cheshire hesitated. Then he swallowed. 'Aye, John.' He went aft, past Kent who glanced casually at him but said nothing.

So far, so good, Barker thought, rapidly running over his timetable in his mind. No risks taken, no rules broken, and yet every single enemy had been marked down for capture; they were all moving like puppets to his will. And now was the moment to cut their strings. He went down the ladder into the fo'c'sle as the chorus roared out again.

Shiers was sitting on the top deck of a two-tier bunk. Barker tapped him on the foot. Instantly, Shiers pulled out the pistol from under his blankets. He shoved it into Gillespie's face. 'One cry,' he said menacingly, 'and I blow tha head off.' The singing stopped in mid-line.

69

Gillespie, his mouth still open, went white with shock. Before he could move, he was seized and held down by Porter and Lyon. Barker said, 'You two, stay with him. The rest, come with me. In silence, now.'

On deck, Kent looked round for Gillespie, but he was nowhere to be seen. Kent went for'ard, puzzled. Lesley came out from behind the launch and moved into his path, crowding him. 'Go below, soldier,' he said, grinning wickedly. ''Tis a little cold out here on deck.'

Kent stepped back. 'Thankee,' he said guardedly, 'but I prefer to walk a little. I — ' Russen took him from behind and jammed a hand over his mouth. Lesley wrapped his arms round the soldier's body, almost shutting off his breath.

Men began pouring in barefoot silence out of the fo'c'sle. Barker said, 'Good. Take him below.' He looked round for Fare and the mate. The 63rd Regiment of Foot had been routed in less than a minute without a shot or a shout, and nobody as yet even knew of it.

Tait was coming back from the bows with Fare. They heard the convict say, '. . . able to cross the Bar tonight, Mr Tait?'

Tait shook his head, still buttoning his trousers. 'The surf's too heavy and there's still a westerly breeze outside the Gates. I don't doubt — '

William Shiers came forward and Tait stopped in his tracks when he saw the pistol. Russen came back on deck, followed by James Lesley who had armed himself with an axe.

Shiers said to Tait, 'Get below. Quietly now, or you're a dead man.'

Tait's mouth opened but nothing came out. He was shoved below. As he joined the soldiers, Lyon and Porter came on deck. From God knows where, the one-eyed convict had picked up a cutlass with the end broken off.

Lyon said, 'Close the hatch, Jamie, and stand on it. That'll keep the bastards down.'

'My God,' said Lesley softly. 'Look there, lads. Young Will's got the muskets.'

Cheshire, red-faced with excitement, came padding along the deck carrying the four Pattern 1802s. 'John, the bloody key was hanging on a nail. Twas as easy as kiss your arse.'

Barker grinned. 'Well done, lad.' He gave Russen a musket. 'James Lesley, you can put your axe away.'

'I can use both. The hatchet may be handy for smashing in the cabin door.'

Barker passed him a musket. He and Cheshire kept the others. Expertly, he checked the priming. 'Well, lads,' he said. 'Now let's go and nobble the captain.'

'Wait!' Shiers knew what was in Barker's mind; that the best way to deal with the two armed men in the cabin would be to shoot them through the hatchway before they could reach for their guns. 'Let me go. I know Hoy, so — '

'You'll botch it,' said Lesley contemptuously. 'I'll go.'

Damn Shiers' interference, Barker thought. But there was no time to argue. 'You can both go, but you'd best be quick about it.' He listened to the muffled thumps and shouts that came from the fo'c'sle. 'Quick, before the alarm's sounded.'

Shiers and Lesley ran aft. Barker looked down the channel to the south. In the golden glow of sunset, the whaleboat was lying off the point with her oars shipped. The three small figures sitting in her were paying no attention whatever to what was going on aboard the *Frederick*.

'I'm looking forward,' said Barker, 'to seeing Dearman's face when he comes back up the ladder.'

6

In the cramped, stuffy cabin aft, Taw and Hoy had finished supper. The captain was sitting behind his table with his shirt unbuttoned. Hoy, also in shirt-sleeves, sat on Taw's sea-chest close to the table. He was saying, 'The human spine is similar in many ways, Captain, to the keel of a ship in that it must be the strongest member. Now mine, alas, has been weak since birth. Even as a boy I suffered acutely, and my mother found that oil of camphor, rubbed in well, was the only real remedy.'

'Aye?' Taw stifled, but only just, a yawn. At this bloody rate, he thought, I'm going to know my way up and down David Hoy's backbone better than I know Macquarie Harbour. Why in the name of buggery couldn't I have had some congenial soul on board wi' me for this voyage? Somebody who could tell a yarn or two, somebody who —

'It must, I feel sure, be the damp airs of Van Diemen's Land that have aggravated my complaint. I remember once, in Hobart Town — '

I wonder, Taw thought, whether a good boot up the arse would help your complaint? By all the fiends in hell, a man shouldn't have to endure this. Not when he'd forsworn rum while on board. He said gruffly, 'A pleasant place, Hobart Town. Some damn fine women there in the streets.'

'Some excellent doctors, too,' said Hoy eagerly. 'One I know well in — '

There was a polite knock on the door and William Nicholls came down the companion. 'May I clear away, gentlemen?' he asked.

'Aye, do.' Taw leaned back in his chair, fighting off the temptation to drink himself into a stupor. 'What's that blasted caterwauling up for'ard?'

'The crew are singing, sir.' Nicholls started to collect the dirty plates. 'One of James Porter's ballads, I believe.'

'Singing, eh?' Taw grunted. 'Well, Mr Hoy, at least we seem to have a happy, contented ship. As far as pox-ridden gaolbirds go, ours aren't a bad lot. I find them civil, easy to control and full of respect for — '

The cabin door burst open. Shiers took the ladder in one jump, landing on the deck with his pistol levelled at Hoy. Lesley came down behind him with his hatchet in one hand and a musket in the other.

Shiers said, 'We've got the vessel. If you don't give yourselves up, I'll blow your brains out.'

Hoy stood up. 'William Shiers,' he said sternly. 'What is the meaning of this?'

'It's bloody mutiny, that's what it is!' Taw leapt to his feet as if he'd been stung. 'Why, you treacherous, blackguardly scupperscum, get out of my cabin!' He flung himself at James Lesley and seized the forty-two-inch-long musket barrel, trying to twist it out of the convict's grip.

Hoy shouted, 'Help! Corporal Dearman! Help!'

He knocked Shiers' pistol aside and the two of them struggled silently for the possession of it.

'Where's the bloody military, damn and blast them?'

Taw, purple in the face with rage and exertion, shoved Lesley back violently against the foot of the ladder. Nicholls, who had been cowering against the bulkhead with his hands full of dirty plates, dropped them with a crash and hung on to the arm that Lesley had raised to use his hatchet. Shiers, seeing Lesley in trouble, threw Hoy off and put the pistol to the back of Taw's head. Unfortunately, the captain threw his head back at that moment, nearly stunning himself on the muzzle of the gun. Benjamin Russen began to come down the ladder, his musket pointing downwards.

There were now six heaving, cursing men in a cabin that had been originally designed to hold one. At the foot of the ladder, nobody could move. Hoy, breathing hard, kicked down the plank partition between the cabin and the half-deck. 'Corporal Dearman!' he shouted again, peering through the gap he'd made. Lesley, with Nicholls hanging on grimly, managed to deliver a short chopping blow with the hatchet that caught Taw on the left side of the head. Russen, unwilling to fire in case he hit Lesley or Shiers, prodded downwards with the musket barrel and caught the unfortunate captain a glancing jab under the left eye. Then he retreated up the ladder.

'Give me elbow room,' he shouted to Lesley. 'I'll have the bugger's life in a minute.'

Lesley, with a savage lunge, threw Taw off balance, pushed Nicholls aside and went up on deck. Shiers bounded up after them.

Apart from Porter, who was holding down the fo'c'sle hatchway, the convicts were grouped round the skylight above the cabin. Barker was beside himself with fury.

'You bloody fools,' he hissed. 'To be overpowered by three unarmed men! What the hell are you about? Do you wish to ruin everything?'

'Shut your mouth,' snarled Russen, 'or I'll shut it for ever with this.' He jabbed at Barker with his musket. 'They was too quick for us, an' there was no bloody room to fire.'

Barker calmed himself with an effort and glanced at the sky. The sun had gone and the Harbour was cloaked in twilight. 'Very well. Will Cheshire, open up the hatch.'

Cheshire did so. 'Aye, there they are,' he said, peering down. He pushed the barrel of his musket through to hold the skylight open. Lesley, Russen and Barker levelled their weapons at the men below.

In the cabin, Taw had staggered back, breathing in short, wheezing gasps. He leaned on his table for a moment. Then he made for the ladder.

Hoy said, 'Captain! Those are armed men up there. You can't go on deck.'

'Can't? On my own ship?' The captain leaned against the ladder, panting. 'Aye well, maybe 'tis wise counsel. I don't seem to be as young as I was, David, and that's a fact.' He turned round slowly. 'It seems we must sell our lives as dearly as possible, eh? Where are your pistols?' He opened his chest, took out powder and ball, and began to load his musket. 'Fool that I am,' he muttered to himself, 'I should have had it ready.'

He looked up as the skylight was thrown open and the long barrels of one, then four muskets appeared, silhouetted against the evening sky. He heard a confused yelling from above and a voice shouted, 'Fire!'

Hoy was about to open his sea-chest. As he heard the shout he stepped back. There were two explosions, close together and deafening in the tiny cabin, and two plumes of acrid smoke jetted downwards. In front of Hoy, two splintered holes appeared as if by magic in the lid of his sea-chest as the heavy balls smashed into it. Nicholls, crouching in a corner, squeaked with fright and, on deck, there was a chorus of squawks, quacks and grunts from the animals' pens.

Shiers grabbed the back of Barker's shirt, pulling him away from the skylight. 'My God,' he said furiously. 'Do you intend to commit murder?'

Cheshire, white-faced and trembling, said, 'Not I, for one. I didn't fire, Will, my oath on it.'

Jones, Dady and Fare moved forward.

'If there's murder done,' said the man from Liverpool deliberately, 'you'll have to sail your ship, Johnny Barker, minus two seamen — and John Dady here. We'll none of it.'

'Jamie Porter and me are of the same mind,' said Lyon. 'We'll not see men butchered in cold blood. So that's another two seamen you'd be short of.'

'You're bluffing.' Barker looked at them contemptuously. 'You want to escape as much as the rest of us.'

'Not by murder,' said Shiers. 'It can be done without.' He shouted through the skylight, 'Captain Taw! Mr Hoy! You might as well come out and deliver yourselves up. We have the military held in the fo'c'sle.'

'Those blasted tin soldiers.' Taw cocked his musket and aimed it at the hatchway. 'Marching up and down wi' passwords and countersigns . . .'

'If you don't come up,' said Lesley viciously, 'you'll be shot.'

'And if you damage the quadrant or anything else belonging to the ship, we'll shoot you instantly,' added Barker. 'It is of no use contending against us. We have the military and everybody secured.'

Hoy had taken his pistols out of his chest but, when he began to load them, he found he had no ramrod. None the less, he called back, 'I have my pistols, and the captain his musket. We shall sell our lives as dearly as we can, and I'll shoot the next man who tries to put a musket through the skylight.'

Barker cursed under his breath. All had gone like a clock and now — stalemate. They can't come up and we can't go down.

'God preserve me from fools like you,' he said bitterly to the others. 'If you'd shot them while you had the chance, we'd have the vessel safe by now.'

''Tis easy for you to talk so,' said Lesley furiously. 'What have you done but give orders? You weren't down in the cabin risking your precious neck, I noticed.'

'Dearman must have heard the shots.' Jones, at the rail,

peered down the night-shadowed Harbour. 'We'll have him and his mates back any minute.'

'They're unarmed.' Barker wasn't worried about the three in the whaleboat. He was wondering whether he dared risk splitting his command by ordering the deaths of the three men in the cabin. Shiers and his damned scruples he could have dealt with, but now that five others had turned squeamish —

'It's getting dark,' Russen said impatiently. 'We'll be here all night and tomorrow, too.'

Cheshire said, 'Couldn't we smoke them out? Bring along the pitch-pot and lower it down?'

Hoy heard that. 'If you do, I'll shoot any man as he appears at the skylight.' It was, he knew quite well, too dark now to see anybody at the skylight at all. He paused. 'Listen, men. I've known some of you for several years, and you know me to be a man of my word. I will now declare before my God upon the Bible that, upon condition of your giving up the brig, I will not mention it when we reach headquarters, but will give you all good characters.'

Barker said contemptuously, 'We have the brig in our possession and we shall keep her. So it is needless for you to mention further about it, for 'tis liberty we require.'

'I don't think,' said Taw heavily, 'we'll get far on that tack, David. There's only two courses open to us. We either shoot it out wi' them — and it's one musket against four. Or we go up there and hope they don't shoot us.'

From above, they heard voices raised in argument.

Somebody said, 'Let's shoot the buggers instantly. They can't kill us all.' Then there was a confused shouting over which they heard Shiers call, 'Captain! Mr Hoy! I advise you to deliver yourselves up.'

'If we stay down here, they'll be forced to shoot us, you know.' Taw propped his musket against the bulkhead. 'Tait and the others as well. And we can't expect assistance from anybody, so it's of no use to play for time.'

'I agree. It seems pointless to resist further.' Hoy groped for his chest in the darkened cabin and put his pistols away. He called, 'Very well. We will surrender, if you are not disposed to injure us.'

'My life shall be the forfeit if we do.' There was a note of relief in Shiers' voice. 'We only want our liberty.'

Hoy climbed the ladder. When he was two steps from the top Russen snapped, 'Stand!'

Hoy squinted into the gloom. There was no moon but the night was full of stars and, after the darkness of the cabin, he found he could see reasonably well. Lesley and Russen both had muskets levelled at him.

He said, 'Do you intend to murder me, after all, in this cold-blooded manner?'

There was a pause that seemed to go on for a long time. Then Barker said, with obvious reluctance, 'No. But you must turn round and have your hands tied. John Fare, did you get that bit of cord?'

Fare, with a seaman's expertise, lashed Hoy's wrists together, then John Jones took his arm and led him to the quarter-deck. Porter came aft, swinging his cutlass piratically. 'Fo'c'sle's safe. I told 'em we'd blow their heads off if they showed them outside.'

'Captain Taw,' said Barker. 'Come up on deck.'

Taw stood on the after-deck while his hands were bound, the bitter thoughts running like acid through his mind. It was all one to him whether they shot him or not. He was finished, he knew, as far as government service was concerned. There'd be no plummy Pilot's job in Hobart Town now. Governor Arthur would never forgive a captain who let a gang of convicts take his ship. 'You and you alone will be in charge', Baylee had said. And he and he alone would have to take the blame for this. Suddenly, he felt very old and very tired. He said to Barker, putting up a hand to wipe the blood that was trickling down his cheek from the cut over his eye, 'Who is to be captain of the brig now you have her in your possession?'

78

'I am.' Barker's voice came exultantly through the darkness. 'And, with the assistance of the men, I can navigate round the world.'

Taw grunted sceptically. 'Learnt it all from a book, I suppose? Ah well, tha'll not get far. But that's your affair, eh?' He was shepherded over to the port side, opposite Hoy, as Nicholls was called up from the cabin.

'What do you intend to do with us?' asked Hoy.

'Put you ashore,' said Shiers. 'The weather is mild and there'll be a ship from Hobart Town or Launceston when 'tis known that the *Frederick*'s overdue. You'll come to no harm.'

'You'll leave us provisions?'

'To be sure. Is there anything in your boxes you require?'

'Our coats, if you will let us have them. And I should like some liniment for my back.'

Taw, in spite of his misery and the pain in his injured eye, smiled in the dark. Trust David to think of his bloody spine at a time like this. For a man who claimed to be almost a cripple, he'd put up a damned good fight in the cabin. He said, 'And I could do wi' one of my jars o' rum. In case it gets cold at night, tha knows.'

Barker was fidgeting with impatience. He said acidly to Shiers, 'If we'd known you were going to be so accommodating, we wouldn't have tied their hands. Now, if they're to go down the ladder, we'll have to untie them again.' He moved forward, the musket tucked under his arm. 'I'll take them below.'

Shiers untied the cords. 'I'll go with you.' He didn't trust Barker an inch. It would be easy to say Taw and Hoy had put up a struggle below and he'd had to kill them in self-defence. 'And Jamie Porter, you can come as well.'

Barker shrugged. He had no intention of committing the murders himself. There was another way, and plenty of time for it. 'One of you,' he said, 'had better fire a shot over the stern to recall the whaleboat. Dearman must be either deaf or asleep.' He stood back as the others went down to the cabin.

Taw lit his oil-lamp, put on his coat and rummaged in his chest, taking out a pair of shoes, two shirts and a pair of trousers. He picked up a half-gallon jar of rum. 'The log and ship's papers — I can have those, I suppose?'

'No.' Barker was on the ladder, covering them. He looked at Hoy who had taken down the pea-jacket from its hook and had opened his chest. 'What's that you have there?'

'My watch.'

Standing by the chest, Shiers saw that there were also a pocket compass and Hoy's pistols lying on the top of his clothes.

'Toss it over.' Barker examined the watch professionally. 'Not of the best quality, but 'twill keep time.'

There was the hollow, echoing report of a musket from on deck and a renewed farmyard chorus from the livestock. While Barker was looking at the watch, Shiers pushed the compass into Hoy's pocket.

The shipwright nodded an acknowledgment. To Barker he said, 'May I keep my pistols?'

Barker guffawed. 'Oh, to be sure. So that you may shoot us, eh? Take 'em, Will.' Shiers stuck the pair of silver-mounted pistols into his belt. 'Now get up on deck.' Swiftly, as Barker turned his back, Shiers wrapped a bottle of wine in a shirt and gave it to Hoy.

Lanterns had been lit and Hoy was able to see that Kent, Gillespie and Tait had been brought up from the fo'c'sle and were standing dejectedly near the mainmast, guarded by Cheshire with a musket. Porter stood by the gangway on the port side where the jollyboat was waiting at the foot of the ladder.

'Now,' said Barker, 'over the side with you.'

From the quarter-deck, John Fare called, 'I can hear the whaleboat approaching.'

Barker went to the side with his musket. Tait, Nicholls, the two soldiers and Hoy climbed down to the jollyboat. Taw went last, looking round his deck for the last time. As he went over the side, Porter looked at the captain's swollen eye and said, 'You're a resolute fellow, Captain. You put up a good fight below, I hear. Good luck to you.'

Taw said nothing. There was nothing left to say.

In the whaleboat, Dearman was sick with apprehension. Egged on by MacFarlane, he'd allowed the party to try one stretch of water after another until they were well south of the point when he'd heard the two musket shots that had echoed and rolled from side to side of the Harbour, frightening him almost as much as if the balls had passed close to his head. Then there'd been the lines to take in, and the gear to stow, and the rowing back, so that they'd been barely north of the point when the last shot had been fired. Now, as Barker peered out over the starlit water, he saw the dark blob of the whaleboat pulling towards the brig and about forty yards off her port beam.

'Come alongside,' he said. His voice carried clearly — only too clearly — to Dearman. 'We have the vessel and your weapons. The captain and the guard are our prisoners.'

The whaleboat slewed to a stop.

Gathersole said, horrified, 'My God, Corporal. What's to be done?'

'If you refuse to obey,' said Barker, 'we will fire upon your comrades instantly.'

Dearman sat stunned with shock. He could see it all — the table with the grim, accusing faces of the officers behind it, the escort standing on either side of him — and he could hear first the charge then the sentence being read. *Neglect of duty . . . absence without leave . . .* desertion, they might even call it. Why, that meant a firing squad . . . He fought down his panic. 'Pull for the brig,' he said dully.

And all for a little harmless fishing.

In silence they rowed into the pool of lantern light at the brig's ladder and saw the awful reality — the captain clutching his belongings, Mr Hoy, Privates Kent and Gillespie, Mr Tait, the convict Nicholls, and all prisoners. The side of the brig was lined with grinning convicts, some with muskets. British Army muskets, that had been signed for back at the depot and that he, Dearman, would have to give an account of. And all their regimental clothing and equipment was on board. That meant a Board of Inquiry, as well as a Court Martial. The quartermaster would play bloody hell over this. My God, if they deducted it all from his pay, he was ruined for life. If he had any life left to be ruined . . .

Barker said, 'Into the jollyboat with you. And look smart.'

Dearman, his voice a squeak, said, 'Our regimentals — could we — ?'

'Into the other boat, I said. Row off a boat's-length, then heave-to.'

Numbly, the three anglers clambered over the gunwales and into the overcrowded jollyboat. MacFarlane looked wistfully at the wet, silvery mound of fish he was leaving. It had been such a bonny night's sport, too. Still, there were always other fish to be caught and he'd still be comfortably casting his wee line when yon Barker and the others were brought back for trial and hanging. They were all fools and he wouldn't go with them even if he was asked.

Gathersole slipped an oar into its rowlock. 'And you, MacFarlane,' said Taw. I knew it, thought the little Scot. If there's any bloody rowing to be done, it's Joseph MacFarlane every time. They pulled away from the brig, then sat rocking gently on the star-bright water. Porter and Lyon manned the oars of the whaleboat, Jones took the tiller, and the four armed convicts climbed in to cover the jollyboat with their guns.

'Pull for the shore, Captain,' said Barker.

The smaller craft got under way, the whaleboat following close astern.

When the jollyboat's keel grated on sand, the whaleboat backed her oars ten yards from the shore.

'Out you get,' said Barker to his captives. 'And shove your boat off to us.'

'May we not keep her?' Hoy remembered the compass Shiers had given him. Perhaps Shiers had known it would be needed. Perhaps the convicts had no intention of sending provisions and leaving themselves short. In that case, the shore party would starve long before help arrived from Hobart Town, so they would have to try to get away; in that case, a boat and a compass would be essential.

'No. Take your belongings and shove her out, I say.' Barker had no wish to be surprised in the night by an attempt to re-take the brig. After all, even though the convicts were armed, the numbers — nine in the shore party, ten on board — were almost even. Take no chances, he thought. 'If we have to come and fetch her, you'll get nowt from us.'

The marooned men climbed up a bank and into the thick bush after Gathersole and MacFarlane had pushed the boat off. The convicts took her in tow and rowed back to the brig, where the jollyboat was hauled up into its davits and the whaleboat secured alongside. When that was done, Barker detailed off a guard-roster for the night.

He looked round at the men as he did so. There was none of the skylarking and hilarity he'd expected. No grim determination, either. They all looked like men in a dream, he thought; filled with incredulity that the dream was real, standing with foolish grins on their faces, amazed at the ease with which it had all been accomplished. Even the surly Russen was smiling, and it was he who said, 'Well, John Barker, we hands it to yer. 'Tis done and the brig is ours and not a drop of blood shed.'

'No thanks to you,' said Shiers. 'You could have blinded Taw with your musket.'

'I saw you hit him over the head with your pistol, so there's no — '

'Enough.' Barker handed his musket to Dady, who was to take the first watch with Fare. 'We've not finished yet. There's a strict lookout to be kept this night, and we rise at daybreak. And there's much to be done tomorrow.'

'There is that.' Jones nodded. 'And now, John, maybe you'll tell us where we're bound?'

'Tomorrow.' They were all tired, and Barker didn't want to face an argument. 'Tomorrow will serve for that. We have our liberty, and that's enough work for one day, heaven knows.'

'Aye.' There was a touch of awe in Shiers' voice. 'We're free men now, wi' time and to spare afore us. Liberty Men.' He looked round at the others. 'I think,' he said, 'it's going to be a very fine sunrise tomorrow.'

7

It was a turquoise-and-topaz sunrise, flushed with pink but with no angry reds in it to give the seamen on board cause for misgivings about the weather. Jones sat on deck eating his fish and fried ship's biscuit with the others and watching the early sunlight move down the slope of Wellington Heads. There was no sign of life there. But, Jones reflected, you could hide a regiment in those bushes and none would be the wiser. He pointed shorewards with his knife and said to Barker, 'What victuals are we leaving 'em?'

Benjamin Russen grunted, pushing a greasy lump of biscuit into his mouth. 'I votes we leave 'em none.'

'And leave 'em to starve?' Jones frowned. 'We can't do that.'

'Why not?' Lesley put his empty plate down and licked his fingers. 'What have those buggers ever done for us except feed us like pigs on flour and water, wi' a stinking rotten cabbage leaf or two and maggoty meat once a day?' He jerked a thumb at the shore. ''Tis four murdering redcoats you're talking of giving our victuals to, remember. Our enemies.'

'But to starve them — och, 'twould be worse than shooting them.' John Fare shook his head. ''Tis inhuman.'

'Inhuman?' Lesley jumped to his feet. 'Don't 'ee tell me what's inhuman. Not until the cat's clawed your back as it has mine. Look.' He turned and pulled his shirt off his shoulders. The brown flesh, criss-crossed with long white scars did in fact look as if it had been mauled by a tiger and then badly sewn together. 'Two hundred and seventy-five lashes, mate, that's all the humanity I've had from those bastards. You've never had a taste o' the cat, have you?' He turned to Jones. 'Or you? Or Will Shiers, wi' all his fine talk about letting no blood be spilt?'

'I've had more lashes nor you,' said Porter matter-of-factly. 'More'n any man on board, I've had. An' I still say we leave 'em all the food we can spare.'

'And how much is that?' demanded Lesley. He looked at Barker. 'I say it's high time we was told where we're heading.'

There was a growl of approval.

Barker looked up, chewing a piece of fish, making them wait. At last he said, 'We want to sail fast, wi' a following wind. So we sails wi' the westerlies. And we don't want to end up on a rock in the middle of the ocean, like the *Bounty* mutineers — we want a country as'll help us and not hand us over to the Navy. We want to sail far, far away from anywhere that's British, clear across the Pacific.' He paused. 'We're bound for Chile, lads.'

'Chile?'

They looked at one another. As Barker had expected, it scared them with the fear of the unknown. Half of them had no idea where Chile was. To the others, particularly the non-seamen, the name had a ring of remoteness, of inaccessibility, of infinite hazard over miles of ocean.

'But that's in South America,' said Jones slowly. 'It means a voyage of weeks — months. The Pacific's the biggest ocean in the world. And Chile's all desert and volcanoes, I've heard. That's no place for us.'

There must be no suggestion of coaxing, Barker knew. No hint that he was trying to sell them an idea that might not succeed. He speared another lump of fish with his knife, casual, confident.

'There's deserts and such in Chile, true enough. But, in the middle part, where we're bound, there's a land as green and pleasant as 'any in t'world, full o' lakes and pastures, wi' a happy, friendly people as threw off the Spanish yoke but twenty-four years since to live in liberty. As for the voyage, it'll take eight weeks or thereabouts — but what's that in a well-found ship wi' practised seamen enough to sail her? You heard what I said to Taw: wi' the assistance of the men, I can navigate round the world. And I can, too. The rest of it's up to you, lads.'

They could do it. He'd lain awake night after night making sure the odds were with them, calculating distance against time. It would likely take less than eight weeks, but he wasn't going to tell them that. There had to be a margin of safety, in case they were becalmed or had a stormy passage, and that could happen on any voyage. And, the longer he said the journey was to be, the less support that fool Shiers would get for stripping the ship of provisions to feed men who could testify against them.

Lesley caught on to that. 'Then, if 'tis to be an eight-week voyage, we'll need all the supplies for ourselves. We can spare none for those on shore.'

Charles Lyon put down his knife, laboriously doing sums in his head. They had had provisions for three months, of which one was gone. The shore party was roughly equal in number to themselves. So, if they split equally, each group would have enough food for eight weeks.

'If we have a slow passage,' he said reflectively, 'it would be a close-run thing.'

'Then there's no question of leaving supplies, you'd say?' Barker shrugged. It was the way he wanted it, but he wasn't going to shoulder the responsibility for such a decision. Always, there was the possibility of recapture — of the royals of a British frigate appearing over the horizon in mid-Pacific.

Lesley and Russen wouldn't be shouting murder then. They'd be too busy pointing him out and whining how they'd been led astray by John Barker, the ringleader, planner and first murderer. He'd have none of that. 'Are you all of the same mind?'

'Nay. By God, we're not!' Shiers came to his feet and stood with his back to the port rail. 'My proposal is to share the provisions with them as nearly as possible, and let us trust to Providence.'

'Providence?' He might, as far as Barker was concerned, have said he'd trust to the throw of a dice. 'Are you mad? What if my navigation's amiss and t'voyage takes longer? Providence won't help us much then.'

'But tha said tha could navigate round the world, John,' said Shiers gently. 'Tha navigation won't go amiss, will it? Not when tha'rt the educated man among us.'

Barker glared at him. He'd been a fool to sow doubt by saying his navigation could be at fault. 'There could be storms — ' He stopped. He couldn't afford to frighten them, either.

'True, we all knows that,' said Shiers. 'But we all knows you, too, John, and if tha says eight weeks, we'll most likely do it in six. So there'll be food and to spare.' He paused. 'Lads, if we should be caught, we'll fare badly if we ill-treat our prisoners. Besides, to die in the bush of starvation is a terrible thing. We're at the start of a new life. Do we want a crime like that to live wi'?'

Porter said, 'The sun's well up. If we argue much longer, it'll set on us. Now listen to my proposal: that we give 'em food for a month and leave Joe MacFarlane his fishing tackle. That way, they won't starve while they wait for a ship, and there'll be enough and to spare for us. Who agrees?'

Six hands went up. Then that of Shiers. Finally, even Lesley and Russen raised their hands.

Barker said expressionlessly, 'So be it. Unanimous decision.'

It was a decision they might live to regret, but there was

little he could do about it. He consoled himself with the thought that, if these fools were tracked down and found themselves in the dock facing the very men whose lives they'd spared, he wouldn't be on trial with them. For Barker had no intention of staying in Chile. When the hue and cry had died down, he'd move on — back to England, where he'd take on a new name and lose himself in a big city like Manchester or Liverpool. A little watchmaking business, maybe. Wealth and respectability. Then power; small power, first, as an alderman or summat o' that sort. And (Barker's thoughts raced ahead) one day, wi' the Radicals gaining ground, why, there might be a place for a watchmaker in the House of Commons . . .

'Aye, well.' He stood up. 'Now let's get on wi' it.'

They put a live goat into the whaleboat with some beef, flour, tea, sugar and biscuit. Cheshire added an iron pot and four tin pans from the galley. Shiers fetched a second pair of shoes for Hoy and some bandages and plaster from among the shipwright's belongings, while Porter collected the soldiers' knapsacks and greatcoats from the half-deck. Then, with Lyon and Porter at the oars and Shiers at the tiller, they rowed to the shore, Barker, Jones and Dady armed with muskets.

Hoy had spent a sleepless night racked with backache. At midnight, he and Taw had still been sitting in the clearing they'd made in the bushes, asking each other what they would do if no food arrived. They'd still not arrived at a decision when Taw fell asleep wrapped in his coat and snoring heavily after he'd issued everyone with rum. The soldiers, with the stoicism characteristic of infantrymen, stretched out coatless on the ground and slept, as did Nicholls and MacFarlane who were used to hard lying anyway. At first light, Hoy hobbled down to the water and watched the brig.

The relief he felt when he saw the boat approaching made him want to fall on his knees. He held on to a sapling at the water's edge, trying to see what was in the whaleboat.

Barker called, 'Stand well back. Any tricks, and you'll get nowt.'

'You'll need somebody to help you carry this,' said Shiers.

Hoy turned and went uphill to the camp. Dearman and Gathersole were awake. 'They've brought food,' said Hoy. 'Come and help carry it.'

Dearman struggled stiffly to his feet. 'And our knapsacks, Mr Hoy? Have they brought those?'

'I don't know.' Hoy pushed through the undergrowth on the path they had trampled. At the water's edge there was the goat and a little pile of sacks and pots and clothing. The whaleboat stood about twenty yards out.

Hoy said, 'Men, I did not for one moment expect such kind treatment from you when you have so little on board. I hope God will be kind to you.'

'Amen to that.' Dearman had his eyes on the belts, coats and knapsacks. 'And I thanks you for bringing ashore our regimentals.' That, at least, would ward off some of the blame he'd get. Not bad fellows all through, then, those canaries. 'A safe passage to you,' he said cordially.

'Thankee,' said Shiers awkwardly. 'I hope they send a ship soon for you.'

'I wondered,' Hoy hesitated, 'whether we could, after all, have the jollyboat. If no help comes and we have to cross Hell's Gates — '

'What would you want with a boat?' asked Barker. 'Make your way to the Pilot's Establishment. You'll be snug there till help comes.' It might, after all, be better this way, he thought. We've done all we can for them, but they're on the wrong side of the Harbour and the weather could close in so that no ship can be sent . . .

Dearman had been rummaging with increasing anxiety through the pile of clothes. 'Hey!' He looked up. 'You've brought everybody's kit but mine!'

'Too bad.' Barker chuckled. 'You'll have to make a complaint at headquarters for non-delivery. We ain't a-going back for 'em.'

'Well, I'm damned!' Dearman's bristly face went red with

90

anger. 'Why, you dirty gang of pirates, I hope you founders. What am I to say to the quartermaster when — ?'

'Pull away, lads.' Barker turned his back on them and the whaleboat got under way. The last thing Porter and Lyon, swinging at the oars, saw was Hoy trying to tow the bleating goat into the bush and Dearman standing shaking his fist.

On deck, the others were standing in a group round William Cheshire.

Barker paused at the head of the ladder. 'What have you there?'

Lesley grinned. 'A stowaway.' He moved aside. 'We found him in the hold.' The large black tom cat rubbed its head, purring loudly, against Cheshire's throat. 'We were jettisoning the cargo. No sense in taking that wi' us.'

The boat's crew crowded round Cheshire.

'Where did he come from?' Shiers asked. 'I never saw him at the settlement.'

'Nor I.' John Fare's voice was full of a sailor's superstition. ''Tis a sign, that's what it is. A black cat is aye a good omen.' He scratched it under the left ear and it went stiff with ecstasy. 'We'll call him Lucky. Then we'll always carry our luck wi' us.'

'Lucky it is,' said Charles Lyon. 'But if Will Cheshire is to continue to be cook, let's have a care when he serves us meat pies, eh?'

Cheshire said indignantly, 'I'd never think of — '

'We're wasting time.' Barker, devoid of either superstition or humour, looked over the side while he waited for the guffaws to subside. There wasn't a breath of wind. 'I'll feel happier when we're out of this place and into the open sea. John Fare, I propose you be mate; Charles Lyon to be boatswain. All agreed?'

They all nodded.

Fare said, 'Aye, then in that case we'll need to divide the men into two watches, Charlie, sharing the seamen between us.'

'We'll do that, but later,' Barker said. 'First let's get on wi' lightening the ship.'

It was midday and still a flat calm when they sat down to the meal Cheshire had cooked.

Barker said, 'How do we get out of the Harbour if there's no wind?'

'We kedge her out.' Fare jabbed his knife at the bows. 'We take the kedge anchor out in the whaleboat and drop her. Then we haul on the capstan and take the ship up to the kedge. Up kedge, and off we go again.' He munched a piece of meat. ''Tis bloody hard work, though. We'll no' reach the Gates this afternoon, I'm thinking.'

'But if we wait for a wind we might wait for days. And then get another nor'-wester.' Baker wanted to be off. There was always the possibility that a ship looking for a cargo of timber from the Gordon River might enter the Harbour. Or — he pushed the thought down — it might have been considered a good thing, back in Hobart Town, for the newly-launched *Frederick* to be given a Royal Navy escort on her maiden voyage . . . 'Let's finish our dinners, lads, and begin.'

It was, as Fare had said, bloody hard work. The channel trapped the hot, windless air and everything they touched seemed red-hot. Barker, Porter, Lesley and Russen, stripped naked and with sweat pouring off them, manned the whaleboat with Lyon, lifting the heavy, multifluked kedge anchor, taking it aboard, rowing, dropping it again to have a blessed respite while John Fare's watch strained at the capstan bars to inch the *Frederick* up the channel on the slack of the tide.

It was during one of these pauses that Barker sighted an old whaleboat pulled up on a strip of beach. He ordered the others to pull across and stove it in for, if they were unable to cross the Bar that night, an attempt by the marooned party to re-take the brig was not out of the question. Then they returned to the back-breaking, painfully slow task of moving the brig. When they had progressed six hundred yards to the two islets Cap and Bonnet, John Fare called from the brig's catheads,

'This is hot and exhausting work. Canna you in the whaleboat take us in tow?'

'Exhausting?' Lesley glared up, wiping a shower of sweat droplets from his forehead. 'Trust a bloody Scotsman to call leaning on a capstan bar hard work. This kedging was your idea. Now, if you want any towing done, you can change places with us and do it.'

The whaleboat changed crews, took on a towline, and Fare's men began straining at the oars. At first the brig, whose every detail was reflected exactly in the water, seemed to be embedded in rock. But then a small ripple appeared under her forefoot and her reflection broke as she began to move. Progress was a little better. By two o'clock in the afternoon they were passing through Hell's Gates with Entrance Island to starboard. The Indian Ocean, vast and blue and free, was waiting for them. They changed crews again.

In the glare of late afternoon sunlight, Taw's house showed no sign of life as they passed it with the *Frederick*'s questing bowsprit nodding to the slight swell that was all that remained of the surf of the day before. Laboriously, the whaleboat's oars dug into the sea and, as the heat began to go out of the sun, they crossed the Bar where the gulls called and the sea dropped away to the ocean floor.

Suddenly James Porter felt the sweat-rag he'd tied round his forehead go cold and clammy. 'A breeze,' he panted as his oars came dripping out of the sea. 'A bloody wind, by all that's holy. Cast off the tow-line, Charlie.'

Simultaneously, there was a hail from the brig. 'A wind — a light sou'-wester! Come aboard and we'll make sail.'

As the whaleboat reached the foot of the ladder John Fare leaned over the side. 'Ye can stove her in. Wi' the launch an' the jollyboat, we'll no' be needing her again and the deck's over-cluttered as it is.'

Lyon nodded, taking the axe that Fare passed down to him. When the others had gone aboard, he opened up the bottom of the whaleboat. It filled, drifting away as he swung himself on deck. Already the sun was reddening to ebony and gold the black-and-yellow of the brig's hull. It would soon be dark.

Fare watched his men set sail. 'Man that brace, John Dady! For Christ's sake, Jones, show him what a brace is!' He moved across to help William Shiers. 'Ye'll have to shake down smartly, lads. We're awa' out into the wastes of the ocean where there's no eye to see us but God's.'

Later, sitting at Taw's table in the lamplight and using Taw's pen, Barker wrote in the small, neat hand that contrasted markedly with that of the former captain:

14th Jany. 1834. Toward Evening, took our Departure from Birch's Rocks, setting our Course WSW to steer clear of any Land. Having divided the Hands into two Watches under John Fare, Mate, and Charles Lyon, Boatswain, we set our first Watch at 8 o'clock on a fine, clear Night with light SW Winds —

He put down the pen thoughtfully.

And, if Captain Taw had been there in the cabin, he might have been recompensed in part for the disappointment, injury and humiliation he'd suffered.

For Barker was beginning to feel horribly seasick.

8

The marooned party breakfasted off grilled beef, ship's biscuit, and strong sweet tea. After the meal Taw and Hoy went down to the water, watching the *Frederick* as the cargo was jettisoned.

Taw said, keeping the hurt out of his voice, 'A bonny vessel, David. A pity she had to make such an end as this.'

Hoy said, 'Where d'you think they'll make for?'

'East, wi' the Roaring Forties. The *Cyprus* did so — to New Zealand, then Japan. They'll do the same. But they'll get caught. The Navy has a long arm.'

'And what do we do?'

'Sit tight.' The captain shrugged. 'Wait for a ship. What else?'

Hoy was silent for a moment. 'We might have a long time to wait, Captain. It will be two or three weeks before the Port Officer in Hobart Town discovers that the *Frederick* is overdue at Port Arthur. You know what government departments are like. It could be almost a month before they decide to send a ship. Then she has to be fitted out and make the voyage. If the weather's bad — ' He paused. 'We could be very hungry by then.'

'There's fishing. And there's potatoes still and cabbages, at my house. Mind you, they're the rotten ones nobody wanted, but — '

The shipwright said firmly, 'It is my opinion that we should walk out.'

'Walk?' Taw stared at him. 'Walk, did ye say? David, you're out of your mind, lad. You know what t'country's like hereabouts. This,' he gestured at the scrub behind them, 'is as nothing to the thick, tangled forests we'd have to go through. There'd be rivers to cross, and swamps — to say nothing of the blackfellows.'

'We'd keep to the beaches. Do you remember Jimmy the Pieman?'

Taw shook his head uncomprehendingly.

'He was a convict who absconded in the early days of the settlement. He went north, along the shore. He made nearly fifty miles before he was recaptured at the river that now bears his name — the Pieman River.'

'But where would we walk to, in heaven's name?'

'To the station of the Van Diemen's Land Company at Woolnorth, near Circular Head in the north. A distance of a hundred miles. We could be there in two weeks.'

'A hundred miles?' Taw gaped at him. This was the dull stick who spoke of nowt but his spine; the old ninny who never got drunk or talked of women. The captain recalled the fight Hoy had put up in the cabin, the tenacity with which the shipwright had always insisted on having his ships built in exactly the way he'd designed them. Eh, thought Taw wonderingly. Like we say in Yorkshire, there's nowt so queer as folk. 'And how d'you propose to cross Hell's Gates wi' no boat?'

'There's a whaleboat abandoned on the beach a little way towards the Gates. Are you agreed, Captain?' Hoy turned and began to climb uphill. 'We'd better tell the others.'

'Eh, now, wait on, David lad!' Taw blundered after him.

'Let's go to my house first and discuss this. Over,' he added, 'a tot o' rum.' I'll be needing it, he thought, wi' yon madman to contend wi'.

'Corporal!' Hoy found Dearman sprawled comfortably in the morning sun smoking a pipe and drinking a pannikin of tea with his subordinates. At the snap in Hoy's voice, the corporal came to his feet with a speed that spilt hot tea down his trousers. 'Prepare to march to Captain Taw's house. You men!' MacFarlane and Nicholls were lying on their backs, dozing. 'Clear up the camp and parcel up the food.'

'Yessir!' During the next week or so, MacFarlane promised himself, he'd have his line out every day. He'd sit in the sun and take his ease on the rocks near the Pilot's Establishment. Aye, and there'd be bonny sport wi' —

'You may as well know,' said Hoy, 'that we are to march overland to the north. A distance of about one hundred miles that we shall accomplish in two weeks.'

'David!' Taw was too upset to remember the protocol of surnames in front of inferiors. He'd never walked a hundred miles in his life, and he certainly wasn't going to start now. 'First, let us proceed to my house, eh? Then we can take stock of the situation.'

'Very well. We shall pick up the whaleboat on the way, Captain, if it is seaworthy. If not, we shall have to repair it.'

'To be sure.'

The fact that they had no tools, nails or timber made not a scrap of difference, of course. The man was clearly unhinged and would have to be humoured.

And the journey to the Pilot's Establishment did nothing to change Taw's mind. It took them until early afternoon to cover three-quarters of a mile through the tangle of interlaced bushes, fallen trees and tightly-packed, thin-stemmed saplings. At the top of a ridge, they were able to see down the slope to the beach where the old whaleboat was lying. They were also just in time to see Lesley and Russen stoving it in with the butts of their oars. Taw, his shirt pasted to his back and his face the colour of a beetroot, said, 'Well, David, there goes your boat. And ye've seen during the last hour or two what walking would be like.'

'We would not attempt to penetrate country like this. We will, as I said, walk along the beaches. As for the whaleboat, I don't doubt that it can be patched up sufficiently to take us and our supplies across the Gates. I tell you, Captain, if we wait for a ship we risk starvation.' He looked at Taw's streaming face and torn clothing. 'Of course, if you consider a venture such as I have mentioned beyond your powers of endurance — ?'

'My powers of endurance?' Taw scowled. 'By God, sir, I may be your senior in age by a year or two, but I assure you I can outmarch you any day of the week.'

'Excellent.' Hoy picked up the sack he'd been carrying. 'In that case, we may hope to reach Woolnorth in ten days instead of fourteen.'

They arrived at Taw's house soon after six o'clock and stood on the sloping ground in front of it, watching the *Frederick,* under full sail, stand out into the sunset. The sea was the colour of lavender, shot with pink where it caught the reflection of the clouds that were massing in the west, and the swell breaking on the rocks south of Hell's Gates was showing white streaks of surf. Taw felt the breeze on his left cheek; a surprisingly cool breeze, a reminder that nothing lay between him and Antarctica except sixteen hundred miles of heaving grey water. As the sky faded to slate-grey and the sails of the brig blurred into the dusk, the fire that Nicholls and MacFarlane had lit threw out a welcome warmth, its flames bannering on the night wind. Taw smiled grimly to himself. The sou'-wester was gaining strength. Those bloody pirates who'd stolen his ship were going to need all the seamanship they could muster. As for David Hoy's crazy notion of walking out . . . Taw chuckled at the idea. He'd never be party to anything so mad as that.

*

By half past nine, the wind had increased to force eight and the *Frederick,* running under close-reefed topsails, was plunging into seas that burst thunderously in clouds of spray across her bows. John Fare, in spite of his Scottish stolidity, was worried. Barker was prostrate with seasickness in his cabin; Shiers, Lesley, Russen and Cheshire were retching and vomiting helplessly in the fo'c'sle. Watch-keeping was out of the question. He, Lyon, Porter, Jones and Dady — four seamen and an ex-bricklayer — were left to run the ship with no relief, no cook and no navigator. From below, Fare could hear crashes as the pots and pans in the untended galley were hurled from side to side while the ship rolled dizzily, her masts swinging in great arcs against the stars that appeared briefly among the flying clouds. And, still rolling, the brig lifted her bowsprit to the marching waves, to drop sickeningly into the troughs with a jar that brought a chorus of protest from her creaking timbers.

A fine bloody way, Fare thought bitterly, to begin a life o' freedom — working like a galley slave until a man dropped dead wi' exhaustion.

A shout, almost lost in the keening of the gale in the rigging, took him aft, balancing without conscious thought on a deck that reeled like a drunkard's nightmare.

Lyon, at the helm, yelled, 'I'm havin' me arms torn out o' their bloody sockets here. Can I no' have a bit help wi' the steering?'

Fare hung on to the spokes, feeling the ship fighting him like an unbroken horse. 'Have a wee respite,' he shouted into Lyon's ear. 'Send along Jones and Porter.'

'Aye.' Lyon heaved at the wheel with Fare, ice-cold spray drenching them as the brig tried to fall off to starboard, lying over until her rail seemed about to go under. 'I think ye're over-burdening her, John. Would it no' be advisable to take in more sail?'

'We canna. We must clear Van Diemen's Land wi' all speed.' He shook his head to clear his eyes of spray as a wave struck them like a gunshot. 'And, Charlie, the ship's well-found.'

'She's new though, and — ah well, ye may be right.' Lyon relinquished the wheel and staggered for'ard to fetch his relief.

Short-handed, soaking wet and hungry, they passed a wretched night and Lyon, back at the helm with John Dady, was glad to peer with red-rimmed, salt-caked eyes at the yellow flush of dawn that came up through the scudding clouds. James Lesley was the first to recover from seasickness. Lyon saw him staggering along the deck, his face grey and haggard.

He shouted, 'Charlie, what the hell's John Fare about? We've got to shorten sail. We're leaking like a bloody sieve.'

'Leaking?' It wasn't tiredness then, thought Lyon, that was making him feel that the ship was becoming heavier by the hour. 'Where?'

'In the hold. I've just taken a sounding. We've four feet of water down there. Tis madness to strain a new-launched vessel so.' He clung to the binnacle as John Fare came on deck from the cabin where he'd been trying to rouse Barker. 'We've four feet of water in the hold,' Lesley repeated. 'You're carrying too much sail, you fool. Are you trying to drive her under?'

'We must get clear o' the Colony, man. I'll no' take in an inch of sail.' Fare shook his head stubbornly. 'Fetch John Jones and man the larboard pump.'

Lesley looked at Lyon and Dady. When he got no support he said bitterly, 'Yes, man the pump. And we'll still be pumping when we hit bottom.'

None the less, he went for'ard and, a few minutes later, Lyon saw the two men rigging the pump. They threw their weight on the double handles. Nothing happened.

'The bugger's not working,' screamed Lesley above the gale. 'We'll all drown, thanks to that Scottish madman.' He pumped furiously and uselessly.

'Starboard pump,' said Jones briefly.

100

They crossed the heaving deck and set to work assembling the pump with fingers that seemed to have no strength in them. The first stroke brought nothing up. Lesley cursed obscenely. But on the second, there was a thin spurt of dirty seawater and on the third, a strong jet that was blown into droplets over the side by the wind. Lesley and Jones settled into a steady swing — a palm-blistering, back-breaking rhythm whose *clank-spurt, clank-spurt,* was to stay with them like the tick of some devil's metronome for the remainder of their time aboard the *Frederick*. As each man took his spell at the pump in the days that followed, it seemed as if he had taken his own personal treadwheel with him.

The gale continued all that day and throughout the endless night that followed until the clank of the pump, the kick of the wheel and the keening of the wind in the rigging became a permanent background to their lives. It was not until the morning of the sixteenth of January that patches of blue showed among the ragged clouds and a watery sun cast intermittent shadows on the streaming deck. The wind lessened to a topgallant breeze as the sun moved higher and, at noon, John Barker came on deck to take an altitude observation.

He seemed to have aged ten years. His face, always pale, was now a dirty grey beneath a stubble of brown beard and his eyes had sunk into their blackened sockets. But his hand was steady enough as he took his sight of the sun and made his calculations.

'Alter course,' he said to John Fare. 'Steer east by south.'

'Still south?' Fare frowned. 'If we turned nor'-east, we'd have a following wind.'

'East by south.' Barker put a hand to his forehead. 'We must pass south of New Zealand, away from any track of shipping.' He staggered, clutching at the mate. 'I must go to bed. I am unwell. See to it, John.'

And Fare did see to it, bedevilled as he was by a leaking ship, lack of hands to sail her and by the bitter cold of the Southern Ocean as the *Frederick*'s course took her ever closer to the Antarctic Circle. For two days the wind kept down to a fresh breeze but, on the eighteenth of January, it again increased in intensity and Fare was forced to furl topgallants before they were torn to shreds. The landsmen in the crew who had crawled on deck went back to their bunks so that, for the seamen, the only relief from the torture of the pump was a turn at the helm. Numbed with fatigue, with no warm clothing or hot food, they fought the ship and the seas until it seemed to Fare that they were doomed forever to sail the oceans of the world like the Flying Dutchman, in a wooden prison from which there was no escape.

On the twenty-first of January, their seventh day out of Macquarie Harbour, the biting wind eased. Cold, fitful bursts of sunlight created an illusion of warmth as the brig, under close-reefed topsails, ploughed through the grey-green sea at eleven knots. It was shortly after ten o'clock that Porter, who had the helm with Jones, called, 'John Fare! What's that ahead?'

Fare left the pump and screwed up his eyes against the steely dazzle off the water. For a moment he thought they were approaching a vast, flat island: a green, undulating meadow, treeless and uninhabited, that stretched across their course as far as the eye could see. He shook his head to clear his exhausted brain of the illusion. 'Weed. Masses o' floating weed. Like the Sargasso Sea.'

'Where we could well be, for ought we know.' As a practised mariner, Jones had been driven to the limit during the last week and the strain was beginning to tell.

Porter looked at him, then at Fare. 'We can't go on like this. We don't know where the devil we are, or what lies ahead of us. Barker's of no use. He ain't been on deck these five days.'

Lesley, who had been pumping with Fare, snorted. 'He vowed he could navigate round the world, and, by God, I think he's doing so.'

'He couldna have done much if he'd been on deck, though,

wi' no sun to see.' Fare turned for the cabin. 'None the less, I'll go ask him about yon weed.'

With the skylight clamped down and the door shut, the smell in Barker's cabin was indescribable, making Fare gag after the clean salt air on deck. He stood on the swaying ladder and said curtly, 'Ye'd better come up. We're running through a sea of weed. Where the hell are we, man?'

From out of the gloom Barker's voice came faintly. 'I cannot leave my bed. I'm too weak to stand, John.'

'The men are beginning to think we're lost. You'll have to show your face. I'll send two men down to carry you.'

Shiers, Cheshire and Russen had appeared on deck and were peering at the flat, oddly-sinister landscape of dark-green, swirling sea-plants through which they were sailing.

Shiers, sick and shivering turned from the rail. 'Where in God's name are we, John?'

'If two of you fetch Barker,' said Fare shortly, 'we'll find out.'

Barker, wrapped in a blanket and propped up on the quarter-deck by Shiers and Cheshire, looked at the seaweed, then at the men. 'The weed is harmless.'

It was his crew that frightened him. They'd been no beauties back in the settlement with the scars of their years of captivity on them; now, bearded, their hair matted and their sunken eyes gleaming as they stared at him, they put him in mind of a naked gibbering wretch he'd once seen being dragged off to the madhouse when he was a boy back in Warrington. He must look the same to them. He had to reassure them before, driven to the point of utter exhaustion, they gave up and turned for New Zealand or even back to Van Diemen's Land.

'Men,' he said, 'do not be in the least afraid as to my knowledge or capability of performing what I have in hand.'

'We don't know where we are,' said Benjamin Russen. 'And neither do you, mate. Confess it. We're lost.'

'Far from it.' Barker forced a grin to his white face. 'We

are fifty miles south of Macquarie Island, which we are avoid-
ing because of the sealers who ply between it and Hobart
Town.' He hoped he was right.

'And how,' asked Charles Lyon sceptically, 'can you know
that when you havena taken a sight of the sun for five days?'

'I can take you to South America even without a quadrant.
I can do it by dead reckoning.' He went on quickly before
any of the seamen realized that, buffeted as they had been by
the wind, his dead reckoning would be inaccurate to say the
least. 'In a week, after we have passed south of New Zealand,
we shall change course and be in warmer weather. This,' he
said earnestly, 'is the worst of our voyage.'

They nodded, reassured. Fare and Lesley went back to the
pump and its maddening clank started up again. Cheshire
went below to clean up the galley and prepare the first hot
meal they'd had on board.

They believe me, Barker thought as he was helped below to
his bunk, because they want to. Like ignorant, uneducated
children, that's what they are, in need of their nurse. Well, I
need them too, but only as long as it suits me. Then they can
all hang, for owt I care. Nausea gripped him again as he
went down the ladder. 'Open up the skylight, lads,' he said.
'I need some air.' The same skylight they'd pushed their
musket barrels through — so long ago, it seemed. He pulled
the blanket over himself, wondering how Taw and Hoy were
faring.

*

They were, at that precise moment, trudging along a beach
sixty miles north of Hell's Gates. The party was strung out
along the sand near the water's edge in warm sunshine, following the coast that had been first sighted by Abel Tasman in
1642. Taw, who had drunk all his rum in the first three days
to kill the pain in his left eye, was now recovered and he
sang a little song jauntily to himself as he plodded along, two
pans tied together and slung over his shoulder. Happen things
might not turn out so bad, after all. A military guard was,

104

when all was said and done, a military guard and His Excellency must see, surely, that the whole bad business was that scoundrel Dearman's fault for leaving his post without permission — and that stuffed martinet Baylee's, too, for giving a post of responsibility to such an incompetent jackanapes. Why, look at him now, the clown . . .

Dearman and Gathersole, closely followed by MacFarlane, were marching out in front, 'For fear,' Dearman had said, 'we'm ambushed by natives' and, to prepare for battle, he had armed his men with stout branches to use as clubs. A vanguard, he'd explained, was standard military procedure, as was the rear-guard made up of Kent and Gillespie who were forced, like Gathersole, to carry their clubs at the slope and wear full marching uniforms and equipment, as well as lug along their share of the supplies. Hoy, pale and drawn, limped behind Taw with Nicholls at his heels. Like a dog, Tait thought, eyeing the convict's plump figure as he waddled along.

Tait walked by himself, accepted as usual neither by the convicts nor by their masters. And a fine mess, he thought disgustedly, they've made of it all. There'd been times when he'd thought he was about to be butchered; he would have been, too, had it not been for Will Shiers. He remembered still in his dreams the lust for killing on the faces of Lesley and Russen when they'd taken him down to the fo'c'sle. Well, maybe he was the lucky one, to have got out of it with no more than the loss of his belongings and ship model. Poor old Charlie Taw was a ruined man, that was certain, and he wouldn't like to be in Dearman's shoes, either. And Hoy — why, he'd be crippled for life if he kept pushing them along like this.

A remarkable man, that. Tait was suddenly struck with the memory of the little fishing vessels called hoys that he'd seen in the Clyde. Not much to look at. A bit infirm, sometimes, and creaky in the timbers. But, somehow, they always seemed to keep afloat. Tait grinned, thinking of the fights there'd been between the captain and the shipwright. How Taw had given way at last and agreed to march when Hoy had said he'd go off by himself. Taw had known how it would appear in the official report — the captain sitting in his house on his bottom and letting his passenger risk death to go for help. Then there'd been the crossing of Hell's Gates, with Hoy using every scrap of boatbuilding ingenuity he possessed to improvize patches out of sacks soaked in oil, bits of canvas, timber and nails torn from the walls of Taw's house for the repair of the smashed whaleboat. She'd leaked like a colander, of course, but by baling frantically they'd ferried their supplies across bit by bit. After that, it had been an easy march for the first day or two along a wide beach where the surf thundered and where there were crabs to be caught to eke out their supplies. On the third day, they'd had to halt to construct a raft of branches precariously held together by strips of cloth and creepers so that they could half-wade, half-float across the rock-strewn, sandy estuary of the Pieman River at low tide. They'd had to strike inland when the coast became impossibly precipitous, and there'd been smaller rivers, swamps and quicksands to contend with. But on the whole, they'd made good time, Tait reflected, and Mr Hoy had promised them beds to sleep in within the week, and good food and drink.

Hoy kept his promise. For, on the twenty-fourth of January, the nine marooned men staggered into the Van Diemen's Land Company's station at Woolnorth, sunburnt, blistered and fatigued but otherwise in good health. Three days later, Hoy was in Launceston, making his sworn statement before a magistrate, Mr Alfred William Home. However, in government circles, news travelled slowly. Exactly a week after Hoy made his report, Captain William Moriarty, Port Officer for Hobart Town, wrote to a Mr I. N. Bateman:

The Nonarrival of the new brig *Frederick* having caused an Anxiety as to whether or not some accident may have befallen her in the launching, I have been instructed by

His Excellency the Lieut. Governor to direct that you proceed to Launceston and there report yourself to the Port Officer. Lieut. Friend will be instructed to place under your orders such Govt. Vessel as he may have disposable as well as to see that she is properly equipped for the Service.

You will, upon your arrival at Macquarie Harbour, take upon yourself the Charge of all measures consistent with the Public Service of the Department and I rely upon your zeal to use every effort in bringing the Vessel to Hobart Town without loss of time.

Mr Bateman never sailed. For on the following day, the fourth of February, Captain Charles Taw made his sworn statement in Hobart Town and the whole Colony knew that the bird had flown.

The search for the *Frederick* began.

9

For the next nine days, while the overcast sky prevented noon observations, Barker remained in his cabin. The wind was favourable but freshening and slackening at intervals and his seasickness recurred every time the ship's movement became violent. The crew were once again plunged into doubt and depression, opinion in the fo'c'sle ranging from the view that Barker was lying low because he knew they were irretrievably lost, to the theory that he was dangerously ill and couldn't navigate them anyway. When Russen gave it as his opinion that Barker had fallen overboard and John Fare was trying to conceal the fact to prevent a panic, the mate thought it high time Barker showed himself on deck whether a sighting could be taken or not. On the last day of January, however, the sky cleared enough for Barker to be able to announce that they were well to the south-east of New Zealand. Purposely, he omitted to mention the crossing of the international date line. The moving back of the calendar would not affect in the least the length of their journey, but it would appear to add a day to its duration, thereby having a disheartening effect on men who were eagerly counting the hours to their landfall.

'Alter course,' Barker said. 'North by east.'

'Thank God for that.' Fare looked at the blistered, bleeding palms of his hands. 'Wi' the wind set light and fair, we should be able to spread every wee bit o' canvas we've got. Where do you think to strike the coast of Chile, John?'

'Between Valparaiso and Valdivia.' Barker looked at the haggard faces around him. 'Another five weeks, but in warm sunshine and wi' a following wind. Keep your spirits up, lads. We're over the worst of it now.'

And, for the next ten days, as the *Frederick* climbed up slowly from the floor of the world into warmer latitudes, conditions aboard improved. The ship still leaked, the pump still clanked, but there were more hands to share the work now, and there were beef stews and mugs of scalding hot tea coming up from the galley to keep the cold at bay. James Porter, sitting in the fo'c'sle with the cat Lucky on his knee, even gave a second rendering of his 'Fanny my Queen', which led to reminiscing, with each man making the most of the part he'd played in the seizure of the brig. The tussle in the cabin took on homeric proportions, with Shiers and Lesley braving desperate odds to save themselves from obliteration by Hoy's pistols and Taw's musket. And Tait's being caught relieving himself in the middle of a mutiny was the best joke they'd ever heard.

On the eleventh of February, however, the mood suddenly changed. It was shortly before ten o'clock in the morning. Lesley and Russen were on the pump; Lyon was talking to James Porter, who had the helm. Suddenly, Lyon stiffened. Against the hard line astern where the waste of water cut the eggshell blue of the sky he'd seen, just for a moment, a small point of white. It might have been a distant gull, its wings catching the sunlight as it dived for a fish. Or it might have been the crest of a far-off breaking wave. He stared at the spot, his eyes blurring with the effort of concentrating on nothingness. Porter stopped in mid-sentence, looked over his shoulder and said, 'What is it, Charlie?'

Then it appeared again, clear and unmistakable. 'A sail, by God!' Lyon turned to bawl the warning along the deck. 'Sail-ho! A sail astern!'

Bare feet pattered on planking as the others ran aft. The clank of the pump stopped.

Fare snapped, 'Keep yon pump going! If so be 'tis a pursuer, we canna afford to take on another spoonful of water.'

Reluctantly, Lesley and Russen started up again, peering aft as they laboured.

Fare said, 'Where?'

Lyon was up on the cabin hatchway searching the horizon. 'Dead astern.' Now, there was only the tossing sea and the sky.

'I can see nothing.' Fare snapped open a telescope and squinted. 'Maybe 'twas a whale spouting, Charlie.'

Barker came up from the cabin under Lyon's feet. 'A whale? I thought someone cried, "Sail"?'

Then as the *Frederick* lifted on a crest and, over the horizon, the other ship did the same, they all saw it — a tiny smudge of white, perceptibly rectangular this time — before it sank out of sight again.

Lyon said quietly, 'Whoever he is, he's gaining on us.'

How could they have known? Barker was, for a moment, filled with a superstitious awe of the seemingly limitless powers of the Royal Navy. They'd seen no land, they'd sighted no ship that could have reported their position. And yet here, in the depths of the Pacific, with no land for thousands of miles in any direction, they'd been tracked down as effortlessly as if they'd been on the River Thames. Damn them to hell, they must have devils for navigators. But he'd show 'em. He'd —

'Break out the muskets,' he said savagely. 'Arm yourselves wi' any weapon you can find.' He stared astern as if the hate and disappointment in his mind could somehow shrivel up their pursuer. The sail was continuously in sight now, shortening and lengthening as the two vessels took the wave-crests simultaneously and sank into the troughs. ''Tis liberty or death,

110

lads. We die either here or on the gallows. So we'll give no quarter and take none.'

Fare looked round. 'Will Cheshire. You're the youngest and likely to have the sharpest eyes. Take the glass and go aloft.'

Cheshire nodded. Tucking the telescope inside his shirt, he swung up into the shrouds and climbed like a squirrel. Lyon, Dady and Jones went for the muskets and, under Barker's supervision, began loading them. The *clank-spurt* of the pump increased in tempo as Lesley and Russen heaved frantically at it. Only Shiers did nothing. He won't fight, Barker thought, looking up from the guns. But, by God, if he tries to surrender, I'll shoot him with my own hand.

From the maintop, Cheshire called, 'She's a Frenchie, lads. Merchantman, I think.'

'For a merchantman, she's bloody fast.' Jones gave the musket he was loading to Barker and went aloft. A minute later he shouted, 'She's French, right enough. A whaler.'

Fare blew his breath out in a sigh of relief. 'The Lord be thanked. If 'tis only the crappos, we've nought to fear.'

The others put down their firelocks, grinning at one another sheepishly.

'Keep those weapons handy!' No risks, Barker thought. No chances. 'We may need them still.'

Although France and England had been at peace for nearly two decades, there was no love lost between them. And whalers were independent men, liable to take the law into their own hands. It could be that the whaler's skipper might think the brig was poaching in their territory. He might decide to give *les sacrés Anglais,* caught far from the protection of their Navy, a lesson in who ruled the waves hereabouts. Or on a more civilized level he might merely wish to exchange greetings as one mariner to another. Either way, the *Frederick* could not afford to be intercepted, interrogated and reported upon.

Cheshire stayed aloft, watching the French vessel. Jones slid down to the deck and picked up his musket. He said to Shiers, 'You'd not fight, then, Will?'

Shiers shook his head. 'If we were taken, 'twould be God's judgement on us. There's no resisting that.'

'But you fought in the cabin. With Hoy.'

Shiers grinned, his teeth showing white in his black beard. 'He tried to take the pistol off me. That was his right — and a brave act, too. But 'twas no fight.' He paused. 'And the pistol was unloaded. John Barker thinks I didn't know, but I did. I'd never have done it wi' a loaded gun.' He chuckled. 'That's why I was taken as a highwayman back in Yorkshire — I'd nowt in my blunderbuss. All I want is to be left in peace to grow things, not kill 'em. That's what I hope to find in Chile. Peace.' He looked at Jones. 'What about you?'

'Me?' Jones stared out at the circle of water that surrounded them, unbroken except for the tiny sail that, he observed, was now moving north across their stern. 'That's what I want.' He jerked his head at the sea. 'Not Chile, nor Liverpool, nor anywhere on land.' He turned to Shiers. 'There's two kinds of people in this world, mate. Sailors and farmers — my kind and yours. Them as wanders the face of the earth and them as wants to stay still. And John Fare and me — and John Dady, too — why, we're wanderers. We'll not stay in Chile, we've agreed on that. First cap'n as comes along short-handed and asks no questions — we're off.' He stroked the long barrel of the musket. 'I can't live in a cage,' he said quietly, 'whether the door's open or not. I'd shoot myself first.'

For the next three hours, the Frenchman's royals stayed balanced on the horizon as she sailed northwards on a course that diverged slightly from that of the *Frederick*. Barker took his noon sight and told Cheshire to go below to prepare dinner. Soon after one o'clock the sails began to shrink and an hour later they had disappeared completely. Barker ordered the men with muskets to stand down, and Fare's watch went to dinner.

The weather became warmer, as Barker had promised. The agony of standing watch with numbed fingers and toes was over. But to offset that, a turn at the pump now meant that

112

a man was pouring with sweat in the morning when the sun, unshielded by the sails as it was in the afternoon, struck along the deck from over the bows. Barker made minor navigational corrections, but the brig followed a mainly nor'-easterly course with the wind fair behind her.

It was on St Valentine's Day when John Fare's forenoon watch saw cloud overtaking them from the south-west; a solid white blanket that spread swiftly across the sky to shut off the sun. Barker, fully recovered from his sickness, was taking a turn at the pump with John Dady. Fare checked the course at the binnacle and said to Jones, who had the helm, 'We're in for a change in the weather, I'm thinking, wi' yon cloud.'

Jones grunted. 'Wind's steady enough. And warm. It may be — God in heaven!' His voice rose. 'Will ye look at that?'

Fare turned and stood, petrified. Out to starboard the sea had gone mad, churned into a white wall of spume a hundred feet high that was racing in a hideously frightening silence towards the brig.

'A white squall!' Fare shouted. 'For the love of Christ, John, hold her!'

It was too late to shorten sail, alter course, or do anything but hang on. Fare screamed a warning to the others, then wrapped his arms round the binnacle. With a howling roar the squall struck.

For a moment, the air was so full of water that Fare thought he'd gone over the side. He spluttered and gasped for breath, his eyes shut against the stinging salt, clinging desperately against a blast of spray-laden wind that tried to prise his arms loose. There was an appalling crash from above. The *Frederick* shuddered from stem to stern and something fell like a tree into the sea behind him. He felt himself falling, still clinging to the binnacle, as the deck began to tilt beneath his feet. He scrabbled with his bare toes on the planking but the horizontal deck was turning into a sloping roof and his weight was being transferred from his legs to his arms so that he felt as if he were hanging in space. Dear God, he thought. She's going

113

over. Above the roar of the wind he could hear minor crashes
and screams. Jones, wrapped round the wheel, was cursing at
the top of his voice. Fare opened his eyes. The world seemed
to be full of canvas and particles of spray that stung his face
like ice. And as the spray cleared and the shriek of the wind
diminished, he saw the horizon. It was almost parallel with the
mainmast. The brig was on her beam ends, the tips of her
yards barely clear of the water. Fare shut his eyes again, waiting for the sea to take him.

But slowly the *Frederick* righted herself as the wind fell off
to a mere gale. Fare felt the deck under his feet again and he
let go of the binnacle, staggering. He bawled, 'All hands on
deck!' hoping there'd be somebody left to hear him.

The only casualty, however, was the *Frederick*. The spanker
boom had fractured and been carried away, its immense
weight passing over the heads of Fare and Jones to fall into
the sea to larboard in a chaos of canvas and rigging. Fare let
it be while he got on with the main task of shortening sail:
furling the main course and fore-topsail, taking a reef in the
main topsail and striking topgallant yards so that the brig was
scudding under single-reefed main topsail and foresail. It was
heavy, exhausting work with the wind strengthening and the
brig taking it green over her bows as she butted into the rising
seas. Fare sent Cheshire to the helm to assist Jones as the
movement became more violent. Barker and Dady stayed at
the pump while the others began the task, difficult enough for
an adequate number of trained seamen in a calm sea, of hauling inboard the fractured spanker boom, fishing its two broken
pieces together with some quartering that was on board, and
re-rigging it.

Before they could make a start, Lyon shouted into Fare's
ear, 'John, I've just taken a sounding. The leak's worsening —
water's pouring in. Ye're forcing her too much.'

Fare shook his head. ''Tis a following sea. It'll poop us if
we dinna keep ahead of it.'

'It'll bloody well swallow us if we go on like this,' shouted

Lyon angrily. 'We're lost, mon, if ye don't exercise a wee bit o' sense.'

'Sense?' Fare, fatigued to the point of collapse and worried almost out of his mind, glared at him. 'I never thought to see the day when a fellow-Scot was scared of a rough sea.'

'I'm no scared of the sea.' Lyon's temper flared. 'It's you I'm scared of, ye great buffoon, wi' your bit seamanship that couldna take a spoon across a bowl of porridge.'

Shiers put his large hands on their chests and pushed them apart as they began to crowd each other. 'Easy,' he bawled above the wind. 'Are you mad? Charles Lyon, we agreed to take John Fare's orders as mate, and we'll do it. Now let's get on wi' our task.'

Sulkily, Lyon and Fare went to work, holding on with one hand and working with the other — a hand for yourself and one for the King, as they said in the Navy — until by late afternoon the spanker boom was in place and secured.

The gale lasted nine dreadful days and nights. This time, even the tough little bricklayer John Dady went down, and the burden of running the ship fell on Fare, Lyon, Porter and Jones — two on the helm and two on the pump twenty-four hours out of the twenty-four. As James Porter wrote later, 'What in the pumping and keeping a strict lookout after the Vessel which was necessary in such a heavy Seaway and being short of Hands, so many being sick, the remainder of us were nearly exhausted unto Death.'

They learned to sleep while pumping, to eat dry biscuit at the helm, to forget there had ever been such a thing as dry clothing. When on the ninth morning the wind began to ease and Dady and Lesley came on deck as a relief, Jones dropped in his tracks at the helm and had to be left unconscious on the deck since they hadn't the strength to carry him below.

Thenceforth, it was a race against time — to reach land before the *Frederick,* taking on water faster than they could pump it out, sank beneath their feet. For two days they sailed in sunshine with the deep blue waters of the Pacific about them and a warm, gentle breeze at their backs. With the inbuilt resistance to hardship and fatigue they'd acquired at the settlement, they recovered physically. But all the time the clank of the pump, audible throughout the ship, rasped their nerves to breaking point, as if they were listening to the heartbeat of a dying man.

It was on the twenty-fifth of February, at six-thirty in the evening, exactly six weeks after leaving Hell's Gates, that John Dady, the lookout, stared to the east, shaded his eyes with his hand, stared again.

Then, at the top of his voice, he bawled, 'Land-ho! Land on the starboard bow!'

10

They crowded into the bows, into the rigging, up on the rail, shouting at first and slapping each other on the back, pointing — as if, instead of being on board ship, these bronzed, bearded men in tattered rags of clothing were castaways who had sighted a sail. But then a silence fell on them in which the sea, purpled with dusk, gurgled and slapped under the *Frederick's* forefoot as she wallowed, ominously heavy and sluggish in the water, to meet the night that was coming out of the east. Ahead, under the pointing finger of the bowsprit that canted over with the ship's list to starboard, the horizon was banded with an uneven ribbon of black that was neither sky nor sea.

"'Tis land, right enough,' said John Fare. He spoke softly. If he raised his voice, the vision might disappear. 'Tis South America. Where's Johnny Barker?'

'Here.' Barker, the only one who had not raced for'ard except for Russen the helmsman, was standing with his arms folded by the foremast. 'Do you want us to sink? Why has the pump been abandoned?'

They turned to look at him in surprise.

'We've sighted land,' said James Porter. 'You've made your landfall, John. That's Chile ahead.'

'Chile be damned.' Barker strode forward. 'That's cloud you're gawking at, you fools. We're still five hundred miles off Valparaiso. Get back on the pump.'

'It be land.' Lesley raised his voice angrily. 'It must be.' He stared ahead, his eyes straining, but already the sea had turned black and melted into sky where the first stars had appeared. 'It was there. Damn you, it was — we all saw it.'

'You saw what you wanted to see. Our course is east-nor'-east wi' five hundred miles to sail. It'll be two, maybe three days before you see Chile, lads.'

Fare, up in the shrouds, said, 'I'm shortening sail.'

'Shortening?' Barker stared up at him in the darkness. 'Why?'

'Because I've no wish to run the ship aground, that's why. John Jones, I'll want you and Dady in the catheads wi' your eyes skinned.' Fare swung down to the deck. 'At the first sight or sound of surf, gi'e the alarm.'

'You realize we must make all speed if we're to reach land before we founder?'

'Aye. But do you realize that, five hundred miles off the Chilean coast, there's a group of islands — one of them Juan Fernandez, where Alexander Selkirk lived? We could strike in the dark and drown, or spend our days as Robinson Crusoes.'

Barker turned without saying anything and went below.

It was at ten that night that the cry came again.

'Land-ho!' Fare, on deck in an instant, leaned over the bow. Jones, on the starboard cathead, the heavy lateral beam that took the weight of the anchors, said, 'It's no cloud, John. Ye can see it plain.'

To the east the sky was hung with stars that seemed unnaturally large and bright. The sea was luminous with their reflections. And, between the sea and the stars there was a

118

shadow — a shadow that rose in peaks, outlined sharply against the sky.

Fare shouted, 'All hands on deck to take in sail!' To Jones he said, 'It's no' an island, neither. It stretches clear across the horizon. We'll heave to and see what the morn brings.'

Daybreak brought a flamingo sky and a long strip of coastline that rose and fell in beaches and headlands backed by pine forests and distant mountain ranges. It was dangerously close and under their lee. Fare hoisted sail, sweating at the thought of what could have happened had the wind freshened during the night. He was in a quandary. To stay within sight of a coast that, if it was in fact Chile, was visited frequently by the British Navy was suicidal. But, to put too far out in a vessel that was slowly but surely filling was equally dangerous. He compromised by hauling off until the land was a purple rim along the horizon under the morning sun.

'That clever one, Johnny Barker!' said Lesley at the pump. 'Five hundred bloody miles out in his reckoning!'

'Be fair, man.' Lyon swung on his end of the crossbeam. 'Twas his first attempt, and that on a long voyage wi' all manner o' trials to contend wi'. We're here, aren't we?'

'Aye. But where?'

At noon Barker told them, trying to conceal his chagrin. 'Forty-one degrees twenty south.' They were hove-to in a light sou'-westerly breath of wind and the hands were sitting in the shade of the launch between the masts, munching tough beef and biscuit. 'About a hundred miles south of Valdivia.'

'A hundred miles south?' James Lesley tapped a biscuit on the deck to dislodge a weevil, looking round at the others with mock perplexity. 'Well, now, I must be hard o' hearing. I could have taken my oath our learned navigator told us our landfall was to be to the north of Valdivia — between Valdivia and Valparaiso, I thought he said.'

Barker ignored that. 'Therefore, we shall abandon the brig here.'

'Abandon the brig?' Lesley stopped chewing the meat that,

119

after six weeks, they preferred neither to look at nor smell as they ate.

'What else? Wi' her hold full o' water —'

'But — here?' Shiers, the farmer, looked longingly at the distant coastline. Like all the others, he was a non-swimmer and to him the water meant only a slow, choking death. 'Shouldn't we take her into port while she floats still?'

'Perhaps,' said Barker sarcastically, 'you reckon as we should take her into some Chilean harbour and let her sink in the middle of it? We've stolen her, and she is the evidence of our theft. With her, we may be considered to be thieves and pirates. But without her we are shipwrecked mariners and may hope to be received as such.' He rapped on the hull of the ship's boat they were sitting against. 'We must take to the launch.'

Stowed on chocks between the masts amidship, the launch weighed two and a half tons and was in fact a small, sea-going vessel in her own right, being decked, with small hatches, and fitted with the mast, boom and spar of a gaff-rigged sloop. She had her own suit of sails and for bulwarks Fare decided to use the bad-weather cloth that had been provided for the whaleboat to keep her dry in a choppy sea.

Getting her over the side was no easy task at any time, and the heavy swell that developed during the afternoon made it an arduous, dangerous business. They rigged purchases on the *Frederick*'s fore- and main-yards to lift the launch and sway her outboard and, with the brig rolling crazily, they paid out lines to prevent the launch from swinging uncontrollably once she was clear of the deck. There was one bad moment when she struck the brig's hull with a splintering crash on the way down and a plank above her waterline caved in. But at last she floated. Everybody except Shiers, Lesley and Cheshire swarmed down into her to rig her masts and Fare let her drift clear of the *Frederick*; she was bouncing like a cork and liable to split apart if the two vessels collided.

With the deck seesawing wildly, the rigging of the launch

was not completed until after sunset. On board the *Frederick,* the three men left behind had been opening up the hatches to make sure she would go straight to the bottom. Shiers peered down into the hold. With the pump out of action, the sea had gained rapidly during the afternoon and, in the dying light, the black water seemed to be about to slop over on to the deck as the brig rolled.

'Lesley,' he called urgently. 'Look here, will you? She's filling fast.'

James Lesley came to the lip of the hatchway and swore softly.

'Give Will Cheshire a hand to get the supplies up on deck. She's ready to go.' He went to the side. 'John Fare,' he bawled out into the dusk. 'For Christ's sake, come and take us off. She'll sink at any minute.'

Up to the ankles in water in the gloom of the galley, Cheshire grabbed an armful of sacks and pots and heaved them up to Shiers, listening all the time to the sounds made by the dying ship: the sucking gurgle of water, the almost-human groans of the over-stressed timbers, the clatter of an empty bottle rolling to and fro across the deck. A sudden surge of water that came up to his knees made him stagger and Shiers shouted, 'Will, come up! Save yourself and leave the rest!' Terrified, Cheshire raced up the ladder to find the launch rolling alongside and Lesley throwing down the muskets, ammunition and breakers of water. The cat, Lucky, sat by the mainmast, mewing piteously. Cheshire grabbed him and followed Lesley and Shiers over the side. Even as he did so, there was a crash like a cannon-shot from somewhere below as a bulkhead went and, ponderously, the brig lay over in the heaving sea until her channel plate was awash.

'Get that bloody sail up,' yelled Fare, 'before she comes down on top of us!'

And so, in darkness and a rising sea, they left the *Frederick,* her brief life over, her first and last voyage ended. She lay with her black-and-yellow trim salt-caked and sun-bleached, surrendering herself to the sea. She died alone with no man to see her final agony: the air-bubbles coming out of her as she gasped out her life, the spars reaching skywards like imploring arms, the final foaming whirlpool that was washed away by the next wave as she plunged to the ocean floor. 'A bonny vessel,' her captain had said to the man who had created her. 'A pity she had to make such an end as this.' None of the men who had helped build her looked back as the launch, her sails cracking in the wind, sped towards the land.

The wind continued to rise, harping in the rigging of the launch and forcing its crew to shorten sail. Fare, at the tiller, shouted, 'We'll go as close in as we dare, then heave-to until — ' The rest was cut off as they took a tremendous wave over the stern that almost tore his hands loose. Before he could draw breath, he was swamped by another. He could feel the deck awash up to his knees before it drained.

Porter scrambled aft. 'She'll fill if this continues, John. We must keep the seas from pooping us.'

'Aye.' Fare spat seawater. 'Come and sit beside me. And you, Charlie — and you, John Barker. Now, sit close and hang on.' Another wave smashed at them, the force of it feeling to James Porter like a stroke of the cat. But very little water came into the launch.

All that long and bitter night they sat in the sternsheets in turn, watch by watch, making a human wall with their backs to keep out the pounding seas. At first the icy shock of each blow made them catch their breath and they waited, wincing, for the next assault. After a while there came an agonizing all-over burning as the salt got into their skins. But finally a merciful numbness took over; when a man's watch was over, his relief had to drag him, stiffened into a sitting position, away from the stern to lie kicking feebly until the circulation returned in his back and legs. It was a night that stayed forever in their memories, a night of torture in which some of them, their minds blanked off by cold, pain and fatigue, were not sure at times whether they were alive or dead. When the sun came up over the peaks that blended into the clouds in the east, they sat with their beards and hair white with salt, their lips cracked and bleeding, revelling in the warmth. The cat crawled out of a locker and sat in the sun, licking his matted fur into shape.

It was then that they discovered they had yet another enemy to do battle with. The two big seas they'd shipped had soaked the contents of the few sacks Cheshire had salvaged into a pulpy mess. The beef had been too far gone beforehand to be damaged by salt water but, even with its liberal coating of drowned white maggots, it was only enough for one meal.

Fare pointed to the land and croaked, 'We'll close in. Find a village. Look for a bay, lads.'

He headed nor'-east, steering to meet the coastline that rose up to starboard.

There was no sign of life ashore. They lay a mile off and sailed north, the wind still buffeting them but slackening as the day wore on; they saw nothing but low cliffs, mile after mile of empty rocky beaches and forest that came down to the sea's edge. By four o'clock in the afternoon the wind had dropped to a light breeze and they hoisted the mainsail, bowling along parallel with the coast at seven knots over a sparkling sea. Half an hour later Barker, up in the bow, said, 'There's a bay of sorts ahead. I vote we put into it.'

It was a shallow depression in the coastline, nothing more, but with a curving reef of rocks like a breakwater to the north. They steered under its lee and dropped anchor with a cloud of outraged seabirds screaming and wheeling round their heads.

'Where there's gulls,' said Jones, 'there's food. Let's go and see.' He dropped over the side and waded to the rocks. 'Who's for the foraging party?'

'There may be Indians.' Barker busied himself with the muskets. They were soaked and useless, but fiddling with them gave him a reason for not going ashore. 'Some of us must stay with the boat.'

Porter, Fare and Dady followed Jones. Balancing precariously, the feel of solid ground strange to them, they went along the reef in single file and to the beach, hopping as the hot sand burnt their soles, and threaded their way among pools set in shelves of rock until they came to the under-growth that flourished riotously among the trees. They pushed into it but there were no paths, no clearings, no sign that any-body had ever been there before them. They went back and tried further along the beach and found nothing.

'Best go back.' Jones leaned against a tree, alarmed at his lack of stamina. 'It'll be dark in a couple of hours. No sense in getting lost.'

They trudged back to the launch, their lengthening shadows trailing behind them.

Porter stopped beside a rock pool. 'Hey, look!' He plunged his hand into the clear, still water and came up with a brown, spiny object the size of a coconut. 'Shellfish.' He smashed the sea-urchin open and nibbled the pulpy orange contents cautiously. 'Tastes strong, but 'tis good.' He bit off a lump and stood chewing happily.

Jones went back to the launch. 'There's no sign o' life.' He stood outlined against the sky, leaning on a boulder and breathing hard. Weak, he thought to himself, that's what I am. I can't stand much more of this. With his grey beard streaked with white salt, he looked nearer sixty than forty-two. 'But there's shellfish in the pools. What if we stay here for the night?'

'If you're sure 'tis safe to do so.' Barker stared about dubiously. 'Those woods could be full o' wild beasts as well as — '

'We'll stand watches.' Fare had come back to the boat. 'The lying'll be easier on the sand.'

'We'll light a fire.' Cheshire splashed excitedly ashore. 'Pass me those pots, Charlie. I can make a soup out of those shellfish. And there may be fruit on the trees. Bananas and pineapples and breadfruit — '

124

'Pineapples don't grow on trees,' said Barker coldly. 'And the banana is a tropical fruit. As for breadfruit — '

But Cheshire had already leapt across the rocks and was running along the water's edge, kicking up sheets of spray and yelling like a hooligan.

They recovered, that night, something of the picnic atmosphere of the fitting-out of the *Frederick*. There was little wind and the stars came out like lamps as they lay, ten men and a cat, on the deliciously soft sand with the driftwood fire blazing and their stomachs full of the thick soup that Will Cheshire had concocted out of the mussels, sea-urchins, scraps of beef and the more edible parts of the salt-soaked flour and biscuit mush. Charles Lyon told of a girl he'd smuggled aboard the *Union* ketch that his strict Presbyterian father had sailed out of Leith, and of the waste of effort it had been, since the lass had been paralyzed with seasickness the whole voyage. But most of their talk was not of the past, but of the future. Russen and Lesley had decided to set themselves up as partners in a boat-building business; how they planned to acquire the capital, they wouldn't say. Only James Porter had no plan, no ambition.

'Me? I've already got what I want, mates,' he said when they asked him. 'A full belly and the open sky above me. I don't call no man my master, and I don't have to cheat for money and then fear it'll be taken from me. The more you get, the more you stand to lose. Me, I've nothing at all, 'cept my liberty. And if I wish to stay here tomorrow and let you lads sail off without me, then I'm free to do so. But one thing I would like to do.' He lay on his back, his hands behind his head, staring unseeingly at the sparks that jetted up from the fire. 'I'd like to set down an account of our voyage, that's what I'd like; and maybe I will, one day.'

'You?' Barker gave a superior chuckle. 'You that can neither read nor write?'

Immediately, Porter wished to God he'd kept his mouth shut. 'Ah, 'twas but an idle thought.' It was truly better to

125

have nothing. Even a dream can be taken away from you, or destroyed. 'Now, lads, what about a song or two?'

Next morning they were up before the sun, spreading out along the beach to gather the protein-rich seafood from the rock pools. They washed out their sacks and filled them with shellfish and hung them over the side of the launch to keep their contents fresh. The sea was so calm that they had to row out beyond the reef, but as the sun rose so did the breeze until they were spanking along under full sail at a good nine or ten knots. They sat soaking up the sun, refreshed, relaxed and, for once, with nothing to do except steer and keep a lookout for the harbour, whatever it might be, that they were confident they would reach that day. At nine o'clock they saw a long point of land rise, misty blue, over the horizon. It was a long way off and seemed to extend far out to the north-west. Fare scanned it through his glass. It would take them all of the day to round it.

'There may be a bay beyond it,' he said slowly, as he peered. 'Or there may not. If so be there isn't, we'll be on the far side of it by nightfall, at the mercy of a nor'-wester, should one spring up. It'd be another bad night for us.' He snapped his telescope shut. 'The question is, do we round it or anchor for the night under its lee?'

'We stand on for it and take our chance.' Jones looked round at the others. Nobody, not even the prudent Barker, disagreed. 'If we waste time loitering in every cove we come to, we'll never reach port.'

He tapped the water breaker at his feet. They all knew what he meant. One water container was empty already; the one he'd struck sounded ominously hollow. If they lived off shellfish in a salt-laden atmosphere and hot sunshine, they'd need far more than the few pints of water they had left.

They steered for the point and rounded it at half-past two in the afternoon, having shared out raw shellfish and half a pint of water per man at midday. Fare estimated that they had two pints left; less than half a mugful per man. He stared

126

expressionlessly through the glass at the shoreline; there was no place as far as the eye could see where they could put in with safety.

'Keep going, lads,' he said encouragingly. 'We can't be far from Valdivia.'

They only had Barker's word for that, he thought grimly. The word of an amateur navigator who'd been wrong in his calculations by almost the length of the British Isles. Fare pushed down the hideous doubt that had been growing all day in his mind — that Barker's landfall had been pure guesswork and that, for all he knew, they could be north of Valparaiso instead of south of Valdivia. In which case, they were now sailing into the deserts that lay to the north of Chile. No water there. Only a slow death from thirst, drinking salt water or your own urine until —

'A few hours' sailing,' he shouted cheerfully. 'No more.'

They sailed on — with no more joking, no more chat about what they were going to do with their liberty. They watched the shoreline as it unrolled slowly to starboard like a parchment scroll that carried no message for them. Until, suddenly, Fare picked up a break in the monotony of rocks, beach and green undergrowth.

'A bay!' He steadied himself against the mast. 'I can see two tall rocks wi' an opening between. Put the tiller over, Charlie, an' we'll go closer in.'

The rocks were strange; eroded smoothly by the wind and sea until their faces were planed flat and they were almost perfect pyramids. The launch turned in between them. Beyond, there was a vast flat shelf of rock, covered with basking seals. For a moment, hundreds of whiskery muzzles and huge popping eyes were turned towards the intruders. Then, in a groaning chorus of alarm, the sleek brown animals heaved up on their flippers to waddle clumsily to the edge of the shelf and fall into the sea in a cataract of foam. The sea boiled briefly with snorting, rolling shapes, then the seals were gone and the shelf empty.

127

'Gawd,' said young Cheshire, awestruck. 'Did you but see that? Didn't stay to pay their respects, did they?'

'Got out faster than clergymen from a burning brothel,' said Porter, grinning painfully through cracked lips. 'One of 'em put me in mind of Charlie Taw. And, look, there's a good spot for the boat.'

'And a stream!' Dady's voice rose to a shriek. 'Water, thank Christ. Pull for the shore!'

They took the launch into the shallows, grounded it and leapt ashore, falling into the deliciously cold freshwater stream and drinking, splashing, soaking their heads in it. They refilled the water-breakers and Fare and Jones carried them back to the launch. Gradually the others, after searching for shellfish and finding none, drifted back.

Fare said, 'Where's Lesley and Russen?'

They looked at one another.

'They were at the stream,' said Barker.

Lyon said to him, 'Get into the boat and try your hand at making the muskets serviceable. Fare and Jones, pull away from the beach. No sense in losing the launch.'

'You think there may be Indians about?' Barker scrambled over the gunwale.

Lyon ignored him. 'You others, come with me. Stick close together and keep your eyes peeled.'

He walked slowly towards the trees, looking for tracks in the sand.

At the same time, the two missing men ran out of the undergrowth a little way to the right, swerved towards the launch and Russen yelled at the top of his voice. 'A hut! We've found an Indian hut!'

11

'Keep your voice low, blast you,' hissed Lyon.

Porter said, 'Bit late for that, mate. Unless we have deaf Indians hereabouts.' He turned to the launch. 'Will the muskets fire?'

'One only.' Barker passed it across. 'T'others are rusted.' He jumped into the shallows, shoved the launch out and scrambled back on board. Fare and Jones rowed her out twenty or thirty yards.

The seven men on the beach followed the faint track of flattened grass and trampled undergrowth that Lesley and Russen had made. Lyon, third in line with the musket under his arm, said softly, 'Did you go close to the hut?'

Lesley shook his head. 'We saw the roof, turned and ran. It might be a village, for ought I know.' He held out an arm. 'Here 'tis.'

Ahead of them was a clearing with, in the middle, a wattle-and-daub hut with a thatched roof. But the roof was holed and sagging and the grass in the clearing had grown halfway up the walls. Lyon moved forward. 'Empty. The grass is un-trodden, see?' He ducked inside, wrinkling his nose at the smell of some small unidentifiable animal that had crawled inside to die. There were some broken fragments of earthenware, but nothing else. Lyon came out and glanced at the sky. 'Let's awa' back before sunset for fear we have visitors. And I vote,' he added thoughtfully, 'we don't sleep ashore this night, either.'

The launch took them aboard and, as the shore greyed into dusk, they rowed out into the middle of the bay, dined off shellfish and clean water, and set an anchor watch for the night.

They awoke, ravenously hungry, at daybreak. The shellfish were keeping them alive, but they needed fats and carbohydrates to fill their stomachs. They obtained both on the beach. The seal they found had perhaps been separated from the herd and come ashore to find them. It may have been too old or feeble to swim far away. At all events what happened was not pleasant, with the men whooping like savages and, like savages, rushing to find rocks and sticks while the beast, the fear of death in its soft brown eyes, tried pathetically and unavailingly to shuffle on its flippers to the safety of the sea.

They lit a fire, not caring now whether there were hostile natives about or not, and cooked huge hunks of flesh, with the flippers, heart and liver as delicacies, gorging themselves to bursting point. It was the first fresh meat, apart from the livestock they'd had on board the *Frederick,* that they'd eaten for weeks. Even Lucky was fed until he could eat no more and rolled over in the hot sun and fell fast asleep. They skinned the seal and used the hide to repair the plank that had been stove in when they'd left the brig. Then, glutted and belching, they staggered aboard and rowed out of the bay.

It was a morning similar to the previous one; very little wind until the sun was well up, then a favourable breeze that enabled them to make a good seven knots northward. There were more bays now and, late in the afternoon, they dropped anchor in one with the intention of sheltering for the night. But even while they were discussing whether to go ashore or spend the night in the launch, the wind shifted to the nor'-west.

130

And with the wind came a wall of water curling in from the Pacific — the first of a series of great waves that picked up the launch, anchored though it was, and hurled it towards the beach. Caught on a lee shore, they had to row like madmen to keep the vessel from splintering into driftwood on the rocks. As fast as they made ten yards, the swell would come roaring in and take it from them. At last, Fare managed to steer them under the lee of a reef where they spent an anxious and uncomfortable night, and next morning it took all their combined strength to row the launch out of the bay. With a perversity that put their tempers on edge, the wind then fell away to a flat calm so that they had a day of laborious rowing close in to the shore until, at about four o'clock, they were able to hoist sail and let the wind take them to what they afterwards discovered was the mouth of the Rio Bueno. Here they found saplings that had been cut with a saw; evidence, Jones said, that sealers had called in to make mats for their whaleboats.

And here their cat deserted them. Before, when they'd gone ashore, he'd mewed to be taken with them. He'd played in the sand, slept in the sun and stayed near them all the time. Now, as soon as Will Cheshire carried him to the beach and set him down, he bounded off into the bushes and never returned. He, too, wanted his own kind of liberty. And besides, they'd run out of food.

They'd lost their mascot; they were hungry; and others apart from John Fare were beginning to think that, surely, if John Barker's estimate of their position had been correct, they would have made port by that time. None the less, there was an inexplicable air of light-heartedness among them next day. There was no more rowing. The southerly breeze stayed with them, the sun shone, and the launch cut a white wake into the sea like an arrow pointing to their journey's end. At midday, they came to a point that seemed to be the end of a long peninsula jutting several miles out to sea. They rounded it and saw a high headland at the northern extremity of a bay that it took them all afternoon to cross. They decided to put

131

in for the night after they had passed the headland, but they found no place to anchor on the northern side. At sunset they were close inshore, searching for an anchorage, when they heard the bellowing of a bullock.

They looked at one another. Nobody spoke. Then suddenly and quite distinctly, they heard it again and, with it, the sound of a voice shouting faintly in the distance.

'Thank God,' said Jones softly. 'A haven at last.'

He rubbed a hand across his eyes which, for some reason, were watering annoyingly. He glanced round but nobody was watching him. Shiers, in fact, had his eyes shut and his lips were moving silently.

'Where would ye say it came from?' Fare peered at the shore. The light was going, and already the beach was blurring into the rocks and trees behind it.

'Further on.' Lyon pointed. 'Round yon wee reef o' rocks, I'd say. Let's pull for it.'

As soon as they rounded the reef they saw the fires; several of them, like beacons twinkling in the dusk. They shouted. At first, there was no reply but then somebody, then several others, shouted back at them. They sounded confused and alarmed, as well they might, with the voices in a foreign tongue coming to them out of the empty sea at night.

'Let's put in to shore,' said Lesley impatiently. ''Tis useless crying back and forth like this.'

'Wait.' Barker looked at the fires. 'If we come upon them suddenly in the dark, they may mistake our intention. I vote we anchor and wait for daylight.'

'To hell with that,' said Russen. 'I'm famished. There's food ashore there — and wine, maybe, and women, and all for the asking. Take an oar, Jim.' He and Lesley began rowing.

But the decision was taken out of their hands when they found no place where the boat could put in. In the darkness they bumped and grated over reefs that, had there been any kind of swell, would have taken the bottom out of the launch. Finally, frustrated and angry, they had to drop anchor and

132

spend the night offshore. Nobody slept. They passed the hours in a fervour of anticipation, their bellies rumbling and their mouths watering in a torment of hunger as they translated the bellowing of the bullocks into fresh beef — roast and sliced thin and succulent, or grilled as steak with onions, or made into a ragout, perhaps, with vegetables and spices. They almost drove each other mad with stories of gargantuan meals they'd had from beef, each one bigger and better than the last.

There was a full moon that night and the sea was as smooth as a pond — which was just as well, since they'd taken no precautions whatever for the launch's safety and, on a lee shore, they would have been lost had a wind sprung up. But none did. The day dawned clear and pearl-grey over the far-off Cordillera and they pulled in to the shore at the place where they'd seen the fires the night before. As if they had been watching and waiting for them, small brown men began moving slowly out of the trees down to the beach — men with straight black hair that sat sleekly on their heads like helmets; men with faces from which all the hair had been plucked by shells.

Fare said, 'Easy all. We'll lie off a wee while and see what they have to say.'

The Indians called gutturally across the water.

Lesley looked at Barker. 'Come on, now, Johnny. You're the educated one. What are they saying?'

'Well — ' Barker looked judicious. 'Tis plain, they're asking questions. Want to know where we came from, and the like.'

'Well, answer them directly,' said Lesley impatiently. 'Tell 'em we're famished and want food.'

'And drink,' added Benjamin Russen. 'Served by some dusky beauty as I can cuddle a bit. Go on, Barker, tell 'em.'

Barker felt as if he'd been asked to write to Santa Claus in Chinese. He looked at the expectant faces in the boat. Then he cleared his throat. 'Moo!' he said loudly. 'Moo! Baa!' He pointed to his open mouth.

'What the devil are you about?' asked Fare wonderingly. 'They'll think ye're crazed, mon, if ye continue so.'

'I'm telling them,' said Barker with dignity, 'that we want beef and lamb because we're hungry.'

'Well,' said Porter, 'I'd say you don't seem to be having much success.' The Indians continued to shout, clustered in a group at the water's edge. 'Hullo! Look at the size of that fellow there!'

A man had walked slowly out of the trees and now stood surveying the scene on the beach. By the standards of the men in the boat he was enormous, being well over six feet tall with shoulders that were proportionately broad. His face was as brown and impassive as if it had been carved out of teak, and he wore a woollen poncho, tasselled at the corners and brilliantly dyed, with a pair of blue woollen trousers. His right hand rested on the hilt of the large knife he carried stuck into his belt. As he walked down the beach, the other Indians fell back, chattering to him excitedly, and left him an open space at the edge of the water. He stood immobile, staring at the launch, with his hand still resting on the hilt of his knife.

Jones picked up a hatchet from among the clutter of belongings at the bottom of the boat, held it up, and tossed it lightly onto the beach. The tall Indian picked it up, examined it, then waved it in the air, grinning. Then he beckoned to the men in the launch.

'He wants us to go in,' said Barker.

'Truly?' said Lesley sarcastically. 'I'd never have thought it. Well, I for one am not going. I don't like the look of that bastard.'

'Nor I.' Russen spat over the side. 'Nor his bloody knife.'

'I'll go.' Shiers rooted in the bottom of the boat and came up with some needle and thread. 'Pull in, Fare, will you?'

The launch moved in slowly, Lyon with his hand on the musket below the gunwale. Without taking his eyes off the Liberty Men, the Indian giant made a sweeping gesture that sent all the other natives back up the beach. Fare took the boat in to a patch of seaweed among the rocks that seemed to offer a possible landing place.

He said, 'Will, you shan't go alone. I'll go with you.' He looked round. 'Who else?'

Jones, Dady and Cheshire nodded.

The five men climbed ashore and moved hesitantly up the beach. The Indians followed, keeping their distance, with their chief taking up the rear; the whole party disappeared into the trees.

Lyon turned. 'Take her out again. I hope to God we havena seen the last of our mates.'

A quarter of an hour later, the five came back alone. The Indians, they said, were called Mapuches. They were friendly, but more ready to receive presents than give any. The chief had accepted the needle and thread but, in spite of all their efforts, they'd been unable to get anything to eat out of him.

'Sweet Jesus, and me near ready to die o' famine!' Lesley jumped over the gunwale. 'Here, let the rest of us try, taking our man o' learning wi' us. He'll soon get our bellies filled, eh, Johnny?'

Porter, Lyon and Russen climbed out after him with Barker following reluctantly. They went up the beach, through a screen of trees and into a large clearing where a stream ran sparkling in the sunlight and where huts, well-constructed and spotlessly clean, stood beside a patch of cultivated ground. A man and a boy wearing bark loincloths were ploughing with a pair of bullocks yoked to a wooden plough by the horns. Women nursing brown babies stood watching in doorways as the chief met them and led them to a hut markedly larger and more ornate than the rest. He took them inside, sat them down on mats, and waited expectantly until they handed over the buttons and pins they'd brought as gifts. These he tossed into a corner of the hut. Then, courteously, he ushered his guests outside.

'Why, damme,' said Lesley. 'He thinks we came here on purpose to hand over our goods to him. Ask him for a bite to eat, Barker, for the love of God.'

Barker went through his farmyard pantomime again, joined this time by the others.

'There's none so deaf,' said Porter bitterly as the Mapuches smiled amicably and nudged them firmly back to the launch, 'as those who won't hear.' Before he climbed into the boat he turned and smiled winningly at the chief. 'You greedy villain,' he said, bowing politely. 'You selfish, black-hearted rogue. I hope you do yourself an injury with that bloody axe we gave you.'

The chief smiled back, rattled off a staccato sentence, and stalked away.

'He's most likely saying he's done you brown and please to call again with more axes and such,' said Lesley furiously. 'They've made fools out of us. Look at that old crone grinning over there.'

An ancient Indian woman, wrapped in a faded robe and with a face like a walnut, was standing at the water's edge, nodding and showing her toothless gums. She came closer, cackling, as she saw they were talking about her.

'I hope,' said Lyon, eyeing her with revolted fascination, 'they have better-looking females than that in Valdivia.'

'Valdivia?' The hag cackled again. 'Valdivia.' She pointed to the north, grinning with senile pleasure at her own cleverness, and held up three fingers. '*Leguas!*'

'By God,' said Fare in amazement. 'She understood you, Charlie. She says — '

'She says,' cut in Barker hurriedly, 'that Valdivia lies three leagues to the north.'

'Three leagues,' said Shiers softly. He raised his voice. 'Well, come on, lads. Why do we wait here?'

They pushed off, away from the seaweed that clogged their oars, and made sail.

The wind was tantalizingly light and the shore seemed to crawl past as they wallowed slowly northward, close in. It appeared to stop moving altogether when they had to haul off to weather a point of land, and they hung for an age always approaching the point but never reaching it. At three o'clock in the afternoon, however, they eventually rounded it.

John Fare, his telescope to his eye, said slowly, 'I can see a flagstaff, lads. And a fortress at the mouth of a river.' He turned, grinning foolishly through his reddish-brown beard. 'We're there, thanks be to Christ. It can only be the river Valdivia stands on. We're saved!'

Pandemonium broke out, the launch rocking wildly as they jumped up and down: a boatful of ragged scarecrows, their hunger and weariness forgotten as they yelled and pumped one another's hands. Only Barker kept aloof. He sat in the sternsheets, methodically parcelling out their few possessions — some half-guinea pieces he'd found in Taw's cabin, clothing, a blanket or two. David Hoy's watch wasn't all that bad, as watches went. He kept it for himself. Then they steered for the river mouth.

It was, William Shiers thought with a strange sense of familiarity, very like Macquarie Harbour. The estuary, set with islands, was wide and lake-like, and low hills tumbled away from it into the distance to rise into mountain ranges. There was a fort on the largest island with a twelve-gun battery, and there was a flagstaff like the one on Sarah Island, with red-white-and-blue national colours flapping in the light breeze. But here the water was the brilliant blue of a kingfisher's breast; the forests were green with pine, not like the dusty grey-green of Van Diemen's Land; the flag was the flag of the Independent Republic of Chile. And the soldiers in the ill-fitting blue-and-white uniforms were friendly, grinning and waving, showing them where to put in as the launch lowered her sun-bleached sails for the last time. There was the tired sigh of the keel grounding on sand. Shiers climbed out.

It was the fifth of March 1834, and four in the afternoon. It was over.

*

137

On the same day and at the same hour, three British Army officers were sitting at a table in a high-ceilinged room in Hobart Town, considering the evidence they had heard on this, the first day's sitting of the Board of Inquiry into the seizure of the brig *Frederick*. Captain William Moriarty, RN, Port Officer for Hobart Town, had been examined and had stated categorically that the brig had never come under his charge. A letter from Mr Foster, Chief Police Magistrate, had been read giving a general outline of the affair as narrated by Captain Charles Taw and David Hoy. Now the clerks had left and late afternoon sunlight slanted into the room through the white-painted, muslin-curtained window. General Roberts, Deputy Assistant Commissary and senior officer present, leaned back in his chair.

'Well, gentlemen,' he said. 'Damme if this isn't the oddest kettle of fish I've come across in a long day. Brig stolen — pirated — but she don't seem to belong to anybody. As far as the records go, she don't even exist.'

'Worth £1200 with all her tackle, though, sir.' Lieutenant-Colonel Leahy, of the 21st Fusiliers, stroked his moustache. 'Lot of money to belong to nobody, eh, what?'

'Navy don't have anything to do with her.' Roberts shook his grey head. 'Damnedest odd business, you know.'

Captain MacKay, the Town Adjutant, said, 'I would suggest, sir, with all respect due to the Navy, that they've been damned dilatory about the whole business. Those chaps in the 63rd were left quite alone. No support whatever.'

'Should have had a naval escort, eh?' Roberts nodded. 'I knew Baylee, y'know. Damned fine feller. Fought with distinction at Martinique and Guadeloupe. Iron discipline. First-rate chap.'

Leahy said, 'His Excellency is much displeased, sir, by the extraordinary attitude taken by the Navy in this matter — wants a statement from Captain Lambert of the *Alligator* giving his reasons why he didn't go in pursuit of the blackguards.'

'Bad business all round.' The general came to his feet, the two juniors rising respectfully. 'And damned odd, eh? That feller Taw — captain of the brig. Seems to have been damned lackadaisical too. No armed guard. Troops spread out all over the place. Fishing, by God, in the middle of a mutiny.'

'Not the men's fault, though, sir.' Mackay opened the door for the general. 'Corporal said he'd asked repeatedly for orders. Got none.'

'Yes. Taw was in command.' Roberts looked round the room before he left. 'Be interesting to see what he has to say in his deposition. Try to saddle the Army with the blame, I shouldn't wonder. Can't have that.' He snorted. 'Fishing, gentlemen. His troops extended in the presence of the enemy. Damnedest odd business I've met, by God.'

It was another fortnight before the Board completed their investigations. After Charles Taw, who was in Sydney, had sent his affidavit and David Hoy had been examined, the Board found:

> . . . that no culpable blame attaches to the Guard, it having placed itself under the directions of Captain Taw. The loss of this Vessel can be accounted for only by the number of resolute Convicts having associated together so as to have enabled the Organization of the Plan to take the 'Frederick', and to the blind Confidence placed in these People by Mr Hoy added to a like Confidence on the part of Captain Taw whilst considering them as Crew to which Misfortune (this misplaced Confidence) the Court are of the Opinion the Success of the Attack so easily carried is attributable.

Taw was dismissed from the service of the government.

12

Willing hands helped the men haul the launch up the beach to a rapid fire of Spanish. Laughing and chattering excitedly, the soldiers escorted them to the fort. Porter hung back when he saw the thick stone walls, the ponderous iron-bound gate, the fixed bayonets of the sentries. It all came back: . . . *Prisoner, how do you plead — guilty or not guilty? . . . The sentence of this Court is . . . lashes . . . treadwheel . . . to labour in chains on the roads* . . . But the flag overhead wasn't the Union Jack; the soldiers weren't redcoats; the air smelt of pines, not eucalypts. He was a free man — a Liberty Man. He blinked his single eye, squared his shoulders and marched through the gate. Gawd, he thought to himself. It's going to take a bit of getting used to, this hobnobbing with the military.

The military were very ready to be hobnobbed with. They fed their guests beef cooked with beans and spices, fruit and cheese and fresh bread, until it became a game to see just how much these poor starving devils could put away. '*La mejor salsa del mundo es el hambre,*' they quoted to one another. The best sauce in the world is hunger. The only thing they were sparing with was their wine, a rough red that would have laid their guests out cold, in their debilitated condition, if they'd had much of it. Then they were left to themselves in a bare, white-washed guardroom — with the door unlocked.

'Their officers sleep in the afternoon. Siesta, they calls it,' said Barker knowledgeably. 'We'll be taken to him when he wakes. In the meantime,' he looked round, 'we've to decide what story we'll tell.'

Jones belched slowly and lingeringly. 'Jesus,' he said dreamily. 'That was worth starving for, a feed like that. I haven't set to in that fashion for bloody years.' He paused, then looked at Barker. 'What do you mean, what story we'll tell? I thought you said we'd be welcome here, gaolbirds or not, as men who've gained their liberty?'

'And so we may well be.' Barker pursed his lips. 'But we want to feel our way, don't we? We don't want to start our new life wi' every man looking sideways at us to see if his purse or his wife is safe in our presence. I vote we say nowt about the settlement until we've been accepted here as hard-working, honest men.'

'There's something in that.' Fare's Scottish caution was coming to the fore. 'But what if they find out later?'

'Why should they? There's nobody to blab but ourselves. And, if they do, why, by that time we'll have shown ourselves to be so useful to them and so well-behaved that our unfortunate past will be overlooked in favour of our present industry.'

'I see no harm in that,' said Shiers slowly, 'if 'tis a lie that hurts no man in the telling of it. What shall we say, though?'

'That we are shipwrecked mariners from the brig,' Barker paused, '*Mary*. Out of — out of —'

'Liverpool,' said Jones promptly.

'Liverpool, so be it. Bound for Valparaiso. On the night of the twenty-fourth of February, we struck a bank in latitude forty-one degrees twenty minutes south. We took to the launch and, after many privations, arrived here. And,' Barker paused, 'if we're starting a new life, I'd like to start mine under a new name. From now on, I'm to be Benjamin Smith, mariner.'

New names? They looked at one another. It was fitting; like being born again, in a way.

'Aye, a good notion, that, lad,' said Charles Lyon. 'I'll be — ' He stopped. For the life of him, he couldn't think of any name but his own. 'James,' he said, looking at Porter. 'James Smith, that's who I'll be. Pilot.'

Lesley sneered. 'Can't you think of anything different from the name Barker's chosen? Me, I'm going to be,' he paused for effect, 'George Fortune, mariner.'

'By Christ, that's a good name,' said Russen, impressed. 'Can you think of one for me?'

'Price,' said Lesley, grinning. 'Because of the one on your bloody head. James Price, mariner. How's that?'

'I'll be William, as I am now,' Cheshire said. 'I'd never answer to another given name. I'll be William — William —'

'William Williams, then,' said Barker impatiently. 'Then you'll have no difficulty in remembering.'

They'd barely finished their re-christening when a soldier appeared at the door, beckoning, and they followed him to a room where a young lieutenant, unshaven and with his coat undone, sat behind a table. He spoke some English and, after asking politely whether they had had enough to eat, listened to the story Barker had concocted.

'So, Señor Smeeth, you are shipwreck?' He poured wine into two pewter mugs. 'You 'ave suffered much. But now,' he handed Barker a mug, 'you are safe an' we care for you. But there are formalities, you understand? First, you must report yourselves in Valdivia. I suggest that you an' per'aps two, three friends do this. Go by canoe — it will be easier and quicker. The others, your boat also, can stay 'ere until a decision has been made by my superiors. You agree?'

Barker nodded, drinking his wine. To row the launch nine miles against the current would be exhausting; to make sail on an unknown river might be disastrous. He would go and tell his story, taking Lesley and Russen with him in case they got drunk or started fights with the soldiers if left here. Will Shiers could come, too; his bloody scruples would make a good impression.

'You must, of course, surrender your arms to us. As for your boat — ' the *teniente* made an apologetic gesture with his mug. 'It might be as well if your men kept a watch on it. Unfortunately, some of my men, of the lower class, are not — ' He shrugged.

True, Barker reflected. The penalty of being a free man and a man of property was that you had to keep your hand on your wallet. The world had come to a pretty pass, he thought indignantly, when a man couldn't even leave a boat he'd stolen lying about for fear of some rogue pilfering from it.

Next morning, the four of them set off upriver under a grey overcast sky in two canoes paddled by two impassive, dignified Araucanian Indians whose impassive dignity did not, to Barker's disgust, prevent them from demanding a generous payment for their services. The other six Liberty Men spent the day in the luxury of having nothing whatever to do except eat, lounge about and drink with the soldiers. They found, as the day wore on, that languages were not nearly as difficult to learn as they had thought. All you had to do, Porter discovered, was put an 'O' at the end of every word, and the result was perfect Castellano. If he said, 'Drinko', and held out his mug, it was instantly filled. If he said, 'Vittles-o', and pointed to his mouth, food appeared. 'I wonder,' he said, sitting propped against the wall of the guardroom with a plate of some kind of spiced fish in one hand and a mug of wine in the other, 'how long it'll be before Johnny Barker returns?'

'Who cares?' Will Cheshire patted his stomach. 'For my part, I could stay here until the supply of provisions runs out.'

Barker did not return at all. On the following day, a cutter came downriver to take them and the launch to Valdivia. These men, in charge of another Army lieutenant, were less inclined to be friendly and spoke no English. Even Porter's new-found linguistic talents were useless for extracting information; in the presence of a brother officer, their own English-speaking lieutenant was cautious and non-committal and so the six Liberty Men started up the Rio Valdivia late in the afternoon in misty rain with vague premonitions of disaster.

With no wind to assist them, rowing was hard work. Green, uninhabited forest enclosed them like a wooden wall, sombre and forbidding under the grey sky, and the air was full of the scent of pine trees. The light began to fade. There was no sound except the hiss of rain on the water, the monotonous plunk of oars, and an occasional rapid exchange in Castellano from the men in the cutter that was following them. They rowed on, silent and apprehensive, swinging in a lethargic rhythm backwards and forwards as the darkness closed in on them, never seeming to move at all. Until Fare, at the tiller, said, 'I can see lights ahead. Looks like a town.'

They could make nothing of it, this place they had had on their minds for so long, as they came alongside the wharf — only yellow, twinkling lights, the smell of cooking-fires, a baby crying somewhere, the barking of a dog. Surrounded by soldiers, they were helped ashore and escorted along narrow streets in the thin drizzle, followed by a small, shrill-voiced crowd. Lights showed through chinks in the shuttered windows of the houses they passed, but they could see little of the houses themselves. They soon saw all they wanted, however, of the building to which they were being taken. Torches, spitting in the rain, burned in old-fashioned iron sconces on either side of the gateway and the six men halted in the flickering reddish glare, staring in dismay at the thick stone walls, topped with spikes; the small heavily-barred windows.

'No!' James Porter's voice was a horrified whisper. 'Not back to chokey again. Not after all we've — '

Somebody put a hand on his shoulder and propelled him firmly through the gate. It thumped shut after them and they heard the all-too-familiar sound of the bar being dropped into place. There was the prison smell that none of them would ever get out of his nostrils, the echo of boots on stone flags, the rattle and creak of a cell door being opened, the slam as it closed behind them.

Out of the frying pan, Fare thought bitterly, and into the bloody fire.

It was a large cell, whitewashed and lit by candles in brackets on the wall. There was clean straw with which to make beds and a pile of blankets, for the evening was chill and damp.

Barker said matter-of-factly, 'Well, lads. Here we are together again, it seems.'

He was sitting on a pile of straw, a blanket round his shoulders, playing cards with Shiers, Lesley and Russen.

'Aye. Together again in prison.' Fare stared gloomily round the cell. 'A fine trap we've walked into.'

'Trap?' Barker stood up. 'Nowt o' t'kind. Watch.'

He tossed his cards down, went to the door and thumped on it. Instantly a slide snapped back and a swarthy, grinning face appeared. Barker produced a coin. '*Vino, amigo,*' he said, '*pronto.*' He turned to watch the effect on the others as the soldier nodded and vanished. A minute later, a bottle of wine came through the peephole.

'We're to have everything we require — baccy, wine, food.' He passed the bottle round. 'We've been examined by a judge and we're to be held here until the Governor returns from Santiago in five days' time. We're not prisoners; we're being detained for questioning, so we has to pay for our keep. But it's all cheap, and the government gives us money — a quarter of one of their dollars a day.' He looked rather sourly at Fare. 'Since I named you, John Fare, alias John Thompson, as mate, you are to receive a dollar. Lyon, as boatswain, is to be given half a dollar.'

'Trust the bloody Scotsmen to come out of it on the right side.' Porter was grinning with relief. 'I vote they pay for the wine and baccy and each man pays for his own food. Pass that bloody bottle!'

On the morning of the thirteenth of March, they were

awakened early and, after breakfast, they made themselves as presentable as they could. They were taken through sunlit streets where most of the houses seemed to be made of wood and where passers-by smiled amicably at them as they went along. It was a warm, clear day, and they caught a glimpse of a distant white triangle, like a blunt arrowhead, that pointed up into the blue — the volcano, they found out afterwards, of Villarica.

Valdivia, they had already learnt, stood at the confluence of the Rio Valdivia with the Rio Calle-Calle where there was an island called the Isla Teja. The Governor's residence faced a small plaza at the northern end of the town. Inside, the house was cool after the warmth of the morning, and rich with Moorish screens, sombre oil-paintings and dark, ornately-carved woodwork. Indian rugs provided colour, and there were many little tables that showed off beaten silverware and figurines in brass and copper. The ten self-styled shipwrecked mariners were taken into a long, low-ceilinged room, bare and white, with a glossily-polished wooden floor that took moist prints of their bare feet as they walked on it. At one end of the room stood a heavy mahogany desk; above it a portrait in oils of a high-ruffed, helmeted Spanish grandee stared haughtily at them as they waited. A clock ticked somewhere, and the lieutenant's sword-belt clinked as he stood just inside the door. As a small, elderly man dressed in austere black and white entered, the officers came to attention and rapped out a string of titles in Spanish.

The Governor paused inside the doorway, his shrewd black eyes flickering over his guests before he smiled and inclined his head. 'Gentlemen.' His English was heavily-accented, but perfectly comprehensible. 'I am Don Fernando Martell, Governor of the Province of Valdivia. I must offer you my apologies for not being here to welcome you when you arrived. I hope you have been well treated?'

'Very well, thankee, Your Excellency,' said Barker. 'Most handsome treatment we've had.'

146

'I am happy to hear it.' The Governor inclined his head again. 'And I must also offer you my sincere condolences on the sad loss of your ship.'

'My thanks to you, Your Excellency.' Barker bowed.

'And, of course, on the even more painful loss of your captain.'

'Captain?' said John Fare.

'But of course.' Don Fernando walked across to his desk and picked up a sheet of paper. 'I am informed by Judge Ortega that only the mate, boatswain, and eight seamen of the *Mary* were saved. I assume your captain perished. A sad loss.' He stroked his neat white beard. 'What was his name, by the way?'

'Dearman.' Barker took the first name that came to mind. 'A fine man, Your Excellency.'

'Undoubtedly. You were bound from Liverpool to Valparaiso, yes? With what cargo, may I ask?'

'General cargo, Your Excellency.' Barker hadn't bargained on a detailed cross-examination. Damn this dried-up dago, he thought. If the judge accepted our story, why can't he?

'And you must be the mate, Señor Thompson, yes?'

'No.' Barker was beginning to sweat a little. 'I am but a mariner by trade.'

The Governor raised his bristly white eyebrows a fraction. 'So? Then why does not the mate, as your senior, speak for you all?' When nobody answered he said, 'Who, if you please, is Señor Thompson?'

'I am,' said John Fare.

'Then perhaps I might be allowed to address myself to you.' The Governor smiled charmingly. 'You must be a very modest man, señor, to allow a seaman to speak for you, eh? Who is the owner of your ship?'

'Owner?' Fare floundered. 'Er — the owner, of course, is — why, to be sure — '

'Mr William Owens, merchant, of Liverpool,' said Barker.

The sharp black eyes switched back to him. 'Thank you. And your name is?'

'Smith, Your Excellency. Benjamin Smith.'

The Governor nodded. Then he looked straight at Russen. 'And yours?'

Russen had forgotten his pseudonym.

There was a hideous silence until Barker said, 'Your Excellency, the man you have singled out is a harmless idiot. His faculties, never sound, were severely impaired by the shock of taking to the boat and our subsequent privations.'

'Idiot?' said Russen, outraged. 'Why, I'll show you who's the idiot, Johnny Barker, when — ' He grunted as Lesley dug him sharply in the ribs with his elbow.

'He has my sympathy,' said Don Fernando solicitously. 'Not only does he not know his own name, but he seems to think yours is Barker. No doubt the British Consul-General in Santiago will arrange some suitable hospital for him.'

Barker went cold. 'The Consul-General?'

'But naturally.' The Governor smiled. 'You are all British subjects, yes? It will be my duty to inform Señor John Walper of your arrival and he will make arrangements for — '

'Your Excellency, there's really no call for you to trouble yourself so,' said Barker rapidly. 'We ourselves can arrange to take ship back to where we came from and — '

'I see.' Don Fernando's voice cut like a knife. 'You really wish to return to the place you came from? To Van Diemen's Land?'

Nobody said anything. There were no more lies to tell. They stared at the courtly, straight-backed old man dumbly, the truth of what he implied confirmed on their faces, waiting for him to call the guard and put them in chains. Instead, he smiled gently.

'Gentlemen,' he said reprovingly, 'lies I can understand. But they must not, please, be an insult to my limited intelligence.' He sat down behind his desk, checking off points on his long fingers. 'You are shipwrecked, but not one of you manages to

148

save anything that can identify you or your ship. Well, that is possible; as is the loss of your captain, the vagueness of your cargo, and the fact that you have a mate who cannot speak for himself and who does not know the owner of his ship — and a seaman who forgets his own name. But, most important of all, the mention of the British Consul-General strikes you with fear, not with the relief of men hoping for succour from their own kind.' He leaned back in his chair. 'The truth,' he said curtly, 'or I will have you instantly thrown into prison — without the comforts you have so far enjoyed — pending instructions from Señor Walper in Santiago.'

Barker told him everything, including their real names, watching the Governor anxiously as he talked, but the long aristocratic face gave nothing away. When he'd finished, Don Fernando said, 'And so you committed no murder in making your escape?'

'None, Your Excellency. We put the others ashore with provisions, as I told you, to await a ship.'

'I can, and I will, check the truth of what you have said.'

'Do so, Your Excellency, and you will find that, this time, we have kept nothing back.'

'Tell me one thing. Why did you decide to come to Chile?'

'For the same reason — ' William Shiers' Yorkshire voice made Martell turn his head sharply, 'that your countrymen decided to fight against the Spaniards. For liberty.'

The Governor stared at him for a moment, then nodded. 'Believe me, I will not take yours away from you if I can avoid it.' He stood up. 'You understand that I must communicate with my government in Santiago. The final decision will not be mine. But my recommendation will be that you should be allowed to stay in Valdivia as free citizens. I will assign to you an interpreter, a gentleman of good reputation named Captain Lawson.' He walked to the door. 'In the meantime, I fear that you will have to remain in custody until I receive further instructions. Good day to you, gentlemen.'

Captain William Jose Miguel Lawson turned out to be an

149

engaging mixture of the Latin and the Anglo-Saxon; the twenty-year-old son of a Guards officer who had married a Spanish girl during Wellington's Peninsular Campaign of 1812. He sat on their beds, his back up against the wall of the cell, drinking and gesturing energetically as he told them something of Chile's history: of Pedro de Valdivia, the aristocratic Spaniard after whom the town was named, who had tried to tame the untameable Araucanian Indians and who had been captured by them and put to death by, it was said, being forced to drink molten gold; of the wild son of an Irish father and a Spanish mother, Bernardo O'Higgins, who played so great a role in the liberation of Chile from Spanish rule and became the Republic's first President.

'The British will know you are here as soon as His Excellency communicates with Santiago,' he said. 'They will undoubtedly try to reclaim you. But do not fear. If we take you under our protection, no harm can come to you.' He grinned all over his olive face. 'It may encourage you to know that the Governor is not over-fond of the English as a nation. He will not give you up without good reason.'

'But how long are we to remain locked up?' Charles Lyon turned from the barred window. 'There are girls out there, and — '

'The most beautiful in the world.' Lawson put his forefinger and thumb together and blew a kiss into space. 'Ravishing creatures, as ready to be set afire as tinder from a spark. Lips like wine and brown supple bodies that — but I am forgetting.' He fumbled in the side pocket of his coat and pulled out a paper. 'I have a petition here to present to His Excellency, signed by some of the leading citizens of the town, asking for you to be set free. We build boats here, you know. They have heard that some of you are shipwrights and could be of use to them.'

And, on the next day, they were taken before Don Fernando again, their filthy rags replaced by new shirts and trousers, their faces oddly white where their beards had been shaven off, in contrast with their deeply sunburnt foreheads. Lawson was present, tall and sleek in his bottle-green Army uniform.

'I have considered this request.' The Governor sat at his desk, the petition in his hands. 'It is reasonable, and carries much weight. But should I be instructed by the government to hand you over to the English, I must do my duty without regard for my own personal feelings. You understand?'

Barker said, 'Sir, rather than be handed over, we'd consider it an act of charity if you took us out and had us shot in the town square.'

'Precisely. You would do anything rather than be returned to your countrymen.' Lawson nodded. 'That is what concerns His Excellency — that, fearing an adverse decision from Santiago, you might take it into your hands to escape if he sets you at liberty. That would place him and our government in an extremely difficult position.' He paused. 'If, however, you would give your parole not to leave Valdivia — '

'Aye, we'd do that.' Barker looked round at the others. 'Agreed, lads?'

'Only until word comes from Santiago,' said Shiers. 'I'll promise no more than that.'

'Captain Lawson has also given his word as a Chilean officer that you will not escape.' The Governor and the captain exchanged a glance. Meaning, thought Barker, that we're to be watched; maybe shot if we try. 'He will assist you to find lodgings. If you drink, be temperate and avoid trouble. When you are able, you will pay back to the government the money that was allowed for your subsistance while you were in custody.' He stood up and smiled. 'Otherwise gentlemen, until the dispatches arrive from Santiago, you are at liberty to do as you please.'

13

'Captain Lawson!' James Lesley had to raise his voice to a shriek above the blare of the band and the roar of four hundred yelling Valdivians. 'Tell those fellows to watch what they're about with their sledgehammers, or the bloody ship's going to enter the water on her beam ends.' He bawled across to Shiers, 'All well on your side, Will?' Shiers lifted a hand. Lesley turned to the Valdivian overseer. 'All ready, *amigo*.' He made a pushing movement with his hands. 'Let go!'

The Liberty Men had had no difficulty at all in finding employment. On this, their first day of freedom, a four-hundred-ton barque was being lauched to the accompaniment of a trumpet-and-drum band, fluttering flags, and a crowd that was howling itself hoarse with excitement. The sun shone warmly, wine bottles passed freely from hand to hand, and His Excellency himself stood in the shade, smiling benignly at the uproar. There was a sudden hush as the vessel began moving down the slipway, then an ear-splitting roar from the crowd as she hit the Rio Valdivia in a flurry of foam.

'Just like old times, eh?' Porter had to shout into Lyon's ear. 'Pity Charlie Taw's not here to call for three cheers for

152

the Governor.' He imitated Taw's rough Yorkshire voice, slurred with drink. 'Why don't you cheer, you dog?'

'And, by God, so I will!' Lyon looked round. 'Lads,' he bellowed. 'Three cheers for His Excellency! Hip, hip!'

The cheers sounded thin against the yelling and the blare of the band, but Don Fernando heard them and bowed, smiling. A fat, swarthy Valdivian in a top hat and cutaway coat ran up to Lawson and delivered an impassioned speech, shrieking at the top of his voice and gesturing furiously at the Liberty Men.

'Somebody,' said Fare morosely, 'doesna want us here, evidently.'

But when Lawson translated, it seemed to be the fat man's opinion that the newcomers, criminals or not, had been sent by the blessed saints themselves; they could do the work of thirty ordinary men, and the fat man (the owner of the newly-launched barque) wished to hire them for the fitting-out at fifteen dollars per month per man.

'Tell him,' said Fare cannily, 'that if he'll throw in our provisions, he's on.'

The corpulent one listened, nodded eagerly and turned to the crowd, shouting until the veins stood out on his forehead. He then, to John Fare's utter revulsion, kissed him on both cheeks, grabbed the first woman he saw, and began dancing wildly in front of the townsfolk. Grinning, the band switched from march to dance time. Yelling encouragement, dancers formed circles round the ship-owner; a man with a guitar joined the band, then another, with brightly-painted gourds filled with seeds which he shook. In less than a minute, the whole formless crowd had shaken itself into the orderly pattern of the dance. The rhythm got into the blood, into the mind; a fast beat that was echoed visually by the swing of the girls' skirts, the gesture of the men's arms as they pirouetted and leaped. Two girls, giggling and blushing, ran across, seized Will Cheshire and Shiers and dragged them into the nearest group.

Jones said to Fare, 'My God, John, will ye look at that?'

An enormously fat woman dressed in black silk, her face coated thickly with powder, had approached John Barker like a ship-o'-the-line in full sail, curtseyed creakily, and towed him away. Lawson, an arm round the waist of a tall, sloe-eyed señorita, paused to say, grinning, 'Your friend's made a conquest, it seems. The widow d'Oliviera, the richest woman in Valdivia.' They watched Barker hop forward, smiling fixedly, lose his balance and bounce off the widow's vast bosom like a billiard ball off a cushion. Then Lawson was pulled away and Fare, Jones and Dady were drawn into the vortex by three purposeful middle-aged women.

Charles Lyon stood with Porter, Lesley and Russen.

James Porter said, 'Come on, Charlie. Let's go quietly with these two beauties.'

Two girls, one curvy and voluptuous, the other slim but with magnificent breasts, rushed up, laughing; but Lyon moved behind Lesley and let him and Porter be dragged off.

Russen said, 'What the devil, Charlie? I never thought to see you backward when there was this kind of work afoot.'

Lyon said, 'I'm going for a stroll, Ben. You go and join in.' He walked away across the square, away from the shipyard.

She was standing at the corner of a white-painted house at the edge of the square as if she'd just happened upon the scene by chance. She'd been for water — there was a pitcher standing beside her that she'd been carrying on her shoulder when Lyon first saw her — and her bare feet were still wet, with a little mud sticking to them that she'd picked up as she walked. She was wearing a dress that, although clean and carefully mended, had faded long ago from its original red to a delicate rose-pink, and it was obviously the only garment she had on.

Lyon said quietly, 'Would ye like to dance?'

Her body was breathtakingly lovely under the thin cotton. The long smooth line of the hip flowed into the smaller curve of her waist as she stood, her weight on her right foot, looking

154

up at him. Her breasts were small but full and erect, with long, firm nipples.

Lyon said, 'What do they call ye, lassie?'

Her hair was blue-black and reached down to her waist. It shone in the sun like the feathers of a blackbird, and her skin was the colour of honey. She looked up at him with slightly-slanting brown eyes that were flecked with topaz; eyes that were wide with — what? Lyon asked himself. Shock? Fear? Surprise? He was reminded of a deer he'd come upon in a glen, once, when he'd been a lad.

He said again, 'Will ye dance wi' me?' and took her hand.

She snatched it away as if he'd burnt her. Her full lips parted as if she were going to scream, but she didn't utter a sound. The devil take her, he thought angrily. He felt a bloody fool, standing with his hand still held out to this half-crazed slut who stared at him as if he was about to murder her. He let his hand fall, and turned away.

He felt her long, warm fingers close on his arm. He looked down at her. She didn't smile coquettishly or lower her long black lashes. She gave a strange little animal sigh and let him take her into the dance. She moved like a cat when she walked, all hard, flowing muscle; she danced as if she and the fast, insistent rhythm of the music were one — as if, Lyon thought confusedly, she were talking to him through that taut, supple body that swayed and spun before him. She never took her eyes off him. She never spoke and she never smiled — not until the dance was over and he stood grinning at her. Then she smiled — a slow smile that began in her eyes and transformed her face from defensive reserve to open friendliness.

Lyon said, 'Whew! What wi' the springing about and the day's work, my throat's like sand. Can we no' see if we can find something to drink?'

She stared at him, the smile vanishing as she frowned intently, trying to understand what he was saying.

'Drink,' he said. He curved his right hand into a cup and held it to his mouth.

Instantly her face lit up. She turned, ran away, and the next minute he saw her lifting her pitcher of water effortlessly to bring to him. He ran across to her.

'No, no. Not that sort of bloody drink.' He thought a minute. '*Vino*.' He'd heard Barker use that word in the prison. '*Vino*. That's what we need.'

She didn't react, except that all of a sudden her eyes misted and a tear, trembling and translucent, trickled down her cheek. She turned away from him, buried her face in her hands and sobbed silently.

For Christ's sake, Lyon asked himself, what have I done? Luckily, the orchestra had struck up again and a couple were out in the middle dancing all alone while the crowd stood round them and clapped out the rhythm. Nobody was watching. They'd think I'd insulted her, he thought, remembering his nightmare experience in the hayloft back in Hobart Town when Abigail had turned from hot, naked desire to a terrified sobbing wife fighting for her honour when her husband appeared.

'Listen, lassie,' he said in his soft Scots voice, 'I'm no' going to hurt you. I'm your friend. *Amigo*.' It was the only other word in Spanish he knew.

He might as well have spoken to the pitcher for all the response he got. Cautiously he put a hand on her firm, smooth shoulder. If she screams, I'm as good as dead, he thought. Even my mates willna believe I didna try to assault her. She turned, her head down, and buried her face in his shoulder, sobbing in great, hoarse gasps. He stroked her hair, baffled. What, in God's name, had he said? Did the word *vino* mean something inexpressibly insulting when you used it to a woman? He stared round helplessly. Captain Lawson, holding his girl by the hand, was watching him from across the square, his face set in a hard, expressionless stare. He bowed to his partner, released her and came over with his long, loping stride.

Lyon said hurriedly from over the top of the girl's head,

156

'Captain, I meant no harm, I assure you. All I did was — '

Lawson said harshly, 'What, in heaven's name, made you pick this girl to dance with?'

'She seemed lonely. She had nobody to dance wi'.' How could I say, Lyon thought, that as soon as I set eyes on her it seemed she'd been standing on that corner since the beginning of time, waiting for me?

'Of course she's lonely. She's a Mapuche and an outcast from her tribe. A woman with no family. A vagabond. She makes a living running errands, peddling water. Charles, leave her and find another girl to dance with.'

Lyon stared at him. 'And I thought this was the land of freedom and liberty! I tell ye, Captain, I too am an outcast from my tribe. I've no family and I'm a vagabond. I make a living as best I can. If this lassie's an Indian and a servant, why, it makes no difference to me.'

He looked down at the girl. She'd stopped sobbing. The remote, expressionless look he'd seen on her face was back again as she watched Captain Lawson.

'Nor to me,' snapped Lawson. 'Here in Chile, little regard is paid to the colour of a person's skin. But you forget I am responsible for you, and I cannot allow you to — ' He stopped. 'Forgive me, Charles. How could you know? It is merely that I do not wish you to be involved in an impossible situation with this woman.'

'Impossible? Know what?'

'That she is a deaf-mute. You will never be able to speak to her, nor she to you. She is a body, nothing more; a female body that has served the purpose of many men. She has no name. In the town they call her "*La Silenciosa*", the silent one. Now will you leave her? I can find you — '

'Then, at least,' said Lyon, 'I willna have the labour of teaching her English.' As the Chilean frowned, then shrugged and walked away, he turned to the girl, grinning. 'And you'll never be able to nag me, eh?' As she smiled back at him uncertainly, he said, 'But ye'll have to have a name, lass.

What can we call you?' He flicked back through the names of the women he'd known. No, that'd never do. But then one name came into his mind — a woman's name that he'd known only too well when he'd been shut away from the world like this girl. The name of a place for outcasts. 'Sarah,' he said aloud. 'That's your name from now on, whether you ever know it or not. Sarah.' He picked up the pitcher and, in front of her horrified eyes, poured its contents onto the ground. 'And now,' he said, 'we're going to take a real drink together.'

It was, thought John Jones, like nothing he'd ever seen before in all the ports he'd visited. Not much of a one for dancing, he'd abandoned his matronly partner for a bottle and a seat on the ground in the shade where he'd been joined soon after by Dady and John Fare. Now the three of them watched in astonishment as tables were dragged out from nearby houses, set with white cloths and loaded with food that seemed to materialize out of thin air — great bowls of beef broiled with spices and vegetables; roast chickens; legs of lamb. Fresh, crusty bread with slabs of butter, plates of little sugary cakes, piles of fruit. And wine — bottles of it, wine-skins full of it, earthenware pitchers running over with it. 'Be temperate,' Don Fernando Martell had said. But with every man in the town wanting to toast them, pledge them, drink their healths, how could they refuse? There were Lesley and Russen, their shirts already red-splashed ruins, abandoning mugs and glasses to tilt bottles to their mouths as they sat in a circle of giggling girls. There was Johnny Barker sitting on a bench beside his huge, billowing widow who, an arm posses-sively round his neck, was topping up his glass as fast as he swigged from it and feeding him bits of chicken out of a bowl. Shiers was with a girl who seemed to have brought her entire family along; there was her squat, muscular father who, Jones had heard, was a blacksmith called Carvenia, a stout, shrill-voiced mama and enough brothers and sisters to keep a Lanca-shire cotton-mill running. Porter was playing hopscotch with some of the brats. Young Will Cheshire was nowhere to be

158

seen; either he was flat on his back with drink, or his girl was flat on her back with him, as Fare had coarsely remarked. And Charles Lyon . . . now that was a right queer business, if you like. Instead of some flash, big-breasted hussy ripe for bed, he'd taken up with a woman who, although beyond doubt the most shapely lass present, was a beggar-maid. An Indian woman, from the look of her. She never spoke nor did he, and she never took her eyes off his face. They just sat, quiet-like, having a drink and a bite to eat, and smiling and touching one another. Eh, a right queer business, that.

And the sun set as if the world were on fire and candles were brought out, hundreds of them, until the night sky was a black lake that reflected the still, yellow candle flames in myriads of twinkling points of light overhead. Fresh relays of musicians took over. The dancers, refreshed by the cool, pine-scented night air, leapt and spun with renewed vigour. But Charles Lyon didn't dance. He sat watching the candlelight on the face of the girl beside him — a face so still, so smooth, that it might have been that of a statue cast in bronze had it not been for those warm, smiling eyes. He saw his friend Jamie Porter lead a girl out of the dance and try to speak fair to her in his parody of Spanish, getting a scream of laughter and a torrent of incomprehensible Castellano in return. Porter tried a gesture and drew another scream, this time of outrage, and a swinging buffet across the face. Then Lyon squeezed the hand of the girl he'd name ' Sarah, and felt his own hand squeezed quickly in return. What more, he asked himself, do you need in the way of talk?

She, knowing no words, had no names for her emotions. There was a coldness in the belly sometimes, fast breathing, pounding blood; they were brought on by a man bent on rape, the river she'd almost drowned in as a child, a snarling dog. That, for her, was fear. There was having no food, no warmth, no shelter; that was unhappiness. And for her, hap-piness had always been a negative state; it had meant not being cold, not being hungry, not being beaten. Until now.

Now there was this all-pervading warmth, a feeling of being in hot sunlight. There was the wonder she'd felt when she'd watched a rainbow, a spider's web sequinned with dew, the loveliness of a *copihue* flower. She thought as an animal thinks — in pictures, sensations. The words 'man', 'protection', 'love' were as unknown to her as any others. She, as a female animal, watched Charles Lyon as devotedly and untiringly as a stray dog will watch someone who befriends it. She didn't fetch his food or his drink; she knew that if she went away from him and tried to take some, she would be driven away and beaten and there would be the angry, bitter faces of the women who, for some reason she could never understand, hated her on sight and who would urge on their men to beat her. Some of the men did beat her. Others waited until their women were out of sight and then did other things to her. Once, she had objected to this and pushed the man off, but that had resulted in a thrashing she had never forgotten. Now, she let the men do what they liked. It was a matter of indifference to her and, being Indian, she knew how to prevent herself becoming big-bellied with child if she did not wish to be. So she kept close to Charles Lyon — his shadow when he went to bring wine and meat. But when, towards midnight, he yawned vastly, she stood up and took his hand and tugged it gently.

Looking often over her shoulder to make sure he followed, she led him through the little town and south along a track between vegetable gardens where cicadas whirred in the cool summer night. The cultivated land petered out until they were walking on a centuries-old cushion of pine needles between tall straight-trunked trees that soared up to shut out the stars. And then they came to a native hut — one deserted by its builders, Lyon thought, noting the crazy walls, the great rents in the roof. Inside, in the starlight that came through the gaps in the thatch, he could see that it was pitifully bare, with only a pile of fresh hay for a bed. She stood watching

160

him for a moment, her dark eyes gleaming in the starlight. Then abruptly she bent, took the hem of her dress, straightened, and drew it off over her head.

She was a living sculpture, a goddess of the forest, beautiful beyond belief in the sweet curves and planes of her body. Her small perfect breasts rose and fell as she watched him anxiously, hoping for his approval. When he didn't move, she walked across to him and began to unbutton his shirt. When he was naked she moved against him, gently, like a cat rubbing itself against its master. She felt him come erect, and she took his hands and drew him to the bed, watching him all the time. She turned him round and gave him a small nudge with her breasts to tell him to lie down on his back. She stood over him, astride his body. Then, slowly, she sank down on her knees, taking him deep inside her, and she began to move rhythmically above him, faster and ever faster, with her eyes still on him and her long hair flowing over her shoulders. She had never done this before, but this was how she knew it had to be. Other men had taken her. This time, she wanted to tell this male that she was accepting him — taking him as her mate.

And so, in the starlight and with the scent of clean hay in his nostrils, Charles Lyon heard Sarah talking to him for the first time.

14

The Presiding Officer waited until the door had closed behind the four prisoners; the other members of the Court Martial turned towards him deferentially. In the silence that followed the hoarse commands of the escort, a tree outside the window scrabbled at the glass and the wind, the first of the equinoctial gales that would buffet Hobart Town that autumn and sprinkle the peak of Mount Wellington with snow, blew a puff of smoke down the chimney.

'So there you have it, gentlemen.' The president glanced irritably at the cloud of smoke that hung over the fireplace. 'We have found the prisoners guilty. It now remains for us to determine the sentence.'

The Judge Advocate nodded, watching his clerk's pen fly across the paper before him.

'I think, sir, we must take into consideration the extenuating circumstances involved before sentence is passed. The corporal of the Guard is not a man of great intellect or initiative. He was put under the command of a man who, it appears, is of like character. Captain Taw is — '

'A civilian, sir!' The elderly colonel on the Presiding

162

Officer's right smacked a hand down on the table. An inkwell jumped and was steadied by the junior officer present. 'By God, sir, this is what comes of placing the military under the command of civilians. Ha! I remember, gentlemen, when I served under General Picton — '

'I agree, sir.' The Presiding Officer cut in smoothly. 'This trial has, among other things, cast doubt upon the whole question of giving command of the Army to civilians.' He looked round. 'Dammit, gentlemen, the House of Commons is enough to bear, God knows, without having the Captain Taws of this world thrust upon us.' He waited for, and received, his tribute of guffaws. 'It is clear from the findings of the Board of Inquiry that Captain Taw must be held responsible for this outrageous piracy. He set no adequate guard, he gave no proper supervision, he took no precautions of any kind against it. His sole defence is that, since he regarded the convicts as the crew of the vessel, he allowed them the freedom consistent with that status. The blame, surely, lies at his door. But,' the Presiding Officer paused, frowning, 'these four wretched men before us — Dearman, Kent, Gathersole and Gillespie — must be disciplined.'

'By God, sir, indeed they must!' The elderly colonel glared round the table as if suspecting the four miscreants of hiding behind the chairs. 'Otherwise we're going to have every blasted private in the Army saying he couldn't do his duty because some damned bum-boatman or other told him not to.' He thumped the table and, once again, the junior officer had to grab for the inkwell. 'Confound it, gentlemen, neglect of duty is no light matter. I recall General Picton saying on — '

'Precisely, sir. But on this occasion I am inclined to the opinion of the Judge Advocate. There are, to be sure, extenuating circumstances, and we should, I think, temper justice with mercy.'

And temper it they did. Their sentence was, by its mildness, an indication of the Army's unwillingness to be blamed for a situation that, in their opinion, had been brought about by

163

civilian — and naval — incompetence. Dearman lost his corporal's chevrons, of course. A part of the cost of his missing equipment and of the four lost Pattern 1802s was stopped from his miserable, and sometimes irregular, pay, and all four men were severely reprimanded. Then they were packed off to India to rejoin their old comrade-in-arms Colour-Sergeant Mayhew. That, in their opinion, was the most horrible punishment that could be inflicted on them.

But it was not nearly enough for that man of integrity and intolerance, Lieutenant-Governor George Arthur. Although an Army man himself, holding his commission in the 91st (Argyllshire) Highlanders, he was not concerned with triangular squabbles among the Army, Navy and civilian officers under his command, and he took no sides. His constant concern was the reduction to zero of the number of bushrangers operating in Van Diemen's Land; and every escaped convict was a potential bushranger. Already, on the seventh of February, as soon as the whole laxity of the *Frederick* affair had been made known to him, he had slammed the stable door shut by promulgating in his *Standing Orders for Masters of Government Vessels carrying Prisoners* that convicts were to be kept in heavy double irons, checked morning and night; that no axes were to be allowed within reach of the prisoners; that no vessel carrying prisoners was to put in to shore during a voyage, and several other discouraging ordinances.

'Confound it!' His long face pink with anger, his thin mouth set, he strode up and down the long room in Government House where he was dictating letters, the Court Martial papers in his hand. As always, he wore a semi-military coat, with a red seam down the outside of his trousers and a high-necked stock. 'At Port Arthur, we have every conceivable means of thwarting the escape of a convict — semaphores, man-traps, patrols and dogs. The expense of their maintenance is enormous. And yet these fellows, a pilot and four nincompoops, almost present a gang of convicts with a government vessel worth twelve hundred pounds!' He shook the reports of the

164

Board of Inquiry and the Court Martial at his clerk, who made himself as small as he could behind his table. 'Any man who allows a convict to abscond has, in my opinion, acted as a recruiting sergeant for the bushrangers and has assisted, however indirectly, in any consequent rape, murder or plunder of the people for whom I am responsible. Send this to the Honourable John Burnett, Colonial Secretary.'

The clerk wrote furiously; Arthur dictated, striding up and down the room:

> I think, from the Documents herewith forwarded, it is sufficiently evident that the Capture of the Brig has been principally owing to the total Neglect of any military Guard being kept or of the most common Precautions having been taken for her Safety.
>
> Indeed, it would appear from the Master's Deposition that all the Convicts were considered by those on board as forming part of the Crew. It is scarcely possible that the loss of the Vessel could have occurred had a proper Lookout been kept for, of the seventeen Persons on board, ten only were concerned in the Piracy. [In his agitation, the Governor made a small slip; there had been, in fact, nineteen men on board the *Frederick*.]
>
> The Master appears to me to have conducted himself personally well after the Attack was made but to have been very blameable in not having taken the slightest Precaution to prevent what has unfortunately happened, nor do I learn that he ever required the Military to assist him in the Protection of the Vessel by mounting a Guard, although I submit that to the Conduct of the Corporal in charge of the Party the loss of the Vessel may be mainly attributed.

So His Excellency blamed everybody, but principally Corporal (now Private) Dearman. Taw blamed Dearman. Dearman, supported by the Board of Inquiry, blamed Taw; so, indirectly, did the Court Martial. The Port Officer for Hobart Town,

Captain Moriarty, washed his hands of the whole business while David Hoy dined out on his experiences and bought a share in a shipyard. The Navy maintained a lordly unconcern; Captain Lambert, of the *Alligator* frigate, when taken to task for not pursuing the *Frederick,* stated roundly that he took his orders from their Lordships of the Admiralty and not from a pack of prison warders.

For the Navy in its wisdom knew it had not yet finished with the Liberty Men.

They, by mid-April, had settled down very comfortably in Valdivia. No word concerning their future had come through from Santiago, but already they were accepted in the town and John Barker in particular was on the way to becoming a pillar of Valdivian society owing to his shrewd brain and his association with the whale-like but wealthy widow d'Oliviera. She, in fact, was hinting coyly to her friends that, as soon as *Juanito,* her *novio,* was made a citizen, there would, perhaps, be a surprise in store for them all. Barker, his long nose twitching at the thought of the widow's money, did not in the least object to being forcibly married; nor did the fact that he already had a wife and two children at Stokeneath in Cheshire deter him in the slightest. James Lesley, with a wife in England, was also contemplating bigamy, having fallen madly in lust with a big-bottomed, raven-haired siren who worked as a serving wench in a tavern. Charles Lyon, after changing lodgings several times, had found a landlord who did not object to the presence of Sarah in his house, and the two of them lived together in silent harmony. All the Liberty Men worked hard at the fitting-out of the barque. It was work they knew blindfold, and hard labour was something they had had beaten into them for years. They ate well, they put on weight and John Fare, as a true Scot, began to amass a small pile of savings.

It was on the twenty-fifth of April that the first small cloud appeared on their horizon; a cloud that, for a variety of reasons appeared and disappeared before they were even

166

aware of its presence. Private Pedro Rodriguez, lookout at the fort on the Isla Mancera in the estuary of the Rio Valdivia, saw it first — a small white speck that gleamed in the cool morning sunlight far out to sea before it winked out of sight. He ran for the telescope and focused on the speck when it heaved up again beyond the hard blue line of the horizon.

'*Barco*!' He beat the brass gong to summon the guard. 'A ship,' he said as the duty officer appeared, buckling on his sword-belt. 'To the north-west.' He pointed.

'Gunners! To your posts!' A little loading practice, the *teniente* thought as he took the telescope, wouldn't do those fat sons of unmarried mothers any harm. 'Sergeant Gomez! We load with ball!' After all, this was supposed to be a fort for the defence of Valdivia and not a home for semi-inebriates. 'All guns, load!' He peered through the glass, waiting for the ship's hull to come up over the horizon. Then he snapped the glass shut. 'English. A frigate. His Majesty's ship *Dublin*. I've seen her before.'

'She comes here, sir?' Private Rogriguez wriggled with anticipation. 'We fire the guns? In salute?'

'It is possible.' The lieutenant began to worry about the number of guns he ought to fire — the English were very touchy about such matters. And, *nombre de Dios,* he'd loaded with ball . . .

But the lieutenant need not have troubled himself. For the *Dublin*, having been relieved by HMS *Blonde* on the South American station, was on her way home to England via the Horn and was not disposed to potter about in obscure Chilean ports. Her captain glanced cursorily through his glass at the fort, used it to check his position on the chart, and then *Dublin* was gone, her sails bellying as the northerly drove her onwards.

The Liberty Men didn't know that the shadow of the White Ensign had passed over them until the guard was changed at the fort three days later. By that time it was too late to worry — and any apprehension they might have felt was dispelled on

167

the last day of April when a courier came down from Santiago with despatches giving them permission to stay in Valdivia as free citizens. There was a *fiesta* to celebrate that.

But the resultant hangovers were as nothing compared with the Bacchanalian series of celebrations that followed in rapid succession in May when first Barker, then Lesley, were married. Barker's wedding was a grandiose affair, with relatives and friends of the bride coming from as far as Santiago and Valparaiso. Don Fernando Martell himself danced decorously and stiffly with the Black Widow, as Porter irreverently called Barker's spouse after he'd heard about the size of the female of that species of spider compared with the male, and her practice of dining off her mate. Lesley's nuptials lasted a week and it was during those celebrations that Benjamin Russen, drunk as an owl, proposed marriage to the bride's sister — a muscular señorita with a moustache and a pronounced squint, who had the presence of mind to accept him in front of witnesses before she rushed off to burn candles in astounded gratitude to her favourite saint.

Matrimony was becoming all the rage. Or maybe, as John Fare cynically remarked, the nights were becoming a wee bit chilly and a wife was cheaper than a blanket. At all events, Will Shiers made an honest woman of Señorita Carvenia, the blacksmith's daughter, and William Cheshire married (or was married by) Maria Belasco, the plump, giggling girl he'd seduced (or been seduced by) at the launching party.

And through it all Charles Lyon and Sarah held hands and watched and danced and lived for each other. She was now a well-dressed girl, apart from the fact that she could never learn to wear shoes. But her clothes, her lace and the ribbons in her hair that Lyon loved to buy for her were as good as those of any woman in the town. He taught her to use a knife and fork and spoon, to eat and drink slowly and not as if every mouthful were about to be wrenched from her lips. He bought a slate and chalks and began, from his own limited literacy, to teach her to write, printing CHARLES and pointing to himself,

then SARAH and touching her gently. He was always gentle —
except sometimes when they made love and she would arouse
him to bursts of savage animal lust that seemed necessary to
her; it was as if she wanted him to know, by the pain and
ferocity of his love-making, that she was all his, to do with as
he wished. Then, when he fell asleep out of sheer exhaustion,
he would wake to find her washing his body, oiling it, brushing
and combing his long hair. There was always food ready
instantly when he came home after his day's work; she discovered by trial and error what he liked best to eat, how he
liked his shirts to be ironed, where he liked best to walk when
they went out together wrapped up against the chill of the
evening air as winter approached. He clowned for her and she
laughed silently, clapping her hands with pleasure. And when,
after many patient lessons, she wrote shakily on her slate
SARAH LOVES CHARLES and kissed him, he thought he would
die of happiness.

James Porter came to visit them frequently at first and took
a great deal of interest in Sarah's writing lessons, cocking his
one eye at the symbols chalked on the slate and running his
finger over them thoughtfully. Then, abruptly, his visits stopped and he shut himself up in his lodgings in the evenings —
teaching himself, Lyon discovered, to read and write from an
old copybook of Captain Lawson's.

Inevitably, the Liberty Men were drawing apart. The
married men were caught up in their wives' worlds, Barker in
his fine clothes being particularly remote and no longer involved, of course, in anything so menial as manual labour.
Rumour had it that he was to have a handsome sum of money
settled on him as soon as he got his Black Widow with child;
Jones, prepared to wager that Barker would kill himself trying
to earn his stud fee, found no takers. Shiers had gone into the
blacksmith's forge with his father-in-law. It helped the older
man and, since it paid better than the shipyard, Shiers was
able to put away good Yorkshire brass for the farm he'd buy
one day. Lesley and Russen, too, were trying to amass capital

— to buy into the boat-building business; they spent every evening spending money in the tavern and discussing how they'd do it. Cheshire, entirely wrapped up in his plump, amorous bride, was never seen at all except at work. Like the other married men, he was soon fluent in Spanish and he adapted quickly to the local way of life. Lyon and Porter, the bachelors, who lived in the same house and spoke English together and had less social contact with the locals, were slower to learn the language and settle in.

Winter came, cold and wet, and the town was filled with the smell of burning wood by day and night as the smoke gusted from the chimneys and was held down by the pouring rain, stinging the eyes and spreading a thin layer of ash on the mud in the streets. It was chilly work at the barque's fitting-out berth, out on deck in the wind and rain.

'Devil take it,' said John Dady irritably on a particularly wet, bleak morning in late August. He shivered in his damp clothes. 'This place is little better than the Harbour.'

'The pay's better.' James Porter spat a nail out of his mouth and hammered it home. 'And there's less flogging.'

'But the same work, the same cold rain, the same — ' Dady looked at the wall of trees on the opposite bank of the Rio Valdivia, at the Isla Teja almost lost in the weeping rain, 'the same shut-in feeling.'

'But we could leave if we were so minded.' James Porter paused in the act of reaching for more nails and stared at Dady. 'Is that what you're thinking of?'

Dady nodded. 'That's about the size of it, Jamie. John Fare and I have talked much of it lately. I haven't been a seaman all my life like he has — and Jones. But I feel — well, restless, like.'

'It's the sea.' John Fare stared for'ard, over the barque's bow downriver. 'It gets into a man's blood, the salt water does. I've been telling myself for weeks now that a rolling stone gathers no moss and that I must settle down one day. But 'tis of no avail.'

'So you want to leave, too?' Porter looked from one to the other. It seemed incredible. John Fare, as solid and cautious a man as you could wish. And Dady, the quiet unobtrusive one who never put forward an idea, never showed excitement. Porter turned to John Jones. 'What about you, John?'

For a moment, the older man appeared not to have heard. He gave three quick clouts to the nail he was hammering in, then he stared critically at what he'd done.

'I've been thinking about the *Dublin*,' he said slowly in his thick Liverpool voice, 'as nearly put in here last April. Up in Valparaiso, the Navy must know of our presence here by now. One of these days, they're going to pay us a visit in the *Blonde*.'

'But we'd be protected; 'twas promised us.' Porter put down his hammer. 'The Governor'd send the *Blonde* away with a flea in her ear.'

'The Governor's a good man, but he's not the government,' said Jones. 'All politicians, English or otherwise, are bastards, and their promises aren't worth a pig's bristle. Britannia rules the waves and if she was so minded, she could make the Chileans hand us over fast enough.'

'The Chileans'd never do that.' Porter shook his head decisively. 'They're a proud, free people, not to be bullied either by Spain or England.'

Jones shrugged.

John Fare said, 'If we went, would you come with us?'

'I would not.' Porter turned his one eye on him. 'All I wanted in Van Diemen's Land was my liberty, and that I now have. I like this place, I like the people and I trust them not to betray us to the Navy. I don't feel shut-in here.' He turned back to Jones. 'Where would you go? Don't you realize that the Chileans are the only people in the world who will offer you protection? The minute you leave Valdivia, you'll be a runaway, with every man in every port you come to ready to hand you over to the English.' He paused. 'Don't do it, John lad,' he said quietly. 'I don't want to think of you back in Hobart Town, shuffling along the quayside with the clank of the leg-irons in your ears, and the warders a-shouting, and nothing in your mind but the thought of the liberty you've lost. That would be a sad and bitter end to it all, after enduring so much.'

'We'll take our chance on that.' Jones looked squarely at Porter. 'And you'll not mention this talk we've had to anyone?'

Porter didn't. Not even a fortnight later, when the brig *Ocean West* came up the river, bound for Callao in Peru, to put ashore three men sick with the scurvy. Not even when, on the evening before the brig sailed, he saw Fare, Dady and Jones in the tavern, talking earnestly with Captain West, the owner of the vessel. And, on the following day, when the three failed to report for work and Captain Lawson had gone to their lodgings to find their rooms bare of everything that had belonged to them, Porter still said nothing. He blinked his single eye as he worked, regretting the passing of his friends, and he muttered to himself as he hammered:

Ten absconding pris'ners found themselves in Heaven;
Three went a-roaming, and then there were seven.

15

'Señor Jaime! Señor! Please open the door!'

Shouts from the street below almost drowned the landlord's voice as he beat on Porter's door. Downstairs, his wife was screeching curses on impotent drunkards who woke honest people in the middle of the night to alarm them and rob them of their sleep. Porter, duly alarmed and robbed of his sleep, rolled out of bed.

'What is it? What do you want?' he shouted in Spanish. Out in the street, torches flickered, soldiers' boots tramped, and people from neighbouring houses yelled indignantly at the uproar.

'Open the door!' Another voice joined with the landlord's; a military voice. 'Open the door, in the name of the Governor! And quickly!'

It was the tenth of February — five months after Fare, Jones and Dady had disappeared — and a hot summer's night. The barque had long since been fitted-out, and Porter had come home tired and sweating after a week's pine-felling at a lumber camp up the Rio Calle-Calle. He'd begun work a few weeks previously on his account of the escape of the Liberty

173

Men, and after spending an hour or two on his narrative, he'd fallen into bed exhausted. Feeling as if he hadn't slept at all, he opened the door.

'Whatever it is you wish,' he said, screwing up his eye in the glare of the lamp held by the landlord, 'would it not be possible, gentlemen, for you to return in the morning?'

'Regrettably, no.' The officer was courteous but unsmiling. 'Please do me the favour of dressing yourself and accompanying me.'

'In the middle of the night? Where to?'

'To prison.' As Porter opened his mouth, the officer added, 'It is useless to ask me questions, señor. I am merely carrying out my orders.'

It was all a bad dream. Yes, that was it; he was over-tired and dreaming about what had happened to him nearly a year ago. And, once again, he found himself being marched through dark streets by night; once again, the gates of the prison yawned open to receive him, and the torches cast their red glow on the olive faces of the soldiers. The same stone-flagged corridor . . . the same prison smell . . . the same creak of a cell door being flung open. The very same cell, at that.

And in his nightmare he saw Barker, Shiers, Lesley and Russen sitting on the straw beds. But they weren't in rags, and they weren't playing cards, and Barker was no longer in control of the situation. When he asked why he was being detained, the officer told him curtly that he would find out in due course.

'But you know me,' said Barker. He pulled out a bag of money. 'I am well-known to the Governor. Go to him and — '

'My orders, señor, come from His Excellency himself.' The officer went out and slammed the door. And locked it, Porter noticed.

Barker turned to the others. 'This is an outrage,' he said peevishly.

Porter, who hadn't seen him since his wedding, was staggered at the change in his appearance. The *Frederick*'s former

174

navigator had grown immensely fat and pallid, and his pointed dark-brown beard made him look like a Moorish money-lender.

'My wife is to be brought to bed at any time, and she requires my support.'

Lesley said, with a sharp look at Russen, 'So you've got your money, then, Johnny lad?'

'I think,' said Barker with dignity, 'that, in view of our altered circumstances, it would be more fitting if you called me Mr Barker. As for — '

The cell-door opened and Charles Lyon was ushered in.

'Well, Charlie,' said Porter. 'What brings you here in the middle of the night? Or don't you know either?'

'No.' Lyon looked round at the others. 'And my Sarah's nearly going crazed because she doesn't understand what's afoot any more than I do. Has it anything to do wi' Fare and the others absconding, d'ye think?'

'That was last September,' said Barker. 'And His Excellency told me he would take no action against us because of it. He is a very tolerant man.' He looked at Lyon disparagingly. 'Tolerant even of the immorality of certain of our number who take advantage of ignorant natives.'

'And is he tolerant,' asked Lyon pleasantly, moving closer to Barker, 'of fat, crafty convicts who commit bigamy to line their pockets?'

'Have a care,' said Barker sharply. 'I'm a free citizen, not a convict, and I — '

'A fat, crafty free citizen, then,' said Lyon. 'And if you call my Sarah an ignorant native again, I'll beat you into blubber, may God help me.'

'That'll do!' Lesley climbed to his feet, followed by Russen. 'Just leave Mr Barker alone, Charles Lyon, and mind your manners.'

'Mr Barker?' Lyon stared at him. 'And how long have you been his bloody lapdog, may I ask?'

'They've just heard,' said Porter, grinning, 'that Barker's

earned his stud fee.' He ranged himself alongside Lyon. 'Which one will you take, Charlie?' He examined the faces of Lesley and Russen, blotched with drink, their eyes muddy and uncertain. 'Or should we draw lots for who's to take on the pair of them?'

'Enough.' Shiers spoke placidly without standing up. 'We seem to be in enough trouble without starting a mill in here. Sit down, all of you, and let's try to decide what's amiss.' As the others moved apart he said, 'Has any of you stolen owt, or done owt else against the laws of this country?'

'Not me.' Russen shook his head. 'But what about Will Cheshire? He should be here. Maybe he's absconded. Has anybody seen — ?' At that moment, the cell door was flung open and Cheshire walked in, followed by the Governor and Captain Lawson.

As Shiers came to his feet, Barker said in Spanish, 'Your Excellency. If any one of us has committed any crime, I wish it to be known I was no party to it. You know me to be — '

Don Fernando cut him short.

'I think,' he said coolly, 'that we should speak in English for the benefit of those whose Castellano is not as good as yours. And nobody, as far as I am aware, has committed any crime. I have had you brought here because there is an English naval vessel anchored off the mouth of the river.'

'The *Blonde* frigate!' Barker's pale face had gone even whiter. 'And you intend to hand us over. After our months of good behaviour? You could, at least, have given us a chance to escape.'

'Exactly the reaction I expected.' The Governor's long Spanish face was an expressionless mask. 'I knew that, as soon as you heard there was an English man-o'-war in the vicinity, some of you would have had no faith in me. Fearing betrayal, you would have fled into the forest and there you would either have died of starvation or been murdered by the Indians. So I had you brought together here. I must apologize for the lack of comfort, but at least you are safe.'

176

'Sir, I assure you I did not doubt your good intentions for one moment,' said Barker quickly. 'But, if the captain of the *Blonde* should use force —'

Lawson said, 'In that case, you will be sent inland to the chief of a Mapuche tribe whom we can trust.' He looked directly at Barker. 'Novel as the idea may seem to some of you, we Chileans believe in keeping our word. It is, for His Excellency, a matter of personal honour that you should not be taken by the Royal Navy.'

Commodore Mason, of the *Blonde*, had other ideas. Stout, red faced and choleric, he had served as a midshipman aboard the *Shannon* under Captain Broke in the American War of 1812-14, and had been one of the party that had boarded and captured the *Chesapeake*. Compared with that feat of arms, the winkling of ten frowsy gaolbirds from a lice-ridden South American village should, he thought, present no difficulty at all. However, with the diplomacy insisted on by the Consul-General in Santiago, he had already sent, via the lieutenant in command of the fort, a letter to Don Fernando Martell:

Your Excellency: Having received the Information that several Men are in Valdivia that have come on the Coast in a clandestine Manner, I am commanded by my Government to request you to permit these Men to come on board His Majesty's Ship *Blonde* in order that they may give in their Declaration how they came on the said Coast. I have the Honour to be, Sir, Your Obedient Servant, H. Mason, Commodore RN, South American Station.

The commodore, far more at home on his quarter-deck than behind a writing desk, considered his epistle to be a masterpiece of suave cunning.

'And when the scum are brought aboard,' he said happily to his First Lieutenant, 'I want the buggers double-ironed directly and held in the orlop deck under armed guard.'

He walked his deck in the morning sunlight and waited

177

confidently for the boat containing the ten ruffians to appear at the mouth of the river.

All morning, the little fort on the Isla Mancera slept in the warm sun, the flag of the Independent Republic of Chile hardly stirring at its staff. Beyond, Mason thought irritably, there seemed to be nothing but bright green trees — like bloody parsley, mounds of it, as far as you could see. Full of heathen Indians, no doubt, all practising revolting obscenities when they weren't otherwise occupied in shrinking one another's heads. There'd be plenty of cover along the river bank, too, for any disgusting natives who wanted to use their bows and arrows and those filthy blowpipes of theirs. A landing-party could be a tricky task, pushing ten miles upriver under fire. Very tricky indeed, by God. But, fortunately, it wouldn't come to that. When the Navy said, 'Jump!' then, by the Lord, people jumped, and —

'Canoe in sight, sir! Pulling away from the fort!'

Mason snatched the spyglass out of the hands of the pointing midshipman and focused it across the sparkling sea. A canoe? How in the name of fortune can ten men fit into a canoe?

There were two men, not ten, and they were both Mapuches. Passing up a package, they stared disdainfully at the sailors lining the rail, spat into the sea, and waited for an answer. Mason's eyes bulged as he broke the seal and glanced at the letter.

'Damn and blast it, it's in Spanish. How in the name of hell am I expected to read this dago scrawl?'

After half an hour with a Chilean mess-boy, he managed to arrive at a rough translation. His Excellency thanked Commodore Mason for his letter and sent his sincere good wishes concerning the Commodore's health, that of the Consul-General, and also that of His Britannic Majesty King William the Fourth. The Commodore's request was perfectly reasonable and, in the light of the excellent relations that prevailed between the Governments of Chile and Great Britain, His Excellency would be delighted to assist the Commodore in any way possible. ('Good,' snarled Mason. 'The old fool's coming to the point at last.') But it would be a gross breach of hospitality if His Excellency did not receive the Commodore on this, his first visit to Valdivia. Therefore, the Commodore was most cordially invited to call upon His Excellency and, at the same time, interview the unfortunate men concerning whose welfare the Commodore was so rightly concerned. The Commodore would understand that, owing to the small size of the boat — regrettably the only one available — he would have to travel alone.

'In a bloody canoe?' Mason screwed up the letter and hurled it to the deck while the mess-boy flattened himself against a bulkhead. 'Damnation take his insolence!' The Commodore may have been lacking in subtlety, but he got the point of the letter. 'He's not going to give them up, confound him. He's defying me, curse him.' He glared at the terrified mess-boy. 'Get out. And request the First Lieutenant to come to my cabin.'

His first inclination was to reduce the fort to rubble but that, unfortunately, was not practicable. John Walper, the Consul-General in Santiago, had said that, at all costs, a breach between the governments of Chile and Great Britain was to be avoided. Very well, thought Mason craftily. Very well. We'll play these damned impertinent onion-eaters at their own game.

When the First Lieutenant came into the cabin he said, 'Mr Oxenbold. You are to take an armed party upriver and fetch out those ten blackguardly runaways. If you set out directly, you should return by nightfall.'

'Aye aye, sir.' The First Lieutenant, a thin man who had seen no active service, stiffened dutifully. 'The Governor has agreed, then, to surrender them as you requested?'

'No, confound him, he hasn't. We'll just have to ignore the old rogue and drag them from their pigsties unaided.'

'Aye aye, sir.' Oxenbold hesitated. 'And if there is resistance?'

179

'From the convicts? Stun them. If you are molested by Indians, shoot the vermin. But there'll be no resistance from the Chileans. They may bluff, but they'd never dare cross swords with the Royal Navy.'

'No, sir.' Oxenbold coughed and shuffled his feet. 'But, sir, they're an excitable lot. Suppose they get carried away and open fire?'

Mason swallowed, hardly able to get the words out. 'Then, dammit, man, you retreat. Those are my orders -— to risk no conflict. But I think a show of force will be sufficient for the purpose. Look fierce, Mr Oxenbold! Bluff the bastards!'

Oxenbold, it was true, didn't look particularly fierce, but to send some fire-eating midshipman on an errand like this could result in a wholesale massacre, war with Chile and his, Mason's, Court Martial, in that order.

'Just brandish your muskets, and you'll find the dagos'll take to their heels the minute they set eyes on you.'

From the fort, Lieutenant Enrico Barregales watched anxiously. What was in the dispatch he'd sent out to the English frigate, he'd no idea. But his own orders were clear: he was to prevent any Englishman other than the captain of the frigate from entering the Rio Valdivia. On the other hand, an open breach between the Republic of Chile and Great Britain was to be carefully avoided. 'Use no force,' his orders said. 'Let no man's blood be shed. If our gallant fighting men but show their teeth, the English will retire in confusion.'

The confusion, however, belonged exclusively to Lieutenant Barregales. He was, with all modesty, he told himself, a brave soldier. He was ready to give his life for Chile, to die gladly in the blazing ruins of his fort. But what he couldn't do was visualize these fighting fiends of English, the victors in so many sea battles, being prevented from entering a river by a few bared teeth. He watched through his telescope as the long-boat was lowered and the sailors (as evil-looking a gang of desperadoes as he'd ever seen) swarmed aboard followed by their officer — a thin, rapier-like man with a mouth set in grim

180

determination who, doubtless, was running through his mind the unspeakable cruelties he would inflict on the townspeople when the fort had been obliterated by cannon-fire. All the boat's crew were bristling with weapons — muskets, cutlasses, pistols. The boat pulled away from the *Blonde*.

Oxenbold eyed the sinister, squat bulk of the fortress, his jaw clenched, not in grim determination, but to prevent his teeth from chattering. He was running through his mind the possible effect of a thirty-two-pound ball striking the longboat amidships. Would he be killed outright? Would he, hideously torn and mutilated, be thrown into the sea to die between the jaws of a shark? Or even if by some miracle they passed the fort, would he meet his end from the diabolical poison on the tip of an Indian arrow? 'Stop that confounded talking there,' he snapped edgily. The bow oarsman, who had been debating with his mate the possibility of their having enough time in Valdivia to be accommodated by a couple of the local whores, muttered an obscenity.

'What was that?' squeaked Oxenbold.

'Beg pardon, sir, I'm sure.' The man heaved on his oar. 'Twas Seaman Bennet's cutlass, sir. It caught me in the private parts and made me — '

There was a chorus of sniggers.

'Damn you, will you hold your tongues?' Oxenbold hissed. 'I'll see the next man flogged who opens his mouth.'

They were well within gunshot now. He could see the twelve huge muzzles in their embrasures, the officer on the battlements with his telescope trained. These coastal batteries always had their arcs of fire ranged to an inch. Brandish your muskets, Mason had said. The First Lieutenant picked up a cutlass and waved it feebly in the air.

Holy Virgin, thought Barregales with a shudder. They must be lusting for blood. The officer flourishing his sword, snarling at his men; telling them to hurry, probably, to the devil's feast of rape and murder ahead. And the men laughing like savages as he outlined the atrocities they were about to

181

perpetrate . . . *Something must be done, and quickly.*

'Sergeant Gomez!' He ran down to the battery. 'Put a shot across the bows of the English!'

'Of the frigate, *teniente?*' Gomez, pot-bellied and smelling strongly of cheese, peered out of the embrasure. 'I do not think she is within range, and — '

'The ship's boat, imbecile! She will be under the walls at any moment!'

Dancing with impatience, he watched Gomez flapping his hands as the gunners heaved the fat muzzle round and depressed it. An eternity passed as Gomez made fussy adjustments. Barregales stuffed his fingers into his ears. Then Gomez shrieked, 'Fire!' and the end of the world seemed to take place as the charge ignited and the huge ball was slammed out of the muzzle. Dear God, thought the lieutenant, blinded with smoke, his ear drums singing. Please don't let that fool Gomez hit the boat.

Oxenbold was beginning to gain confidence. Evidently, the Commodore had known what he was talking about when he said the Chileans were bluffing. There seemed to be a good deal of leaping about in the fort, and there was one gun that was swinging round to follow them. But, already, they were so close to the river that he could see the islands in the estuary, and the — There was a thin cry from the fort. He looked up.

The ball did not go across the bows of the longboat. It passed, thirty-two pounds of solid iron, six feet above Oxenbold's head with a roar of displaced air that blew his hat off and sounded like a ravening lion — a roar that was drowned instantly by the thunder of the gun fired at close range. A dense cloud of black smoke jetted out from the fort while the low-trajectory shot struck the sea half a mile off in a sheet of spray, rebounded, struck again, and disappeared.

It was the only shot fired in the Battle of the Rio Valdivia. The longboat returned rapidly to the frigate. The *Blonde* returned to Valparaiso. Lieutenant Barregales got very drunk that night, and Sergeant Gomez gained the reputation of a master-gunner who could take a man's hat off with a thirty-two-pound ball without touching the man himself.

Oxenbold resigned his commission and went back to England to join his brother in the drapery business.

16

Summer faded into another autumn, the days shortening imperceptibly and the dust in the streets turning to mud with the first rains. Barker's son was born in late February and, soon after the mother had presented herself at church, the event was celebrated with a christening party. It was a stiff, formal affair, and soon over. It was observed that there seemed to be little affection between Señor and Señora Barker; they sat apart during the eating and drinking, she shrewish when he spoke to her, he sullen. Indeed, Barker spoke little to her at all, spending most of his time with Lesley and Russen, who were also on bad terms with their wives. After the celebration, the three of them were together every evening in the tavern, drinking on Barker's credit, and none of them turned up to the small dinner given by Charles Lyon and Sarah on the fifteenth of March, the anniversary of their meeting and of the Liberty Men's first day of freedom.

Shiers was there, but his son was only three days old and his wife unable to attend. Cheshire came alone also; his Maria, who was pregnant, spoke no English. Porter brought a box of coloured chalks for Sarah, who had taken up drawing on her slate. Captain Lawson brought flowers. After Sarah had cleared away the dishes, they sat drinking wine and telling Lawson about the voyage and trying to draw out James Porter into telling them about the progress of the account that he was writing. When that failed, Lawson said, 'I hear that the launch you came in has been sold?'

Porter nodded. 'She's been lying behind Government House for a year, so it's high time something was done with her.'

'Went with all her gear — masts, oars, sails, anchor and cables, so I'm told. I hope you obtained a good price for her?'

'John Barker conducted the sale. I know the boat fetched forty dollars, but I haven't heard anything about the gear.'

'I haven't heard anything about this at all.' Cheshire looked from one to the other. 'I suppose Barker's going to share out? I could do wi' the money, Maria being — ' He twiddled his glass self-consciously.

'Aye, we must speak to him about that. Mind you,' Shiers pointed out scrupulously, 'by rights, 'tis not our boat. But 'tain't Barker's neither.' He looked at Cheshire. 'When's time for you to become a proud father, Will lad? August, isn't it?'

Lyon was suddenly very conscious of Sarah beside him, like a dark flame in the red velvet dress he'd had brought from Santiago for this occasion. He put out a hand without taking his eyes off his guests as he recalled Barker's gibe about taking advantage of ignorant natives. Well, he thought as his hand was eagerly seized, maybe he had, in a way. Maybe he should have married his girl, as his mates had married theirs, and given her a child. But, if he'd been taken away in the *Blonde*, what would have become of her with a bairn to rear, and alone? Shiers' wife had her parents. All the others had friends and relatives to care for them if anything happened to their men. But Sarah had nobody but him. No, they'd come together alone and unencumbered, and that's how it would be if it ended. There was a little money he'd put away with a priest in the town if — He shivered. This was no time for morbid thoughts like that. He said, 'My friends, a Scottish

185

toast. To John Fare, John Jones and John Dady, wherever they may be. To absent friends.'

They drank.

Porter said, 'John Jones was right about one thing — the Navy did come for us as he said it would.'

Lawson looked up. 'That's why they left? Because they thought we would not protect them?'

'No. Because they thought you wouldn't be able to. They never doubted your good intentions.' Porter swivelled his single eye round the table. 'I've never told a soul of this. But they talked to me of leaving. In the shipyard one day, not long before the *Ocean West* called in.'

'And you never tried to prevent them?' Cheshire shook his head. 'Poor devils — they may be back in Van Diemen's Land by now.'

'Maybe.' Porter shrugged. 'But 'twas their choice. Their lives, to do as they pleased with.' He paused. 'I happened upon something one day, Cap'n, in one of those copybooks you lent me.' Lawson nodded. 'An Arab proverb, it was: "Take what you want — and pay for it." You can do what you like, be what you like. But, by God, one day you have to be prepared to pay the price for it. I reckon it's a pretty good rule for a man to live by, that. And John Jones and the others, they were ready to pay by risking their freedom for what they wanted — the sea.'

Lyon glanced at his friend sharply. It was odd how reading and writing had altered James Porter. He'd talked a lot about fate and destiny and such-like of late. 'Take what you want — and pay for it.' Would Sarah and this year of happiness have to be paid for, one day? Again, a chill ran across the back of his neck and he said curtly, 'They were men o' the sea. Jones always said he wouldna settle anywhere on land.'

He watched Sarah as she held up the wine-flask to Lawson. He smiled, nodded, and she poured for him. Truly astonishing, he thought, how little we need speech — how we use a spate of words, most of which aren't needed. By touch, facial ex-

186

pression, a little mime and the use of a slate, there was very little she could not say to him, or he to her. And after the strident, staccato voices in the street, in the shops, all competing for attention, all demanding money or admiration or service, it was so restful to come home to a silence that demanded nothing. He watched the sheen of the lamplight on her dark hair, the swell of her breasts, the grave intentness of her smooth brown face as she concentrated on not spilling a drop of wine. I'd die for her, he thought suddenly. Yes, that's the price I'd pay. For this person, who is closer to me than anyone has ever been, I'd give my life.

'And you others?' Lawson asked. 'Do you ever wish to leave Valdivia?'

'Where should we go?' Cheshire looked round the little room. It was very bare. The plaster walls bulged here and there, and the pinewood door hung slightly askew on its hinges. But, with its spotlessly white paintwork, the raw burst of colour from the Indian blanket across the bed, the soft glow of the ceramic and brass oil lamp lighting the huge spray of scarlet *copihue* blossoms that Lawson had brought, it had an atmosphere of its own — a blend of the old world and the new. Maria's taste, it was true, thought Cheshire, was a little more ornate, with pictures of saints on the walls, but his home was just as pleasant.

'Where should we go?' he repeated.

Lawson smiled. 'Don't you ever think of Birmingham?' He looked at the others. 'Or Scotland, or Yorkshire, or London?'

'Birmingham?' Cheshire shuddered. 'My father, if he still lives, is a cutler. Working from dawn to dusk for a pittance in smoke and flame and dust that's full o' steel filings as gets into his lungs and eyes and skin. Going home, sick wi' exhaustion, to eat pigswill in a house crawling wi' bugs and stinking of all manner o' filth. And, if he's too ill to go to work one day, he has to pay his bastardly employer wasted steam money. Me, I'd rather the gallows nor that.'

'Leeds and Sheffield are t'same. Full o' poor devils deprived

187

of a living in the countryside, as I was, and coaxed into the towns to work their guts out by day and drink theirselves insensible on cheap gin at night. The Aire and the Don full o' muck, and the very air poison to breathe. And, in the countryside, starvation.' Shiers pointed round the table. 'Look at us, Captain. No dandies, to be sure, but well-clothed. Think on the meal we've just had. We're living like kings. And come next Spring, I'll be looking around for a bit o' ground to clear and plant. How could I buy land in Yorkshire today? No, I'd be nobbut a fool to leave Valdivia.'

'No need to ask Charlie or young Will if they want to leave. As for me,' Porter grinned at Sarah, who smiled back at him, 'I've a pretty girl to look at, and friends to drink with, and my bit o' scribbling. Why should I wish to go? I'm happy here.' He paused. 'Aye, we're all happy. And that's a rare enough thing, God knows.'

In the years ahead, they were to remember that moment, all of them, even Sarah who did not know what had been said but for whom happiness was now a dear and familiar thing, easily recognized on the faces she knew so well. It was as if, on that March evening, the joined paths of their lives had toiled uphill to a crest, like a sunlit pass over the Andes, where they could rest and talk and drink a little wine together before going on into the unknown valley that lay ahead. It was as well, perhaps, that Porter did not remember something he'd said that night on the beach where they'd found the shellfish: 'The more you get, the more you've got to lose.'

Lawson drank some of his wine. Then he said casually, 'I shall be the first one of us to leave Valdivia, it seems.'

'You?' Shiers stared at him. 'I've heard nowt o' this.'

'I am a soldier. I am here only as His Excellency's aide. When he leaves, so do I.'

'He's leaving, then?' Cheshire's Maria usually kept him primed with the latest news in the town, but her own interesting condition had absorbed most of her attention of late.

'To take up a post in Santiago before he retires. The new

Governor will arrive in May but His Excellency will stay on for a while to advise him.'

'What's he like, the new Governor, do you know?' Shiers wondered if this change could make any difference to the price of land.

'His name, like that of many Chileans, is English. Thompson. A younger man than Don Fernando, and married. Ambitious, they say. This appointment in Valdivia is a rung on the ladder to high office in Santiago, so he is eager to do well; to improve the prosperity of the town, the port facilities, roads and so on. As for the man himself, I know little.'

'It sounds as if he might be one to encourage farming,' said Shiers.

'And more work in the shipyard.' Cheshire nodded. 'That barque we helped launch last April had been on the stocks three years, did you know that?' He smiled to show he meant no offence. 'Don Fernando's a good old man, but not much of a one for haste, eh?'

'His blood is Spanish,' said Lawson. 'He is an aristocrat to whom any kind of hurry is a breach of good taste. So,' he shrugged, 'perhaps Valdivia is a little behind the times. On the other hand, Don Fernando's personal code, as you have all discovered, makes it a matter of honour for him to keep his word. He would have defied not only the English government but our own as well if he had given an unconditional promise to protect you.'

'Aye.' Shiers nodded thoughtfully. 'We appreciate that. That's summat to respect, that is, in these days when cheats and liars abound.'

'Yes,' said Porter. 'Just what did John Barker do with the forty dollars he got for that boat?'

In the laughter and talk that followed, the topic of the new Governor was dropped. The party broke up, with regrets that Captain Lawson would not be present on the second anniversary, and Charles and Sarah were left alone to make love sleepily and tenderly in the bed with the Indian blanket.

Next day, Shiers accosted John Barker in the street, bluntly asking for his share of the proceeds of the sale of the boat, but Barker, whiter and flabbier than ever, pleaded that he was on his way to buy medicine and could not stop. Shiers then went on to pursue inquiries about the sale of the gear and discovered that the total sum raised had been considerable — a compass, a spyglass and three hundredweight of composition nails that had been used as ballast having been part of the deal. From then on, he haunted Barker, but the Lancashire man lay low and resorted to the homes of his friends Lesley and Russen in the evenings instead of meeting them in the tavern.

The whole thing went into recess when, on the second of May, the twenty-one-gun brig *Achilles,* of the South American Squadron, anchored off the Rio Valdivia and the new governor came upriver in the ship's cutter with his wife. The Liberty Men, now coalesced into two distinct groups, prudently took refuge. Shiers, Lyon and Cheshire went to Porter's lodgings on the edge of the town from which they could escape easily if the Navy came looking for them, and where they would not involve any of the women. Russen, working on the reverse principle, took Barker and Lesley into his house, reasoning that not even the Royal Navy could get past his well-muscled, moustachioed spouse.

It was raining again. Towards five in the evening, Porter peered through his window at the gloomy, muddy street and said, 'D'you know, mates, I don't believe the Navy's interested in us any more. D'you recall last time they were here — how Don Fernando had us shut up in the prison? And how the streets were full of soldiers? Today, he's allowed the bluejackets in without a word and they, in their turn, haven't shown any desire to apprehend us at all.'

'If tha believes that, tha'll believe owt.' Shiers was sitting cosily by the fire. 'Bloody Navy'll never forget. It's just that they've other things to do at present, wi' escorting t'new Governor an' all. And they know Don Fernando, bless his whiskers, would cut up rough if they tried to take us against his will. Happen he might even send for Sergeant Gomez.'

They chuckled, remembering the apocryphal stories of that warrior's exploit in the Battle of the Rio Valdivia that had gone round the town — how the tidal wave created by the hail of thirty-two-pound balls dropped with supernatural accuracy in front of the English longboat had washed it all the way back to the *Blonde*, and how each of the frigate's guns had been neatly plugged and rendered harmless by loaves of bread fired into their muzzles by the phenomenal Gomez.

'There's another thing.' Lyon, at the window with Porter, pointed at the street. A group of women, wrapped against the rain, were haggling round a fruit-seller's barrow. A beggar cowered in a doorway, and two men walked beside a horse that was pulling a cart full of firewood. 'People going about their business. You'd think that, since the new governor arrived only this morning, there'd be the usual *fiesta* in progress by now.'

'In this weather?' Shiers warmed his hands at the fire.

'Did you ever know bad weather stop a Chilean from enjoying himself?' Lyon turned from the window. 'No, mates. 'Tis my belief that the new Governor isn't well-liked by the people. Have you heard anyone speak well of him?'

'No,' Porter said. 'But nobody's said anything against him, either.'

'If it comes to that,' said Cheshire, 'very little's been said — to us. Whenever I've mentioned him, the folk have kept quiet and looked at me. Sort of strange-like. As if there was something it'd be best for us not to know.'

Porter nodded slowly. 'True. I've felt that. But it doesn't mean — ' He broke off. 'Captain Lawson! Coming up the street on horseback.' He went to open the door.

'Alone?' asked Cheshire apprehensively.

'Alone or not, it means trouble.' Shiers stood up. 'I told you the Navy has a long memory.'

Lawson came in quickly, his caped greatcoat streaming wet.

191

'Four,' he said, his eyes going round the group. 'Where are the others?' When nobody answered, he said irritably, 'For God's sake, haven't you learnt to trust me yet? Where are Barker, Lesley and Russen?'

'They'll be either at Lesley's house, or Russen's,' said Lyon. 'Is anything amiss, Captain?'

'Of course not.' Lawson was in a hurry. 'But you must put on your best clothes. You are to go directly to meet the new Governor. It is Don Fernando's wish that he should, from the outset, be under no misapprehension concerning your standing in the community.'

'That's kind of him,' said Shiers awkwardly. 'We were afeard that — '

'I tell you there's nothing to fear.' Lawson made for the door. 'Now I must find the others. I will meet you at Government House in one hour.'

Shiers, Lyon and Cheshire went home. Then, shaved, brushed and dressed in their best, the Liberty Men assembled once again in the long room — now lamplit — with the Spanish portrait where they'd waited, barefoot and in rags, for Don Fernando Martell over a year before. Lawson, trim and lean in his ceremonial dress, was already standing beside the door ready to announce His Excellency. Barker came in last, looking particularly resplendent in a plum-coloured velvet suit and flowing cravat.

Shiers said to him immediately, 'John Barker, I'd like a word with you concerning that boat and — '

Lawson, scandalized, said, 'Please!'

He jerked to attention as Don Fernando came into the room followed by a tubby, sandy-haired man with a pink, smiling face that looked as if it had been freshly scrubbed.

The older man said formally, 'Señor Thompson: may I be permitted to introduce — ' and then went on to present each of the Liberty Men in turn. 'Gentlemen,' he said at last. 'Señor Manuel Thompson, my successor.' He spoke in Castellano throughout.

192

Thompson had bowed scrupulously and taken each man by the hand in turn. Now he smiled broadly at Don Fernando as he switched to an almost unaccented English. 'I think, Your Excellency, that out of courtesy to our guests we should speak their language. With your permission, of course?'

'I meant no discourtesy.' A slight frost had crept into the Governor's voice. 'These gentlemen are perfectly at home in Castellano, and are citizens of our town. But,' he shrugged, 'let our talk be in English, by all means.'

'I am a great admirer of the English and I speak the language whenever possible.' Thompson's blue eyes twinkled round the group. 'My father came from Yorkshire. A county famous for its pudding, I believe?'

'It is, that,' said Shiers warmly. 'Not that it's a pudding as such, o' course, to be eaten after dinner. 'Tis more like — '

'You must tell me more of it later. Perhaps we could introduce it here, eh?' Thompson turned to Don Fernando. 'You say the gentlemen are citizens? They have taken out papers, then, as Chilean nationals?'

'No. They are all subjects of His Majesty King William the Fourth. But — and this is the matter upon which I desire to be perfectly clear to you — they have been taken under the protection of the Chilean flag by our government, and it is my wish that this protection should be continued.'

'But, of course, Your Excellency.' Thompson's Chilean side came out as he spread his hands expansively. 'It is obvious that my duty and my desire to comply with your wishes run together in this. They are all employed, these gentlemen?'

'All have shown themselves to be models of honest industry. Most are married men; two with children. I commend them to your benevolence.'

Thompson turned to the men, his smile vanishing as he said earnestly, 'My friends. Let there be no doubt in the minds of any of you that your unfortunate past will in any way affect my attitude towards you when I am Governor. All that concerns me is that you should continue to work for the prosperity of Valdivia. I give you my word that I will protect you.'

'Sir.' Barker stepped forward, an ingratiating smile on his fat face. 'As former leader of the men here, and as the foremost citizen among them, I thankee for those words and express the hope that we will continue to earn the protection of the government of Chile.' Furtively, he consulted a scrap of paper in the palm of his hand. 'And may I say as we hopes your Governorship will be a long and happy one.'

I wonder, Porter thought sourly, whether he had a second speech prepared in case Thompson promised to clap us all in irons. Aloud, he said briefly, 'I'd like to thank His Excellency Don Fernando for all he's done for us.' There was a murmur of agreement — whether with Barker's speech or with Porter's it was impossible to say.

Outside, in the lamplit portico, Shiers said, with enthusiasm, 'I like the new man. I think we'll do well under him, eh, Jamie?'

Porter grunted. 'Because he likes Yorkshire pud?'

'Don't be daft. He's straight. You could tell from his eyes and the firm way he shook hands.'

'And the way he put down old Don Fernando by speaking English?'

'Twas but a courtesy to visitors — he said as much. Besides, you heard what he said: he likes the English.' He looked over Porter's shoulder. 'Eh, there's Johnny Barker. I want a word with him.'

Porter watched the two of them go off down the dark street, wrangling.

'Yes,' he said to himself. 'Thompson likes the English, to be sure. And that's what I'm afraid of.'

17

Don Fernando Martell left Valdivia on the thirtieth of May, taking Captain Lawson with him. It was another occasion unmarked by a *fiesta*: the entire town stood on the river bank in silence to watch him go, the men bareheaded under the cold grey sky, most of the women weeping, the children awestruck as at a funeral. On the following evening, a Sunday, the new Governor had the leading citizens of the town to dine with him — Barker's wife being first thunderstruck, then furious with her husband because they had not been invited — and on Monday, the first of June 1835, the new governor's policy was implemented in a series of ordinances.

Begging was to be abolished under pain of imprisonment for the first offence, flogging for subsequent breaches of the law. Able-bodied beggars would be added to the labour force on the roads if they could not obtain other employment; the unfit would either become the responsibility of their families, or be required to leave the town. Roads in the town were to be improved and others were to be pushed into the forest for the transport of timber; bridges were to be thrown across the Rio Valdivia and the Rio Calle-Calle for that purpose. The

195

wharves were to be deepened and lengthened to take larger vessels. Loans were to be made available for the construction of ships. The government would acquire land for farming and rent it out to suitable applicants. Hospitals, schools and even a fire brigade were to be made available to every citizen living in Valdivia. The Governor had nothing but the good of his people at heart. Naturally, all these benefits would have to be paid for, and so a special tax would have to be levied. And, since all would enjoy the new prosperity of Valdivia, the tax would be the same for all, regardless of age.

It took a while for the stunned citizenry to realize what a sting there was in the tail. 'Regardless of age' meant just that, from the oldest inhabitant to the new-born infants. Unfortunately, the poorer the Valdivian, the more new-born infants he tended to have. Barker, for example, was taxed on himself, his wife and his child. Señor Giminez, however, who sold firewood, was taxed on himself, his wife, his ten children, his wife's mother, his grandfather, and his half-witted brother, who all resided at the Giminez establishment.

There was a protest meeting which, like most South American protest meetings, tended to be dissatisfied with votes of no-confidence. Voices, then fists, then chair legs, were raised. A well-known and respected mendicant named *El Sucio* — the Dirty One — the father of fourteen brats by a variety of mothers, all of whom lived with him, led a march on Government House. The troops were called out and he was thrown into gaol, which suited him very well since, as a convict, he was required neither to work nor to pay taxes. Next day, one of his wives threw a stone through one of the windows of Government House; again the soldiers were called out and, in the confusion, one of them fired a shot which injured a child. Instantly, the mood of the townspeople which, although indignant, had had a certain Latin enjoyment of the yelling, torch-light processions and general histrionics of revolution, became silent and ugly. A soldier was beaten almost to death in a tavern. Among those questioned were James Lesley and Benjamin Russen.

On the following day, the sixth of June, all the Liberty Men were ordered to report to the Officer of the Guard at the gaol every evening except Sunday at six precisely.

'This is the very devil,' grumbled Shiers. 'The only land I can afford is ten miles out of town. How can I run a farm if I'm to be galloping in and out of Valdivia every night?'

They'd met at Porter's lodgings after their first six o'clock roll-call. He said, 'What about me? I'd obtained a good berth as overseer at the lumber camp. But it's fifteen miles up the Calle-Calle, and I have to live there a month at a time.'

'Couldn't we see the Governor?' Cheshire asked.

'I tried.' Lyon shrugged. 'Permission granted, but His Excellency regrets he canna give a time or date for the interview owing to pressure o' business. His secretary told me the order's designed for our protection because of the unrest in the town.' He sighed. 'I wish to God Lawson was here.'

But John Barker had no difficulty whatever in obtaining an interview with the Governor. Although terrified by the rioting, he had slipped through the dark streets to the gates of Government House where a series of bribes, first to the sentry, then to the sergeant of the Guard and finally to the secretary, had got him into the gubernatorial presence after being very thoroughly searched for arms. Thompson, writing at his desk in the lamplight, rose as Barker was shown in.

'Señor Barker.' He came round the desk, hand held out. 'This is an unexpected pleasure. But I regret that, if it is concerning the recent restriction on your liberty that you wish to see me — '

'No, Your Excellency.' Barker looked solemn. 'I realize that your order's for our welfare and, indeed, I'm grateful you're so concerned for our safety as to issue it.' He paused. 'No, sir. My purpose in coming here is to make you a small present.'

'A present?' Thompson raised an eyebrow. 'Truly? Please take a seat, señor.' He settled himself behind his desk. 'You

197

will, of course, realize that my position here makes it impossible for me to accept gifts of money?'

'Money?' Barker chuckled. This was the kind of game he revelled in. 'Your Excellency, I wouldn't dream of such a thing. Why, I'd as soon try to bribe the sentry at your gate to get in to see you.' He laughed amusedly at the idea. 'No, sir. This would be merely an expression, like, of my thanks for your kindness in promising to protect us. No offence in that, sir, I hope?'

'None at all.' It's his fat wife who's behind this, thought Thompson, depend on it. Under Martell, she'd cut something of a social figure, it seemed. Well, if she thought she was going to oil her way back into Government House, she was sadly in error.

'Thankee, Your Excellency.' Barker, his fleshy face shining with earnestness, hitched his chair forward a fraction. 'Now, I cannot but observe, sir, that you're badly in need of a boat to get you up and down the river — about the wharves and shipyards and such. An' I know two men as can build you a boat that'll delight your eyes, sir. A dainty little thing; four oars, best quality timber, the ironwork of — '

'These men. They will be your friends Lesley and Russen, perhaps? The ones involved in the attack on one of my soldiers?'

'Present at the attack, true, but in no other way involved, sir, I assure you.' Barker knew nothing of their part in the brawl, and he cared even less.

'I accept your assurance.' The Governor smiled amicably. 'When the soldier recovers consciousness and can name his attackers, your friends will, of course, be proved innocent.' What is there to lose? he asked himself. A boat befitting his station would, indeed, be very welcome. It could be of use for pleasure outings, too, next summer. Moreover, it would certainly do him no harm if it were known in Santiago that he was already a popular figure whom the townspeople wished to honour.

198

'Lesley is a boatbuilder by trade. Russen is very industrious. I would buy the materials and employ them at my own cost entirely.'

'Señor Barker, you are really too kind.' Thompson rose. 'Shall we regard your generous offer as a gift to the government of Chile? As such, I accept it with gratitude.'

Lesley and Russen were in their usual corner of the tavern when Barker, after much looking over his shoulder in the deserted streets, arrived. Lesley's wife brought him wine, smiling archly at the visitor and allowing an almost naked breast to nudge his shoulder as she poured for him. He, unlike her good-for-nothing husband, had money and might be disposed to spend a little of it on a hot-blooded, shapely girl who could give him a far better time in bed than could his sack-of-lard wife. Desiring a new dress and unable to get the price of it out of her husband, she had already allowed Benjamin Russen to seduce her, but it was not an experience she was willing to repeat. *Madre de Dios,* it had been like bedding with an alligator.

'Is there any other way in which I can serve you, señor?' she asked, smoothing her dress demurely over her hips.

'*Vé te*, you slut,' said Lesley briefly. As she flounced off, he said, 'Well? What brings you here, apart from the desire to fumble my wife?'

Barker looked pained. 'I came to do you a favour. But, if you're not disposed to be friendly, I'll go.' He stood up. 'I thought setting you up as boatbuilders might interest you, that's all, but — '

'Wait, now.' Lesley grabbed him by the sleeve. 'Don't take on, John, lad. You know that drab always puts me in a bad mood. Here, drink your wine and tell me about it.'

Russen said incredulously, 'You're going to set us up as boatbuilders? Why?'

'To win the Governor's favour.' He drank some wine, watching them. 'He wants a boat built — a light pleasure craft, wi' tasselled cushions an' all. It's not a sea-going boat,

199

so it shouldn't take long. I provide the materials and pay you for your labour.'

'How much are you selling it for?' demanded Russen.

'I'm giving it to him. There's no money in this for me — just the contrary. 'Tis a bribe, see? But, for you — well, if you make a good job o' this commission, there'll be others from folk in the town.' There was nowt to be gained, he thought, in telling them that the money he was going to put into the boat came from the sale of the old launch and that part of it was theirs.

Lesley scratched his head. It sounded damned suspect, like most of Barker's schemes, but for the life of him he couldn't see the catch. But it wasn't going to cost him anything. It meant employment at work he enjoyed and, as Barker said, the prestige of making a boat for the Governor would certainly lead to other orders. He said, 'Where do we work?'

'I'll hire a corner of the shipyard. Tomorrow, I'll go about the town and buy the timber. Old Carvenia, Shiers' father-in-law, can help wi' the metalwork.' He drank off his wine and rose. 'How soon can you have it finished?'

It took exactly a fortnight. Lesley, with all his faults, was a craftsman, and she was a beautiful little boat when she was in the water.

'A lady's boat,' said Porter scornfully when he and Lyon and Sarah came to see it. He looked at the low freeboard, the delicately-curved bow, the curlicued wrought-iron on the row-locks. 'She wouldn't last five minutes in any sort of sea.'

'She's not intended to,' snapped Barker. 'She's a pleasure boat for gentry, not like that hulk you were crew of for Charlie Taw. I'm doing this, and paying for it out of my own pocket, mind, as a means of earning the governor's good will, and you'll benefit from it like the rest of us.'

His Excellency was delighted. The unrest in the town had subsided into a sullen compliance; the streets had been swept clean of beggars as if by a high wind and, already, there was more activity in the market-place, an air of purposefulness in the shipyard. He took his wife up and down the river a little way in his new toy, rowed decorously by four Chilean boatmen. Then he sent for John Barker and thanked him.

'Tis nothing, Your Excellency,' said Barker modestly. 'I'm right glad you're pleased with her, that's all.' He took a sip of the sherry, imported specially from Spain, that the Governor had given him. 'Not too fragile, is she?'

'Fragile?' Thompson shook his head, smiling. 'She seems very well-made.'

'Aye. But I did hear somebody say as she was more of a lady's boat. She'd be no good for — well, going out to a ship anchored off the mouth of the river, for example.'

'True, but we hire native canoes and private craft for that sort of work.'

'To be sure.' Barker glanced at the clock and finished his sherry. 'Ah well, one of these days, when Valdivia's a flourishing port, maybe she'll have her own harbour launch, eh? And now, sir, I've taken up more of your time than — '

'There would, of course,' said Thompson thoughtfully, 'be a saving of money if the government had its own vessel for the purpose.'

'And more fitting to the dignity of our country.' Barker nodded. 'I couldn't but notice, sir, that when you yourself arrived you were brought upriver in a vessel that flew a foreign flag. Now, if Don Fernando had only thought of having a launch built — nothing very ornate, of course, nothing costly — but flying the flag of Chile, then — '

'How much would such a craft cost?'

Barker looked guarded. 'Well, now, Your Excellency, that'd be a different kettle o' fish from a little boat like the other one. I don't know as I could afford — '

Thompson laughed. 'Señor Barker! It was not my intention that you should offer to pay for it. This would be a government vessel, paid for wholly by the state.'

'Ah! I takes your meaning, Your Excellency. You're thinking of a kind of naval contract.' Barker nodded. 'Well, now, she'd need to be something like a six-oared whaleboat, I'd say. Fitted wi' mast and sails; a proper sea-going affair, she'd be. Timber's dirt cheap here, so there'd be no great expense in — '

Thompson also looked at the clock. He rose. 'I think, after your success with the smaller boat, I am able to give you permission to proceed with this one on your own initiative, Señor Barker, provided that you submit estimates to my secretary first. But now I must ask you to excuse me. I have an appointment.' He rang a bell and Barker was shown out.

After reporting at the prison that evening, he waited for Lesley and Russen. They arrived late, argued with the Officer of the Guard, and came away grumbling. Seeing Barker loitering in the shadows, Lesley said, 'Why, 'tis Johnny Barker. Him as is going to make our-fortunes.' He and Russen crowded in on him. 'We'd like the favour of a word with you, mate.'

'To be sure.' Barker peered at them in the gloom. 'And I want to talk to you. I've news for you — '

'And we've news for you, too.' Lesley took his arm. 'Let's take a walk by the river.'

They set off between the houses where lamps glowed cosily behind curtained windows. Wood-smoke coiled lazily from the chimneys into the damp night air with a smell of spices and cooking meat.

Barker said, 'Is owt amiss?'

'Amiss?' Russen grunted. 'Aye, mate. You could say as there's something amiss. The matter of the money paid to you for the sale of our old launch, that's what's amiss. I heard about it only today from Will Shiers. What happened to our share?'

'That?' Barker chuckled. 'I used it to build the boat for the Governor.'

'You used it?' Lesley stopped. 'You mean,' he said, choking slightly, 'you paid us to work with money as rightly belonged to us? You, what could have paid us ten times over with the money your wife gave you to get her with child?'

'Dirty little skinflint!' Russen tugged Barker's arm. 'Let's

202

dip him in the river, Jim, and make sure he don't come out.'

'Wait!' Barker shook him off. 'I had to use that money. That fat cow of a wife of mine gave me nothing. She buys my clothes and gives me bed and board, that's all. I've less nor you in ready cash.'

'No stud fee?' Lesley chuckled grimly. 'Me heart bleeds for you. But now you're going to account to us for the ready cash we've given to the bloody Governor.'

'Listen, mates, 'tis a sprat to catch a mackerel, don't you see? For he now wishes a bigger craft — a six-oared whale-boat, one as can go out to a ship at anchor in any weather.' He looked up and down the empty street. 'Let's do as you suggest and take a walk by the river where none can overhear.'

Across the water, as they stopped, the black bulk of the forest lining the Rio Valdivia stood against the stars. The river flowed black and silent at their feet and a night bird called raucously from somewhere close at hand.

Barker said, 'Now, mates, hear me out. Do you wish to live out your lives in this place?'

'In Valdivia?' Lesley snorted. 'The land o' milk and honey as you told us of once? With that harlot of a wife of mine, and where I'm suspect as soon as a soldier gets cut up in a brawl?'

Barker said, 'Did you do it?'

'We did not, and that's God's truth,' said Russen. 'But the ones who did it are planning to shift the blame on us by means of false witnesses.'

'But when the soldier recovers —'

'He was struck from behind,' said Lesley. 'He can say nought. But we'll be blamed for it, mark my words.'

'I wish to God,' Russen looked up and down the river bank uneasily, 'as we could get away from this place.'

'I must agree,' Barker said. 'It hasn't been all I'd expected. And, under Governor Thompson, I foresee trouble ahead for us all. I think we should follow the example of Fare, Jones and Dady, and leave.'

'They were sailor-men.' Russen pitched a stone into the water with a plunk. 'We couldn't obtain berths on a ship.'

'We wouldn't need to. Not if we had one of our own. A six-oared whaleboat, say.' They stared at Barker in the darkness. 'Fitted out,' he added, 'and paid for by the Governor.'

There was a silence.

'By God!' said Lesley softly. 'But you're a cunning bastard, John Barker.'

'What does he mean, Jim?' Russen's mind, as always, was slow. 'It can't be that the Governor's going to pay us to build the boat we'll abscond in?'

'And for the provisions aboard her, too.' Barker grinned in the gloom. 'Twill all be done legally as a shipyard contract.'

Russen guffawed as the idea sank in.

Lesley said doubtfully, 'But it'll be a risky business, getting past the fort. And they're bound to pursue us.'

'Let them,' Barker said. 'Men who escaped from Macquarie Harbour should have small difficulty in dodging a parcel of Spaniards. Leave the details to me. As for the fort, we'll pass it in darkness and go well out to sea. Then we'll head north. With plenty of food and water, we'll have no trouble in reaching Peru.'

'Peru?' Lesley didn't really care where they went. Peru sounded a far-off sort of place. Up north, somewhere . . . 'We're none of us seamen, though. On the voyage from Van Diemen's Land, we had Fare and others to assist us. As for your navigation — '

'Which will you put your trust in — my navigation, or Governor Thompson's promise to protect us?' When they said nothing, he snapped, 'And not a word of this to Charlie Lyon, either, or any of the others. They're settled here; they won't leave, and they'll peach if they learn of our plan. So let it be known you're pleased wi' your government commission and that you hopes for others. And build this vessel quickly. I've a feeling our liberty's hanging by a thread.'

It was not a feeling Barker liked. As he scurried across the town to pay another call, he reflected that he'd never planned on staying in this damp, uncivilized village, anyway, where he was at the mercy of a pack of garlicky dagos. He'd been thinking of leaving ever since it had become apparent that the ton of blubber he'd married had no intention of letting him get his hands on enough money to decamp with. Now, with the pro-English Thompson in Government House, it was definitely time to clear out. When he reached Peru he wouldn't be such a bloody fool as to give himself up, either. No, he'd lie low, sell the whaleboat and use the money to buy false papers. Then, with a new name, he'd take passage for America. Another rich widow, maybe, he thought, chuckling, as he found the house he wanted where lodged a seaman by the name of Roberts.

Lesley and Russen, walking homewards, were chuckling, too. Lesley had just said, 'Aye, he's a cunning bastard, to be sure, that Johnny Barker. Him saying he's got no more ready cash than ourselves! He's got money hidden away, Ben, depend on it, and he'll be taking it with him. So, as soon as we sights the Peruvian coast — ' He turned to Russen and drew a forefinger across his throat. 'Tis up with his heels and over the side with him.'

They'd forgotten that Barker never took chances, and he certainly wasn't taking any with Lesley and Russen. He needed them to build the boat and help sail it, but that was all. In Peru, they'd be nothing but a liability. So, after spending half an hour in Roberts' lodgings, he paid his third and last call of the evening.

He ordered, on credit, a brace of pistols.

18

Monday, the sixth of July, was a clear, cold day with watery sunshine in the morning that did little to dry out the puddles in the streets or warm Charles Lyon's hands as he stood exposed to the chilly wind and applied varnish to the gunwale of the cutter that was being refurbished in the shipyard. The low hills that surrounded the town were drawn sharply against the ice-blue sky and, far away but seeming within a stone's throw, the snow on the slopes of the volcano Villarica gleamed like a white sail in the sun. Nowhere, Lyon thought, can the air be as clear as it is here. Only the smoke from the lumber camps and the town fireplaces blurred the air, bringing with it the smell of burning timber that, with the sharp resinous scent of freshly-cut pinewood, always seemed to hang about the town.

Porter, running short of money since he'd been forced to quit his job at the lumber camp, was working on the other side of the hull, opposite Lyon. All that could be seen of him was a woollen cap that bobbed out of sight as he dipped his brush, to reappear with a half-audible snatch of song as he sloshed varnish onto the woodwork. 'Have you heard,' he asked, breaking off in mid-verse, 'how Will Cheshire's Maria is doing?'

'Well enough.' Lyon finished a brush stroke and paused. 'Tis Will who's going to suffer most during the next month, I'm thinking. When I saw him on Saturday night at roll-call he told me he was keeping water boiling day and night, in case the child should come early.'

'He told me that. I asked him whether Maria was having a baby or a lobster.' Porter chuckled. 'You'd think he'd invented childbirth, the way he swaggers about.'

'Aye.' Lyon began painting again, faster, as if trying to obliterate the picture of Sarah smiling up at him with the mystic smile of motherhood on her face, cuddling a small bundle that would be the natural culmination of their love for each other. Did she want a child — his child? Was she denying herself, practising her secret Indian ways of controlling her body, because she thought he didn't want to be a father? Every healthy female had the right to be a mother. Lyon stopped work and stared unseeingly at the open space where they'd all danced that day when the barque had been launched — at the corner where he'd first seen Sarah. Perhaps he was completely wrong. Perhaps, if she were left alone, she would always mourn the fact that he'd left her nothing of himself, no child that was half of him for her to cherish. Would that be a worse thing to do to her than to leave her to support a bairn unaided?

'Damn and blast it,' he said aloud. As Porter's head bobbed up, Lyon said, confused, 'Tis nothing, Jamie. I put my hand in the paintpot and —'

But Porter was looking past him at the officer and two soldiers who were half-running, half-walking across the square. While still twenty yards away, the *teniente* shouted, 'The Englishmen Lesley and Russen. Have you seen them?'

'No. They'll be down at the wharf with the whaleboat.' It's that business of the set-to in the tavern, Porter thought. The

207

soldier had recovered consciousness, so they said, and the investigation would be —

'They are not at the wharf.' The officer's brown face was flushed with excitement and exertion. 'And the whaleboat, it is gone!'

Lyon shrugged. 'Well, they'll no' be far away. They've taken a trial run down the river, maybe.'

'Gone. Vanished completely.' The lieutenant waved his arms. 'Also Señor Barker, whose wife has reported him to be missing. Oho, if they have run away, His Excellency will be most disturbed.'

His Excellency was, in fact, ready to foam at the mouth with fury, but nobody, looking at his chubby pink face, would have guessed it. Only a slight whiteness at the nostrils and a metallic snap in his voice showed how the English half of him was holding in the Chilean desire to shriek at the top of his voice and throw his desk furniture at the Army captain who stood before him. For, above all things, Governor Thompson was terrified of losing his dignity. And this situation was likely to make him look very undignified indeed — both in the town that he was just beginning to bend to his will and in high places in Santiago. There were many people in the capital who were envious of his rapid series of promotions and he could hear the vicious, brittle laughter in the corridors and offices of the government buildings: 'Have you heard of Thompson, in Valdivia? Hasn't been there two months and already he's paid out government money so that three ex-convicts could escape in a boat he paid them to build. Yes, truly. He even let them stock it with provisions. The locals are laughing their heads off, of course, and who can blame them? The man must be an utter fool.'

The crisis had struck with appalling suddenness — first the complaint of that fat, sobbing Señora Barker that her husband had been abducted; then, within minutes, the report that the brand-new whaleboat had disappeared from the wharf; then the discovery that those drunken, brawling scoundrels, Lesley and Russen (whom he should never have trusted to build a hen-coop, let alone a boat) had gone.

'You say,' said His Excellency in a voice like a saw going through hardwood, 'that all three reported to the Officer of the Guard on Saturday evening?'

'Yes, Your Excellency.' The captain, terrified out of his wits, stood rigid.

Damn them, they'd timed it well. There was no roll-call on Sunday, so they'd had — he glanced at the clock. Ten a.m. Forty hours' start. Even at five knots, they'd be two hundred miles away.

'And there has been no word from the fort?'

'None, Your Excellency. But a canoe has already been sent downriver with a request for information.'

'We'll receive none.' God, if all else failed, he'd at least have the satisfaction of breaking whoever was in charge of the fort down to acting unpaid latrine orderly. 'Take whatever vessel you can lay your hands on and pursue these criminals. I want — yes, what is it?' he snapped. A sergeant, his salute resembling a hand thrown up to ward off a blow, had appeared in the doorway.

'Your Excellency!' The man stared straight in front of him. 'Another Englishman has vanished — from his lodgings. A man named Roberts, a former sailor. He has taken all his belongings with him.'

'But he is not one of the former convicts.' Thompson began to have the insane feeling that the entire population of Valdivia might be on the move like so many lemmings, all streaming downriver in boats paid for by the government.

'No, Your Excellency. But his landlord reports that he was visited by the Englishman Barker one night, three weeks ago.'

'He has, perhaps, gone with them,' said the captain, eager to assist.

'Of course he has gone with them, fool!' For a moment, the Governor's self-control slipped. He recovered. 'They were not seamen. They have forced or bribed this deluded Roberts to sail their vessel — our vessel — for them. I want them all brought back. You understand? The whaleboat also — that is to be brought back, undamaged if possible.'

'The man Barker,' croaked the sergeant, like a bird of ill-omen, 'is armed. With two pistols brought from Lopez the gunsmith, for which he has not paid. Also ammunition.'

'If there is resistance, shoot to kill. I want these men returned, dead or alive. I care little which.' The quietness in Thompson's voice was more frightening than any shout. 'Go now.' As they reached the door, he added, 'If any more of the English disappear, I will hold you responsible.' They saluted, struggled for a moment in the doorway, and left.

Thompson slumped back in his chair. They would not find the criminals. He knew that. The ocean was too vast, the coastline of Chile too long. Oh, they would be picked up one day, six months, a year from now, in Valparaiso or one of the smaller ports. But for him to retrieve the situation, they would have to be found immediately. In six months' time, another man could be sitting in this chair. A fine beginning, he thought bitterly, to the governorship that was to have been a small step, and a simple one, on the road to power. How, they would ask in the capital, can a man who is incapable of governing a town be entrusted with a share in the governing of the Republic?

And yet, how was it his fault? He had arrived here with the best of intentions, determined to be smiling and genial. All he had wanted had been to make a success of this appointment — to stir Valdivia out of the Spanish lethargy induced by that senile idiot Don Fernando. In fact, now he thought of it, the blame for this outrage belonged to the previous Governor for it had been he who had insisted, God knows why, on accepting into the community those blots on the name of England, those criminals, those sweepings of the prison hulks. He, Thompson, had been handicapped from the start by idle incompetents in the town and by the foolish generosity of a government that had agreed to Don Fernando's ridiculous

210

request for sanctuary for a rabble of thieves. And what had they offered in return, these blackguards? Tavern brawls, drunkenness, the ravishment of innocent Chilean girls (it was an effort to fit Señora Barker into that category, but Thompson managed it) and the theft of government property. His mind crawled with the premonition of further disasters — one of his men being shot by the evil Barker, the rest of the rogues stealing more boats to get away . . .

Very well. He would wait until the search party returned before submitting his report to Santiago. If, by some miracle, the drunken, lecherous robbers were dragged back to the imprisonment they so richly deserved, then the matter might be glossed over. If they were not, he would have to take steps to prevent further incidents.

*

Barker had known all along they would not be dragged back. It had all been too well thought-out, too swift a blow, for the Chileans to parry it. The whaleboat had been built and fitted out, with the assistance of local labour, in three weeks. On the second of July, a Thursday, she'd been put into the water. On the Saturday, choosing a time when Thompson was away inspecting a road-building scheme, Barker had put on his best clothes and gone the rounds of the shopkeepers, ordering provisions, chargeable to the government, that were immediately carted down to the wharf and stowed aboard the launch. In the evening he had reported to the Officer of the Guard; then, with Lesley and Russen, had gone straight to the wharf.

As they stepped into the whaleboat, a burly shadow, cloaked and carrying a kitbag, detached itself from the side of a shed.

Russen stiffened. 'Who the devil's this?'

'A friend.' Grinning, Barker took the stranger's kitbag. 'Harry Roberts, a Welshman out of Cardiff. A former prize-fighter and, at one time, mate of the brig *Eliza*. He's to assist us in sailing to Peru. You said we needed a seaman.'

'But you said nought of finding one.' Lesley stared with

open hostility as the sailor dropped into the boat. 'He might have peached on us.' To put Barker over the side was one thing; to get rid of this hulking fellow was another.

'Indeed, man, 'twas only arranged at the last moment.' Roberts began to wrap the rowlocks in strips of cloth to muffle them. 'Why should I peach, look you, on one who's to let me work my passage out of this dreary place?'

There was little they could do about it. Sullenly, they sat down and Roberts cast off. They let the boat drift with the current at first, slipping in complete silence downriver with the familiar evening sounds — a woman calling shrilly to her child to come and eat, a horse neighing and the clink of harness, the clunk of an axe biting into firewood — dying behind them. Then they began rowing, the feel of the oar strange to Barker's soft hands after so long. There was a moon, but the sky was overcast and the silver luminosity behind the clouds merely made the earth seem darker in contrast. By eight o'clock, they had reached the twinkling points of light that marked the fort on its island in the estuary. They could hear the sea beyond it, and the plangent notes of a guitar being played sentimentally from inside the fort.

'Rest on your oars,' Barker said softly. They were close in to the southern bank of the river. 'Put your coats over your heads to hide the white of your faces, and let her drift.'

The sentry was staring out to sea — and perfunctorily at that — as he sang softly the words of the song Miguel was playing below in the guardroom. Even if he had looked behind him — and why should he? — he would have seen only the blackness of the forest merging into the blackness of the river, with a faint line of light along the distant hills. '*Alma de mi corazón*,' he sang to himself. '*Rosita, enamorada mia . . .* ' The gurgle of water against the whaleboat's hull was lost in his humming and in the endless hiss of the sea so that he neither heard nor saw the shadow that drifted along the line of the shore. So close to the shore that there was a slight jar as it touched some underwater obstruction, then slid free, to

212

begin pitching as it reached the first ripples of seawater.

'Take up your oars, lads,' said Barker. 'We've given them the slip, right enough.'

After half an hour's rowing, they hoisted sail and the yellow lights of the fort fused into one, then were lost in the night. They headed west, making eleven knots with the night breeze from the land pushing them out into the depths of the Pacific, and slept in watches, Roberts genially insisting that he and Russen take one, Lesley and Barker the other. Barker fingered the pistols in his coat pocket and smiled to himself in the dark.

By sunrise, they'd covered a hundred miles. They turned north with a gentle sou'-wester, the boat taking the Pacific rollers well. They ate well, the sun came out and, although the wind varied in strength, it held fair so that, on Tuesday, the seventh of July, they were one hundred and fifty miles off Valparaiso and well outside the coastal shipping routes. Even Benjamin Russen hummed to himself as he sprawled on the bottom boards, enjoying the upward swing as the boat climbed obliquely across a wave, then dipped her bow to slide into the shallow trough. Abruptly, he sat up and put a hand behind him.

'Why, damn me,' he said, 'my trousers are wet.'

'You filthy rogue.' Lesley guffawed. 'Do it over the side next time like — '

But Roberts had pushed past him to go for'ard and pull up a board. Barker sat up in alarm.

'She's a new boat.' Lesley peered at the dirty water that ran and gurgled as the keel lifted to a wave. 'She's bound to leak somewhat.'

'Indeed, yes.' Roberts put a hand down and felt along the hull. ''Tis not serious, mark you. But I can feel,' he prodded, 'yes, there's a strained plank here.'

'The devil there is!' Lesley turned on Barker. ''Tis that bump we felt coming out of the river. You took us too close in, you fool.'

'It's your building that's at fault.' It's the *Frederick* all over again, Barker thought furiously. First John Fare with his mad driving of the brig, now this. Were his plans always to be set at nought by idiots? 'A strong-built craft would have weathered a touch like that without flinching.'

'My building? You poxy little toad, what would you know of — ?'

'Stow it,' said Roberts briskly. ''Tis not serious, look you, so there's little to be gained by arguing whose fault it is.'

It wasn't serious. They watched the leak, baling occasionally, but very little water came in. For six days they headed due north, the invisible deserts and salt-pans of northern Chile moving away from them as the land curved away to the east. By Monday, the thirteenth of July, they were two hundred and fifty miles off the coast of Antofagasta.

'Another three days.' Barker's face, blotched with wind burn and sunburn, looked even redder in the fiery glow of sunrise. 'Maybe four, and we'll be seeing the Peruvian Andes.'

An hour later, as if to spite him, the sou'-wester that had been with them since they'd turned north off Valdivia veered suddenly and increased in strength, bringing with it great banks of leaden cloud. Roberts reefed, then took in the main-sail until they were clawing at the wind with a rag of canvas on the foresail and being pushed steadily off course eastward. The seas built up as the wind rose and rain — icy, driving rain — joined with the spray blasted off the wave-crests in soaking them to the bone as they hung on to the whaleboat for dear life. She soared up the slopes of waves that were higher than their mast, to hang dizzily suspended for a moment before plunging headlong into the foaming green troughs. And, with the sprung plank and the spray and the heavy rain, she began to fill rapidly.

'Bale, man!' Roberts, for'ard with Barker, pointed to the baler in Lesley's hand. The man from Bristol had both arms wrapped round the mast. 'Bale!'

'To hell with that!' To bale meant leaving the solid safety

214

of the mast; to cling precariously to the gunwale with one hand and scoop water with the other. 'Tis of no use, anyway!'

'D'you wish us to founder? Bale, you bugger!'

'Who are you to give me orders?' bawled Lesley above the roar of the gale. 'Bale yourself!'

He threw the baler to Roberts. The wind caught it. Roberts stood up to make a grab for it as it went over the side.

He lost his balance and went overboard. He screamed once, then the next marching wave went over him and he disappeared.

'Put about!' Barker stared disbelievingly at the spot where the Welshman had vanished. 'He must be saved!' Without Roberts, he was at the mercy of the storm — and of the other two. 'Put about, for Christ's sake!'

Russen, at the tiller, grinned and shook his wet head.

Lesley bawled, still clinging to the mast, 'If we turn, we'll be swamped.' The whaleboat was taking the seas at a slight angle on the bow, rearing like a startled horse to each one. To be caught broadside on by one of those grey-green foaming monsters was something Lesley didn't even like to think about. 'He's gone to Davey Jones by now, anyway.' And it won't be long, he thought, grinning abominably, before Johnny Barker goes the same way. He'd had something heavy in his pockets that he'd been trying to conceal for the last week.

Barker saw the look on his face. Terrified beyond reason, he tugged the pistols out of his coat, pointed them blindly at Lesley and squeezed the triggers. There were two clicks as the hammers fell. Lesley, who had seen the rain and spray drenching the two weapons in Barker's hands, laughed out loud. Barker, in an agony of frustration and fear, threw the pistols at him. One missed and flew over Russen's head. The other struck Lesley on the right hand, the steel foresight laying his knuckles open to the bone, making him shout with pain and let go the mast with the injured hand. Barker hurled himself aft, catching Lesley off-balance, tearing his other hand free.

215

If he could shove Lesley overboard now, while Russen was occupied with the tiller . . . Lesley went down with the small of his back across the gunwale, his head almost in the sea and Barker on top of him like a wildcat, clawing at him and pummelling with his fists.

'Ben!' yelled Lesley. 'Get him off me, will you?'

Obediently, Russen let go the tiller and started for'ard.

The wave, twenty feet high and green as emerald, struck the whaleboat and turned it broadside on. Russen, realizing what he'd done, tried to go aft again and grab the tiller, but it was already too late. The boat crabbed sideways down the slope, hit the bottom and overturned. Russen was flung into the sea and gasped out his life for a few seconds, his arms flailing the water ever more feebly as his lungs filled. Barker and Lesley, still locked together, were trapped in the airlock beneath the capsized whaleboat. They were still choking and fighting when the next wave struck, bearing down the heavy hull on to their skulls and crushing them beyond recognition.

216

19

It had been a day of cold winds and heavy rain. A day of new roads blocked by fallen trees, of drowned cattle floating stiff-legged and bloated in the swollen rivers, of bridges washed away: a day of frustrated effort. The townspeople felt it as they put pots and pans under leaking roofs; the sentry at the fort, cloaked against the driving downpour, felt it as he watched the cutter with its crew and six soldiers battle upriver towards the town; Governor Thompson felt it as he sat at his desk and listened impassively to the Army captain reporting a fruitless search. It was Monday the thirteenth of July 1835.

James Porter sat in his room, leaning back from his table and reading what he had just written:

The whole of us thanked the Governor for his humanity to us being total Strangers and took our leave to find lodgings which we soon procured and the next day the whole of us assisted in launching a four Hundred Ton Vessel off the Stocks and showed ourselves very active. The Owner said he would rather have us ten Foreigners than thirty of his own Countrymen which expression pleased the Governor, he being there with a band of Music and nearly the whole of the Inhabitants . . .

How long ago it seemed, that Saturday, their first day of liberty! There had been sunshine then, and music and colour. Laughter and women and wine. Porter looked at the rain streaming down the window. Precious little to laugh at now, with the soldiers, hard-eyed and suspicious, watching them wherever they went, and the townspeople eyeing them with the sympathetic withdrawal they'd have felt for a gang of lepers. Tonight, he'd write up the incident of the *Dublin* frigate that had passed them by; that might prove a good omen. In the meantime, it was the hour for reporting to the Officer of the Guard. He put on his coat and went out.

Shiers was in the forge, helping his father-in-law shoe a horse.

'It is a good piece of land,' he said, in his oddly Yorkshire-accented Spanish, 'and the price seems a fair one.' Carvenia nodded, pumping the bellows until the charcoal roared white-hot. 'If I buy now, it can wait until this order to report every night is — ' He switched to English. 'And devil take it, it must be time now.'

He slammed in the last nail, lowered the hoof he was holding between his knees, and shrugged his coat on hastily, glancing regretfully at the warm glow of the forge before he plunged into the rain.

Cheshire was sitting beside the bed where Maria lay smiling at him, her huge belly forming a hump under the blankets. He held her hand.

'The midwife thinks me over-anxious, but it is as well to be prepared, don't you agree? She says the rain makes no difference, and she can come at any time, so — '

'I think, William mine, that it is time to report.' She squeezed his hand. 'Put your cloak over your head and, when you return, be sure to change your stockings.'

'As you wish, my love.' He kissed her, released her hand,

218

and went to the door. 'I shall not be more than a few minutes.'

Lyon had eaten the spiced chicken Sarah had prepared, and was drinking a glass of wine looking, as he always did when he went out, at the dark loveliness of her hair, at the eyes warm with love that were fixed on his to read his expression, at the softness of her smile. It was a picture he liked to carry with him until he returned to her but, in some strange way, she always seemed to grow more beautiful while he was away, so that when he went back to her she was even lovelier than the picture he had formed.

He was going to do this thing properly, by God. Tomorrow, he'd have a wee word with the German pastor who ran a school in the town; he was a Lutheran, but that was as near as could be to a Presbyterian, the church into which Lyon had been received. Or maybe there was a Presbyterian minister somewhere not too far away? He'd have to ask. In any case, Sarah would have to take up with some church or other before they married, he was sure of that. He grinned to himself, remembering a snatch of Rabbie Burns, the poet his father had loved to recite:

> But gie me a canny hour at e'en,
> My arms about my dearie O;
> An' warly cares, and warly men,
> May a' gae tapsalteerie O!

To hell wi' Governor Thompson; to hell wi' all the fears and forebodings he'd felt of late; he was going to marry his girl. He glanced at the clock; ten to six. He stood up, kissed Sarah and put on his coat. He left his glass of wine half-empty on the table; he'd finish it quietly when he returned to his canny hour at e'en.

The streets were running ankle-deep in thin mud and the rain came in stinging gusts as he plodded, head down, to the prison in the early darkness. The torches that usually burned outside the gates were unlit; there'd be little point in lighting them on a night like this. He banged on the heavy timbers and

219

a soldier, his cloak glistening wet in the light from the guard-room, swung the gate open. He was sullen and did not reply to Lyon's greeting. Lyon shrugged, thinking tolerantly that he, too, wouldn't be all smiles if he had to stand about all night in the rain, opening and shutting gates. He dodged among the puddles in the yard and went into the guardroom where the officer sat behind his table in the lamplight, his record book open in front of him.

'Good evening, *señor teniente*.'

Reading the last three entries upside down, Lyon saw that Porter, Shiers, and Cheshire had already reported in. He smiled inwardly. Cheshire had probably run all the way back to his Maria. Odd, though, that neither Shiers nor Jamie had waited, as the three of them usually did, to have a word or arrange an evening together.

The officer's expression was odd, too. He stared woodenly at Lyon for a moment. Then he made a slight gesture. Lyon turned as the two soldiers who had been standing one on either side of the door came forward and seized his arms.

'Englishman,' said the lieutenant with the boredom of a man who has seen this trick work several times before, 'You are under arrest.' He made a fourth entry neatly in his book.

'Arrest?' Astounded, Lyon didn't even point out that he wasn't English. 'Why? What crime have I committed?'

'It is by the order of His Excellency. Take him away.'

'Wait. At least, let me send a message to —' Lyon stopped. How could he communicate with Sarah when the only words she could read were concerned with themselves and love and household matters? Panic seized him. How, in God's name, was she to be told and reassured that he hadn't been killed in an accident, or that he hadn't suddenly taken it into his head to desert her? He struggled, but the two soldiers had been through all this before with Shiers, Porter and Cheshire, and they'd had enough. Lyon felt a brief agony at the back of his head that exploded in a white flare of light before the darkness closed in on him and he tumbled, spinning, into nothingness.

220

He came round slowly, his mind regaining by degrees its control of his body. First, the eyes. Utter darkness when he opened them. Hearing? A clink from close at hand; water dripping and the patter of rain on the roof. There was a foul smell of urine. He had a fiery ache in the back of his head; he was lying on his back; he was cold and wet. His hands touched wet straw with stone beneath it. His legs — he tried again. Yes. They were immovable. Tied to something, or —

'Is that you awake, Charlie?' Jamie's voice. Above him, and close. 'I tried to sit you up out of the wet but I couldn't move you.'

Lyon bent his knees, sat up, and groped behind him. There was a stone shelf. He hauled himself up backwards and sat on it, clinking loudly. He felt his ankles. 'Is it you I'm chained to, Jamie?' He tried to keep from screaming at the touch of the gyves. 'Or is it the wall?'

'Me. We're ironed two and two together. We're in one cell, Shiers and Cheshire in another. There's no window, the door's two inches thick and bound with iron, and there's a sentry outside it. They're taking no chances with us, it seems.' He paused. 'I heard one of 'em say as they'd be for a firing squad if we escaped.'

'But what, in heaven's name, are we supposed to have done? Surely it's no' on account of Barker and the others absconding? We had nothing to do wi' that.'

'The reasons aren't important. Maybe Thompson thinks we assisted in their escape. Maybe he thinks we're planning to go, too. Maybe he just doesn't like being made a fool of by Barker, and he's having his revenge on us. I don't know. The important thing is that we're here, with precious little hope of doing anything about it. So the only thing to do is wait and see what fate offers.'

How, wondered Lyon as his brain cleared, can Jamie be so bloody calm? Of course, it was all right for him — he had nothing to lose. Out there, in the darkness and weeping rain, there was a farm belonging to Will Shiers, a child about to be born to Will Cheshire, a girl with a half-empty glass of wine waiting for himself. But Jamie? He had gained nothing in Valdivia.

Or had he? It would be strange, Lyon reflected, if James Porter, who had wanted nothing but his liberty, had found something he couldn't lose: himself.

In the morning, they asked to see the governor. Outside the gaol, Carvenia asked to see them. Both requests were refused. They tried to bribe the soldiers who brought them their meals to take messages out; they were told their food would stop if they offended again. They had no news from the outside and were driven half mad with anxiety. Finally, after a week, they were taken, still chained together, to the large cell they'd shared when they'd first arrived in Valdivia, the cell where Don Fernando had told them of the visit of the *Blonde*.

It was as if the clock had been put back, Porter thought. Once again, they were filthy, wild-eyed, bearded. Only this time they were ironed together like wild beasts, and there were fewer of them. Porter, with his love of doggerel, thought about Barker and muttered to himself:

Seven absconding pris'ners on the Chilean shore;
Three stole a whaleboat, and then there were four.

Where, he wondered detachedly, would the macabre rhyme end?

The door opened and Shiers' father-in-law came in with an officer. Two soldiers armed with muskets took up station on either side of the door.

'I am to tell you,' said the officer coldly, 'that not one word of English is to be spoken. If it is, your visitor will be made to leave on the instant.'

Cheshire said, 'In the name of God, how is Maria?' He hadn't slept, Shiers knew, for the best part of a week, and he looked like death.

222

'Very well.' Carvenia glanced scornfully at the military. 'In spite of the efforts of certain people, she is well. And so is your son.'

'I have a son?' Cheshire leaned back against Shiers, his leg-irons clanking. 'May God be thanked. If only I could — ' He straightened up. 'I want to see him.' His voice rose and the soldiers stiffened watchfully. 'I demand it.'

'Peace, Will,' said Porter softly. 'We're not in a position to demand anything at the moment.'

'Rosa sends her love.' Carvenia nodded to Shiers. 'All is well with her and your daughter. They are anxious, of course, but with Sarah to help them — '

'Sarah?' Lyon moved forward. 'My Sarah?'

'But, of course.' The blacksmith spread his hands. 'How could we leave her alone with her grief? She is living with us until you return.' He grinned. 'She is a very fine cook, that one.'

Lyon said nothing. There was more to be said, as he had learnt from Sarah, in silence sometimes.

Cheshire said impatiently, 'Yes, but when is it to be, our return?'

'There is a move afoot among the citizens to have you released. A petition. Such as the one that obtained your release under that good man Don Fernando. To such a request even — '

'Enough,' snapped the captain. 'The visit is at an end.' The four prisoners were taken back to their cells.

There were no further visits. They were kept shut away in darkness that slowly turned their skins to the unhealthy whiteness of a fungoid growth. They were fed on slops made of the soldiers' leavings mixed with water; when they refused to eat, it was made clear that it was a matter of indifference to their gaolers whether they starved to death or not. They stank, since no change of clothing was offered to them; in any case, their leg-irons made the removal of their trousers an impossibility and the gyves, they were told, could be taken off only on the Governor's authority. Their cell stank too, from the bucket that two men had to use and that was emptied only when the officer on duty reminded one or other of the sentries to perform this unpleasant task. They heard no more of the petition.

It had indeed been written out, taken round the town by Carvenia and signed by every influential citizen he could get to listen to him. The Governor received it, thanked the deputation that had presented it, and promised to give it his consideration. It went into a drawer in his desk and stayed there. Thompson had not been trained in the government service for nothing. Always courteous, he answered the inquiries that were made with the time-honoured formula that the petition was receiving attention and that a decision would be arrived at in due course. And, as he knew they would, the inquiries became less and less frequent as the weeks, then the months, went by. Three shipyard labourers and an apprentice blacksmith — foreigners, former convicts — had been taken into custody. That was a misfortune, true, but they would be returned to their families one of these days, without doubt. In the meantime, the stream of life must flow on, eh, señores?

It flowed on. It closed over their heads with scarcely a ripple. And what could an elderly blacksmith, two mothers with children, and a deaf-and-dumb Indian girl do about it?

They did all they could. Carvenia and his daughter made nuisances of themselves in the town until they were shunned as if they had the plague. Maria persuaded the priest to write letters for her to the Governor. And Sarah . . .

She had passed through the stage of voiceless, red-eyed weeping. She retreated into herself, helping Rosa in the house, working like a slave in gratitude for the kindness she was shown. In every spare moment she had, she haunted the prison gates. As a dog will wait for its master until it dies, she waited for Charles Lyon, standing in the rains of winter, the warm sunshine of spring, then in the first heat of summer in the square outside the prison. And the soldiers did what they

224

would have done with a stray dog; they chased her away. She fled, and returned. They yelled insults at her; a waste of breath, since she could not hear them. They threw stones; she dodged them. But, ironically, when the thing happened for which she had waited for over half a year, she was not there to see it.

It was on a morning already warm with the promise of a hot summer's day when Lyon and Porter heard the bolt on their cell door thump back. They looked up, blinking like moles in the dim light that filtered in from the corridor.

'Prisoners!' The officer had two armed soldiers behind him. 'Today, you are to be released from here!'

'Released?' Lyon, moving like a very old man, stood up. 'Jamie,' he said incredulously. 'Did ye hear that? He says we're to be released.' Dear God, he thought. I'm going home to her. Weakened, he stood with the tears running through the dirt on his face and into his matted beard. 'Home to Sarah,' he said as the irons came off.

For a brief instant, Porter saw Sarah Island with the gulls flying free above it and the whipping triangle standing stark in the rain. They weren't going to be released. He knew that. With his mind clearer than he could ever remember in his life, he took his friend by the arm. It was all, he had decided long ago, a matter of making certain choices at certain times and then following the path. Like being in a maze. You turned left or right, and then there was another choice — left? Or right? And on you went, the only rule of the game being that you could never, never turn back. So, if you made a wrong choice ten moves back, why, there was nothing whatever to be done about it. You were at a dead end. You were swept off the board and other players could, maybe, take a lesson from the mistakes you'd made. Now there were no more choices, no decisions to be made. He stumbled out into the sunshine with the others and into the yard where they were surrounded by soldiers. The gate was opened. They shambled out.

There was a crowd . . . Carvenia bawling something . . . Rosa, the tears blinding her . . . Maria trying to reach Will Cheshire and being shoved back by the musket-butts . . .

Lyon said uncertainly, 'Jamie? They did say we're to be released?'

There was Cheshire shouting and struggling, lashing out at the men who were pushing Maria . . . screams . . . Cheshire clubbed senseless, being carried . . . the crowd yelling, surging, but kept easily in check . . .

Lyon said, 'Sarah. I don't see her, Jamie.'

There was Carvenia trying to shout, his voice inaudible . . . Rosa screaming incoherently . . .

Porter gripped Lyon's arm more tightly. 'Charlie lad, it's better she's not here. She'd have been mishandled by the military. Hurt.'

'But, if we're to be released — ' Tightly packed in the phalanx of soldiers, they were hustled through the town on the route they'd taken on the night when they'd landed for the first time in Valdivia. Down to the wharf, where a group of sailors stood at the gangplank of a small schooner that flew no flag.

One of the seamen took a pipe out of his mouth. 'Now, me lucky lads,' he said in broad cockney. 'All aboard the packet and look smart about it.'

Shiers stopped dead. 'Be damned to that!' He turned to the Chilean officer. 'We're to be set free, you said.'

'And so you have been.' The Chilean waved a paper. 'From prison.'

'And now you're off on a pleasant little cruise.' The sailor grinned slyly. 'Tis your Governor's doing. He wants to clear his decks of you, but without his government knowing of it, see? So, since our next port of call's Callao, he's asked us to take you off his hands.'

'Callao? In Peru?' Shiers' eyes gleamed. Porter knew what was in his mind: that it was only a matter of time before Rosa could join him there.

226

'Aye, and it'll be a profitable voyage for us. You see, mates, the Navy can't come into Valdivia for you; the government'd never permit it. But,' he gave a nod and Porter felt his arms seized by two burly sailors, 'there's no reason why we can't earn a handsome bounty by handing you over to the frigate as is waiting for you in Callao, is there?'

It was, Porter thought detachedly, the final irony that they should be taken out of Valdivia as illegally as they'd come in. The bloody Navy, he thought, half-admiringly. They never give up. He knew the answer to his question before he asked it. 'What frigate is that?'

'HMS *Blonde*, to be sure. Commodore Mason in command. Sailed thirteen hundred miles from Valparaiso to meet you, he has.' He cocked an eyebrow. 'Reckon they'll pay a good price for you. They want to hang you for piracy.'

From the schooner's quarter-deck, the captain shouted irritably, 'Mr Pascoe, *if* you please! When you've quite finished greeting your malodorous friends, perhaps you'd ask them to be so good as to step aboard and be ironed. And have that blasted canoe moved, will you? Place is like a bloody regatta.' He pointed for'ard, past the schooner's bow.

She was there, as Lyon had known she'd be. She was sitting in the canoe in a white dress, her hair cascading over her brown shoulders, a paddle across her knees. Two sailors gripped Lyon's arms, shoving him up the gangplank, but he didn't struggle. He looked at her and there was nothing else in the world but the sunlight in her hair, the dark eyes that had gazed up at him in passion and tenderness, the mouth he had kissed so often without ever knowing that each kiss was being subtracted from a final total. He stared at her, imprinting on his mind the face he would carry in his dreams, in his heart, for as long as he lived. She didn't weep. She didn't show grief, or any sign of emotion. She watched him, as she'd watched him since the moment they'd met, to read what was in his face.

227

At last, when she'd spoken to him in the only way she knew, she reached down into the canoe. Very carefully, she lifted something and in the way he'd taught her, in the way she'd seen his friends do, she raised to him, just before he vanished from sight, a half-empty glass of wine.

20

'I remonstrated with the men.' David Hoy gripped the carved rail of the witness box, his eyes fixed on the Solicitor-General. 'I endeavoured to induce them to go to their duty, telling them if they did the matter would be kept a secret for ever.' The palms of his hands, he found, were clammy and sweating in spite of the cold. It was stuffy in the high, narrow courtroom that was packed to suffocation and smelt of ink, wet wool and unwashed humanity. A most unsalubrious atmosphere. He would have to inhale some vapour of camphor later to prevent an infection.

Outside, on this wind-swept April morning, the streets of Hobart Town were buffeted by the rain-squalls that swung the ships in Sullivan's Cove uneasily at their anchors, but the worthy townsfolk were not to be kept at home by a little bad weather. For three days the trial had, in the words of the *Hobart Town Courier*, 'excited considerable interest'; after all, it wasn't every day that the Criminal Sittings of the Supreme Court of Van Diemen's Land had four pirates to deal with. Not that they looked very much like pirates. 'More like,' as one spectator remarked, eyeing with ghoulish fascination their greenish-white faces and skeletal frames, 'as if they snuffed it a year ago and never got buried.'

'And how, sir,' the Solicitor-General gave a hitch to his gown, 'did they answer you?'

'They answered that they had got the ship and would die to a man before they would give her up; they had got their liberty and were determined to keep it.' He glanced at the four men in the dock. They hadn't kept it long; and it certainly hadn't done them much good.

On the two-thousand-mile voyage to Callao, they'd been guarded as carefully as if they'd been the runaway offspring of some duke to whose parental care they were being returned. Commodore Mason, pointing out that the mills of God ground slowly but, by all the fiends in hell, they ground exceeding bloody small, had paid for them in gold and then conveyed them to Valparaiso where — discreetly, so as not to offend the Chileans — they had been transferred to the twenty-eight-gun sloop *North Star*, bound for England. The passage round the Horn had been hair-raising, with the tiny ship battling seas that all but laid her on her beam ends, and gales that threatened to dismast her. All the time, they had been treated with rough naval kindliness. They were, after all, men whose days were numbered, men who were as good as in their coffins.

And they behaved as such — like walking dead, showing no anger, no grief. Porter had retreated into the fatalistic acceptance he had learned in Valdivia. The path had reached a dead end, and that was that. There was no way out, bolted as he was to one floating prison after another by leg-irons that were checked twice a day. He muttered to himself, finding a certain morbid satisfaction in completing his jingle:

> Four absconding pris'ners, their hopes of freedom gone,
> Went to the gallows, and then there was none.

The others, deprived of their dreams, were far from fatalistic. But they, too, were men without life. Cheshire had passed

230

through the agony of hysteria that had led him to try, aboard the *Blonde*, to beat his brains out on the bulkhead to which he'd been ironed. For his own good they'd tied him to a chair bolted to the deck after that episode, and there he'd sat, motionless but for the tears coursing down his cheeks, until the ship's surgeon feared for his sanity. Lyon seemed to be completely divorced from reality, sitting on the deck and not responding by a flicker when he was spoken to. He offered no resistance when they fed him and, when taken on deck for exercise, stood immobile until he was pushed gently. Then he would walk a step and stop again. Like a clockwork toy, said the *North Star*'s captain, that had almost run down.

Shiers, too, sat and never spoke. But he was planning ways of escape. If a man from Lancashire can think up schemes, he reasoned doggedly, happen I can do the same. He searched constantly for a chink in the enemy's armour — a bolt to be loosened, a spar to throw over the side to cling to when you jumped. But there were no loose bolts, and not the slightest chance of jumping overboard. The Navy that had carried Napoleon Bonaparte into exile wasn't going to be outwitted by a quartet of convicts.

In the Thames, they were consigned to the horrors of the *Leviathan* hulk while the clerks scribbled interminably and the dispatches went to and fro. Finally Sir John Franklin, who had been appointed Lieutenant-Govenor Arthur's successor in Van Diemen's Land, was informed by Lord Melbourne, the Prime Minister, on the eighth of November 1836, that 'the four Prisoners taken from Valdivia in Chile to the United Kingdom on HMS *North Star* are to return to Van Diemen's Land.'

The convict transport in which they sailed was called *Sarah*.

She left the freezing greyness of Spithead three days before the Christmas of 1836 with two hundred and fifty-five convicts aboard; her master, Captain J. T. Whiteside, was delighted to find that he had accomplished the passage in a record ninety-seven days, the exceptionally good weather enabling him to dock in Hobart Town on the twenty-ninth of March 1837, with the loss of only nine convicts who had died on the voyage. The trial of Cheshire, Lyon, Porter and Shiers began on the twenty-fourth of April.

It was held before Chief Justice John Lewes Pedder, an upright if not brilliant lawyer who had been Chief Justice for fifteen years and of whose meticulousness George Arthur had once complained that 'life is too short to wait for his opinions and decisions'. It was Pedder who had opposed the introduction of civilian juries into Van Diemen's Land on the grounds that they were unconstitutional. The four accused, therefore, were put to trial by a jury composed of 'seven officers of His Majesty's Forces by Sea and Land', according to the terms of the Charter of Justice that Pedder himself had brought out from England. The prosecution was conducted by a Solicitor-General, representing the interest of the Crown. Since solicitors were not attracted to Van Diemen's Land in great numbers in 1837, professional advice was hard to obtain and expensive. 'The business,' as Commissioner Bigge had remarked fifteen years before, 'has been chiefly conducted by remitted convicts.' The prisoners, therefore, conducted their own defence, helped out here and there by sympathetic tipstaffs and constables. There was, after all, little enough to defend.

There were three counts in the indictment, of which the first was the only one of any significance, carrying as it did the death penalty. It charged them with 'piratically and feloniously carrying away on the 13th January 1834 the brig *Frederick*, Charles Taw master, belonging to Our Sovereign Lord the King, and of the estimated value of £1200, from the high seas, to wit, Macquarie Harbour on the Coast of Van Diemen's Land.' The second charge was that of breaking their trust as sworn mariners — a minor point and difficult to prove. The third was even more of a legal quibble, being exactly the same as the second except that it did not state Charles Taw to be a subject of William IV.

The proceedings began with a plea of Not Guilty from the accused and a presentation by the Solicitor-General of the history of the *Frederick* and of the topographical situation of the place of the alleged piracy. It was established that Charles Taw (who was in Sydney at the time of the trial) had been directed by Major Baylee to take charge of the vessel after she was launched and that the four soldiers had been 'directed to keep watches two and two, the same as a seaman's watch, but not to carry their arms, as there was no necessity for it; they were to keep an eye on the seamen to prevent any confusion and to have their arms at readiness in their berths'. It was on the morning of the twenty-sixth of April that David Hoy took the witness stand.

He was as pale, sombrely dressed and slightly hesitant as they remembered him to be. He gave his evidence fairly, tending to gloss over certain inadequacies of his own — his inability to load his pistols, his concurrence with Taw's lax handling of the convicts — but giving what credit he could to the accused. The Solicitor-General took him through his version of the attack on the captain's cabin and the shots fired through the skylight. 'I tore open the lid of my chest,' said Hoy valiantly, 'and, taking out my pistols, I said I would sell my life as dearly as possible and shoot the first man I saw through the skylight.'

The Solicitor-General nodded. He was building up the picture he knew would appeal to a military jury, that of the gallant officer resolutely defending the King's property with his life against a parcel of ruffians. 'And what threats had you heard uttered, Mr Hoy?'

'I heard someone on deck say they had better shoot the two — ' Hoy paused. 'I do not know whether I can repeat the expression in public.'

'Provide the witness with the means to write it down,' said the Chief Justice. Hoy wrote the word 'buggers' on a piece of paper and it was passed up. The judge regarded it distastefully and handed it to the usher who conveyed it to the Solicitor-

General and to the seven members of the jury. Eyebrows were raised and moustaches twirled at this outrage to good taste.

'And,' said the Solicitor-General, 'there was general agreement to this murderous suggestion?'

'No, sir.'

'No? You mean, there was a silence indicating their approval?'

'No. Someone else said: "We will not commit murder if we can avoid it" or some similar phrase. I think it was William Shiers who said it; I was satisfied of it at the time, and have been so since.'

'Were there any other incitements to murder?'

'No, sir. I then heard someone call out: "Bring along the pitch-pot and let us empty it down on them." I believe it was —'

'Pitch-pot?' The prosecutor glanced at the jury, his eyebrows lifted, to ensure that they had heard this diabolical suggestion. 'Did one of the accused say that?'

'Yes, sir. I am persuaded it was William Cheshire who said it.'

'And you do not consider the emptying of hot pitch upon you an attempt at murder? And a brutal one at that?'

'If you please!' The Chief Justice tapped his desk. 'The learned Solicitor-General should know better than to ask the witness's opinion concerning the efficacy of hot pitch as an instrument of assassination.'

The Solicitor-General bowed. The jury were already muttering indignantly to one another, and he had made his point. 'I apologize, Your Honour,' he said smoothly. 'The question is, of course, inadmissable. I will, with Your Honour's permission, re-phrase it.' He turned to Hoy. 'As a master-shipwright, perhaps you would tell the Court something of the properties of hot pitch?'

'It burns, of course. In a confined space, it would have a stifling effect.'

'Precisely.' The Solicitor-General left a pause to allow the

234

words 'burns' and 'stifling' to work on the jury's imagination.

But Hoy continued. 'It is my belief, however, that the intention was to persuade Mr Taw and me to come up on deck without being fired upon further and without taking our lives.'

'That, sir, is an expression of opinion. Pray confine yourself to replying to my questions.' The Solicitor-General, annoyed, glanced for support to the Bench, but Pedder was writing and did not look up.

The examination continued, the Solicitor-General making much of the tying of the captives' hands and, in the middle of a wrangle over whether the soldiers had been bound or not, His Honour said, 'I think, at this point, gentlemen, it would be convenient to adjourn for luncheon.'

In the afternoon, the prosecution established that three of the accused had carried arms during the attack — Shiers a pistol, Cheshire a musket, and Porter a cutlass with the point broken off. Hoy did not recollect whether Lyon had been armed or not, but the cutlass went down well with the jury as a typical buccaneer's weapon. The Solicitor-General pounced on the theft of Hoy's watch. 'It was taken from you at gunpoint by Barker and Shiers?'

'By Barker. Shiers, in fact, gave me my pocket compass without Barker's knowledge.'

'A generous act,' sneered the prosecutor, 'to give you that which was rightly your own property. Why should Shiers have gone with you to the cabin if it was not to rob you?'

'I think, sir, he intended to preserve my life and that of Mr Taw by interposing between us and Barker. At first, I admit, I thought Shiers to be the ringleader; but later I found more security from him than from anybody else.'

The Solicitor-General sniffed. 'Pray continue, Mr Hoy.'

Hoy described their being put ashore and the arrival of the boat on the morning of the fourteenth of January with provisions. He omitted his speech of gratitude to Shiers; in retrospect, it sounded abject and undignified. At this point, too, he became slightly confused, mixing up the old whaleboat that had been lying on the beach, the brig's whaleboat, and the jollyboat. 'I had been asking all along for a boat but I was told I could not have one. They promised to return in the morning — '

'With a boat? And more provisions than the niggardly amount they had given you?'

Hoy paused again. They *had* promised more provisions at one time or another. And perhaps, at first, they had intended the marooned men to use the old whaleboat . . . After three and a quarter years, and when one had been ill at the time, it was difficult to recall. 'Yes, that was it, sir. They promised us a boat with more provisions after the brig had gone over the bar.'

'And, of course, they sent none.' The Solicitor-General nodded, accepting this further evidence of the convicts' lying perfidy. After taking Hoy through the *Frederick*'s departure, he made the point that, although the prisoners had not been on wages at Macquarie Harbour, they had been considered to be seamen, subjects of the Crown. With that, he concluded his examination of the shipwright.

Shiers cross-examined first, standing with his black hair streaked with grey, and his face, shorn of its beard again, lined and aged beyond his forty-two years. He'd been on trial here, in this very room, once before — in 1828, when he'd been convicted of felony and sent to the Harbour — and he knew a little of legal procedure. His hazel eyes were as full of fight as ever when he said, 'Mr Hoy, how long have you known me?'

'At the time of the seizure of the brig, I had known you from three to four years, that is to say, the time you had worked for me in the shipyard at Macquarie Harbour.'

'And how did I conduct myself during that time?'

'You were orderly, quiet and industrious.'

'Thank you, sir. Now, on the night when I went to the cabin with you and Captain Taw and John Barker, what did

236

I give you apart from the compass?'

'Give me apart from?' Hoy frowned. 'Ah, yes. I recollect. You gave me some flannels for my back, and some dressing.' Hoy turned to the Chief Justice. 'I had — and still have, to this day — an affliction of the lumbar region of the spine.' He put a hand to his back. 'I find that, on cold, wet days such as today it causes me considerable discomfort, relieved only by the application of ointments and warm flannels. You can imagine that, in the climate of Macquarie Harbour — '

'I sympathize. And we certainly do not wish to keep you standing longer than is necessary, Mr Hoy.' Chief Justice Pedder's dry voice cut across Hoy's medical history. There were one or two sniggers from the public. He frowned, then nodded to Shiers. 'Continue.'

'Did not Major Baylee leave some rum for occasional use when he departed from the settlement?'

'Yes, to be sure. He ordered marine rations for the men, and some rum was certainly served out.'

'And did not Captain Taw partake of this rum at the launching?'

Hoy hesitated. 'Yes, he drank some rum. It was a wet day, and — '

'And was he not on a later occasion unwell and confined to the boatswain's hut for the night under the influence of liquor?'

Hoy hesitated again. The Chief Justice tapped his bench meaningly at the buzz of delighted comment that came from the spectators when Hoy said at last, 'Yes, that is so.'

'Did Captain Taw threaten to leave anyone behind because of insolence?'

In all honesty, Hoy could not remember Taw's threat to Charles Lyon. 'I do not recollect his doing so.'

'Now, sir, to the pistol I am said to have presented at you in the cabin. How do you know it was loaded?'

'Your Honour!' The Solicitor-General was on his feet. 'The witness has not, in fact, stated that the pistol was loaded.'

237

Chief Justice Pedder nodded. 'How do you know, sir,' he said to Hoy, 'that it was, in fact, a pistol? Mr Taw has stated in his information that there were no pistols on board, apart from your own. Could it not have been, for example, a bar of iron?'

'No, Your Honour, it had every appearance of a pistol. As for where it came from: the convict Barker was a very ingenious man and had been used to repair arms for the military at the settlement. He might have made it.'

Shiers sat down. He hadn't got very far, he reflected. But 'twas better than sitting here and doing nowt while they were preparing the gallows in the gaol in Murray Street, across the road.

Lyon looked as if he'd been turned to stone, Hoy thought, with his pale face and cold, detached voice that had lost its Lowland softness. His questions were vague and repetitious and the representative of the *Hobart Town Courier* noted down that 'they elicited nothing of any consequence to the material points of the case'.

Porter, as well as Shiers, had appeared in that same courtroom before and had been sentenced to death, only to have the execution exchanged for life imprisonment at the Harbour. He, too, had a smattering of legal knowledge, and took copious notes throughout the proceedings. He first made the point with Hoy that, although the quantity of provisions left for the shore party had been small, they had been proportionate to the amount that had been on board. He went on, referring to his notes, 'You have said, sir, that you saw James Lesley and Benjamin Russen pointing their muskets at you when you came up from the cabin that night?'

'Yes.'

'That Cheshire was standing by the mainmast with a musket, while Shiers had a pistol in his hand at that time?'

'That is so.'

'And that I had a cutlass in my hand, with the point broken off?'

'I did indeed say so.'

'Then how, sir,' Porter leaned forward, his one eye glittering, 'can you account for the fact that you saw all this — and in considerable detail — although it was pitch dark at the time?'

This time, the murmur from the spectators was louder. A voice said quite audibly, 'Because 'e was drunk, like 'is cap'n, that's how.'

'Aye,' said somebody else. 'On the rum he'd taken for his poor old back!'

There was a guffaw. An outraged tipstaff shouted 'Order!' An usher hurried forward as another voice said loudly, 'God bless yer, James Porter, you're a Trojan!'

'If this uproar persists,' said Chief Justice Pedder, dispassionately, 'I shall have the persons who cause it charged with contempt, and the Court cleared.' He paused, then nodded to Hoy.

The shipwright said agitatedly, 'It was *not* pitch dark. It was a clear, starlit night. And the persons I have mentioned were, at one time or another, close enough for me to see them clearly.'

'Is it not true,' said Porter, 'that, when William Shiers and I parted from you on the morning when we took you provisions, you said you had not expected such humanity from us when we had so little to share, and that you hoped God would be kind to us, or some such words?'

'I was grateful to you for not leaving us to starve. I do not recall my exact words.'

Cheshire's cross-examination — halting and prompted frequently by the Chief Justice — elicited the admission from Hoy that Cheshire had always been diligent and well-behaved when he had worked in the shipyard, and that Hoy had promised to keep an eye on him at Port Arthur. 'A weak lad,' commented the man from the *Courier* in his notes.

James Tait, the next Crown witness, had come down from Launceston, where he was employed aboard a government brig. His memory was not good and, while he corroborated

239

Hoy's evidence in most respects, he slipped up on detail. He said, for example, that the two soldiers were already prisoners in the fo'c'sle when he was taken below, and that it was Charles Lyon who had given the order to fire down through the skylight. Battened down in the fo'c'sle as the former mate had been at the time, it would have been utterly impossible for him to have identified a voice among the shouting at the after end of the vessel, but Lyon did not pounce on this. Instead, he took Tait through Taw's drinking habits once again and asked Tait whether the Captain had not spoilt the main course of the *Frederick* by attempting to cut it himself. Tait admitted these points but stated firmly that Taw had been 'in a state of complete sobriety at the time the vessel was captured. If he appeared in any way otherwise, it was because he had received a wound on the head from which blood was trickling.' Lyon merely succeeded in arousing sympathy from the jury for Taw as a hard-drinking, hard-fisted captain who had taken some nasty knocks in defending his ship.

MacFarlane and Nicholls, still serving sentences at Port Arthur, had changed little in the last three years. They added nothing in their testimony to what Hoy and Tait had said. Then the accused stood, in turn, to make their defence.

Shiers called a character witness on his own behalf — an emancipated convict named Harker who was employed as a solicitor's clerk and whom Shiers, soon after arriving in Van Diemen's Land in 1820, had saved from being robbed and murdered in the street by two roughs. Harker's evidence did little to sway the jury who, beginning to think of their dinners, yawned and fidgeted in their seats.

But there were no yawns or murmurs from the spectators as Shiers went on to remind the Court of the inhumanity they had suffered at the settlement, and of the humanity they had shown to Taw, Hoy and the others in return. With blunt Yorkshire candour, he pointed out that, had the convicts murdered their prisoners, Hoy, Tait and the others would not have been able to give evidence against them in that courtroom. There were no guffaws when Porter stood to describe the appalling hardships they had suffered across the Pacific, the happiness they had attained in Valdivia, the wives and children from whom some of them had been torn. There were no sniggers as they each, in turn, threw themselves on the mercy of the Court. Only a breathless hush in which, so the man from the *Hobart Town Courier* wrote, 'His Honour summed up with his accustomed minuteness and perspicacity and, after reserving one or two technical points, left the case to the Jury who retired about six o'clock.'

The seven officers were out for half an hour. They returned a verdict of Guilty against all four accused on all counts. Chief Justice Pedder adjourned the Court for forty-eight hours before passing sentence on the following Friday.

They were sentenced to death by hanging.

21

'The gaol at Hobart Town,' wrote John Thomas Bigge in his *Report on the Judicial Establishments of New South Wales and Van Diemen's Land,* 'was finished in the year 1815. It is placed in an elevated and airy part of the town, and has more the appearance and the accommodation of an hospital, than a place of coercion and confinement. The gaol contains an entrance that is fifteen feet in length by twelve in breadth; two rooms for the gaoler, measuring fifteen feet by eight; two rooms for debtors, sixteen feet by fifteen; a lock-up room, twelve feet by ten; and two turnkey rooms. These are separated from the rooms for felons, of which there are two, and each measuring twenty-six feet by fourteen . . . there are two light and two dark cells in the yard, measuring six feet by five.'

The twelve-foot wall of the gaol dominated the southern side of Murray Street, occupying an entire block between the thoroughfares named after Governors Davey and Macquarie, and facing the three freestone buildings — Treasury, Courthouse and Police Office — that had been designed by John Lee Archer, the colonial architect who was to Hobart Town what Sir Christopher Wren was to London. To the west of

242

these three structures and diagonally opposite the gaol stood St David's Church, its leaden dome soaring above them all.

The condemned men were held in the two light cells in the yard, Shiers and Porter in one, Cheshire and Lyon in the other, while the sentence imposed by the Chief Justice, the verdict of the jury and the Solicitor-General's notes on the case were awaiting the approval of Governor Sir John Franklin. Porter, grinning wryly at the thought that, for the first time in his life, he was a gentleman of leisure, began to rewrite his version of the seizure of the *Frederick* and the voyage to Chile. Shiers prowled his cell like a caged tiger, trying to find a way out. To escape from the condemned cell in Hobart Town Gaol would not, admittedly, be easy but, by God, he was going to try.

It was on a blustery May evening, a few days after the trial, that he got his chance.

It began with a greatcoated figure struggling along Murray Street, buffeted from behind by the sou'-westerly gale that caused the lantern over the stocks at the gaol's entrance to flare and almost go out alternately as the wind caught it. There was a clang overhead that made the man stop for a moment. Then he went on as, above the whistle of the wind, the three-sided clock of St David's struck nine. He reached the gateway of the gaol and hauled on the bell-pull, stamping and rubbing his cold hands together. The wicket gate opened. He exchanged a word with one of the two constables on duty, and went inside.

Shiers was in bed, listening to the keening of the wind, when the constable unlocked the cell and flashed a lantern inside. Porter was also lying in his bunk smoking a pipe, having succeeded in obtaining some tobacco with the connivance of a sympathetic day constable. The cell was full of smoke but, as a matter of form, he tried to conceal his pipe. The constable ignored it. 'William Shiers,' he said. 'Get dressed. You are to come with me directly.'

'Where to?' Shiers raised his head, dazzled by the light.

243

'You have a visitor. Look sharp, now. I can't stand here all night.'

A visitor with money, depend on it, Shiers thought as he climbed out of bed, if he could fetch a condemned man out of his cell at night.

Porter said, 'If 'tis Lady Jane Franklin come to hear one of my ballads, please to inform her I'm not at home.'

'None of your sauce, James Porter, or you'll get no more paper and ink.' The constable let Shiers out into the draughty yard and locked the cell door. ''Tis Mr Harker,' he said as he led the way inside, his lantern flickering as he swung it. 'Him as you called at the trial.'

The freed convict seemed on excellent terms with the two warders and sat by the fire in one of the turnkey rooms, warming his hands. He grinned at Shiers and said to the constables, 'Very good, mates. Now give me a few minutes alone with my client, will you?'

'We'll have to lock you in.' One of the men picked up a bunch of keys from the table that stood under the hanging lamp and, after a nod from Harker, they both went out.

'Sit down and warm yourself.' Harker pulled another battered wooden chair to the fire. ''Tis a bitter cold night, to be sure.'

'Aye.' Shiers knew that Harker hadn't come to discuss the weather. 'How did you get in?'

'Never you mind how I got in. It's how you're to get out as matters, I'd say.'

'Out?' Shiers sat down, staring at him. 'Escape, you mean?'

'From gaol? Don't be green.' Harker jerked a grimy thumb upwards in the general direction of the wall where the hanging platform was erected. 'From swinging, matey. That's the lay, to dodge the hangman. Have yer thought of lodging an appeal?'

Shiers shook his head. 'We took the brig, they caught us, and that's an end to it. They'll hang us right enough, just the same as if we'd murdered Taw and all of 'em. 'Twas in this

244

very gaol they hanged one of the *Cyprus* mutineers, wasn't it?'

'There's been a deal of change in Hobart Town since then,' said Harker quietly. 'Now that Governor Arthur's gone, there's folk who want to make this a place for free souls to live in; a peaceful, pleasant settlement, not an island prison. Why, there's even talk o' changing the name of the Colony from Van Diemen's Land to Tasmania. Sir John Franklin's no prison governor like Arthur; he's a broad-minded, intelligent man of experience. And his lady, bless her, is of the same mould — interested in art and science and such, and bids fair to make this town a very different place to live in. Besides which, there's a power of sympathy about the place for you four. You hurt no man, you treated your prisoners kindly, and all you sought was your liberty. If you lodge an appeal, 'twill be favourably considered, depend on it.'

'But how can we appeal if we committed the act with which we're charged?'

'You didn't.' Harker grinned a yellow-toothed grin, his hands stretched out to the roaring fire. 'You were charged wi' piracy on the high seas, weren't you? "To wit, in Macquarie Harbour on the coast of Van Diemen's Land." But Macquarie Harbour ain't on the high seas. 'Tis an enclosed stretch of water.'

Shiers grunted. 'If that's all you came for, you could have saved your trouble. It's been tried before — and rejected, so I've heard.'

'We can try again.' Harker's grin broadened. 'But that's only a start — our line of skirmishers, as you might say. Our big gun lies in this: that you can't pirate a King's ship what ain't a King's ship.'

'Either tha'rt daft,' said Shiers impatiently, 'or else tha must think I am. How — ?'

'Look.' Harker leaned forward to tap Shiers on the knee. 'There's so many holes in that indictment you could drive a coach and four through it. That brig was said to be the property of Our Sovereign Lord the King. But she was straight

245

off the stocks, wasn't she? Not registered. Not the property of anybody — not officially. You look for a record of a ship named *Frederick* and what'll you find? Nothing. On paper, she never existed at all.'

'By the Lord,' said Shiers slowly, 'no more you would. No log-book or papers — they're on the floor of the Pacific. Nothing in any government statement of accounts — her timber came from the Gordon River and her sails, ironwork and the like were out of the stores at the Harbour. "The new brig" is all she was there. 'Twas David Hoy that gave her her name.' He stared at Harker. 'D'you think we can get away with it?'

That was what Porter wondered when Shiers returned to the cell. It was what the legal fraternity in Hobart Town wondered when Harker cheekily processed the appeal. And it was what Lieutenant-Governor Sir John Franklin, veteran of the battles of Copenhagen and Trafalgar, Fellow of the Royal Society, former castaway, author, polar explorer and practitioner of humanity, wondered when the appeal came to him in his capacity of Appeal Judge.

'My love,' he said to his wife one May morning at breakfast, 'it appears that those fellows who took the *Frederick* have yet another surprise for us.'

'Surprise?' Lady Jane dragged her mind away from the thought of a natural history museum she was planning for Hobart Town. 'In what way, John?'

'The impudent rascals have lodged an appeal. They say the brig, since she was never registered, never existed; therefore they could not have pirated her. Furthermore, they claim that piracy on the high seas cannot be reconciled with an alleged offence committed in a land-locked harbour.'

'How clever of them!' Lady Jane's eyes sparkled. 'I do so hope they may succeed. Poor wretches, surely they have suffered enough for so small a thing as an attempt to be free.' She paused, watching a bird in a tree outside the window of Government House. Even that was free. What sort of bird

246

was it? It was high time someone studied the ornithology of this island. There was a Mr Gould, she'd heard, who . . . She drank a little tea, watching her husband. 'Am I permitted to ask what Your Excellency's opinion might be?'

Franklin smiled. 'You know my opinion as well as you know your own, my dear. I don't wish to see them hanged. But, as His Majesty's representative, I must see that the law functions efficiently. After all, we can't have convicts sailing off in all directions whenever the whim takes them, eh?' He paused. 'But, to be frank, I do not think we in this Colony are competent to judge a fine point of law such as this. It is the Appeal Court in London that will make the final decision.'

'That will take time,' said Lady Jane thoughtfully. 'Even if they arrived at a decision instantly — and, with lawyers, that is hardly likely — it would take six months for us to know of it. In six months, a good many things may happen.' She smiled. 'They may even escape once more.'

But the four Liberty Men did not escape. Sympathetic and amicably disposed though their gaolers were, they watched their prisoners like hawks. And it took eighteen months for the appeal to travel halfway round the world and back again from the red-robed, dry-as-dust judges who sat at the feet of blindfolded Justice and weighed the question in her scales. In the meantime, James Porter finished his Narrative and arranged to have it published in the *Hobart Town Almanack & Van Diemen's Land Annual* for 1838. He had concluded his account by saying:

> . . . We were found guilty and sentenced to be hanged; but which we have every reason to believe will be commuted to transportation for life. And our case has gone home for the opinion of the English Judges.
> Gaol, Hobart Town, 1st. November 1837.

The spring came with blossom like snow on the apple trees that had been brought out with loving care from England, where, it appeared, the old king had died the previous June.

247

There was a queen on the throne now, an eighteen-year-old girl, of all things. A deal of change, as Harker had said, what with girl monarchs and Lady Franklin exploring the south and west of the island, just like her husband, and encouraging painters and botanists and folk who studied birds. The year 1838 came and went, its hours counted tirelessly by the great bell of St David's Cathedral, and Porter's Narrative appeared and was much admired and his hardships pitied.

It was on a morning in the late summer of 1839 that the French barque *Alouette* out of Marseilles and bound for New Zealand tied up at the jetty in Sullivan's Cove opposite the three-storied warehouses that, both in appearance and in activity, were oddly like rectangular beehives. The River Derwent was like shot silk in the mild sunshine and, above a haze of smoke that rose from the fires and forges of Hobart Town where the dome of St David's stood out like a beacon, the hills rose one above the other, dark-green with trees, light-green with open pasture, to the humped four-thousand-foot summit of Mount Wellington.

'*Une belle ville, ça, n'est-ce pas?*' The *Alouette's* mate jerked a woollen-bonneted head at the mellow sandstone and neatly-painted wood of the houses set among the greenery.

'Aye. A pretty town.' The English seaman who was leaning on the rail puffed at his pipe. 'If you don't get too close, that is.' Like a swamp, he thought. All green and smooth in the sunlight. But once you broke the surface, you were into the black slime and the slow death and the stink of it.

'You 'ave been 'ere before?' The mate switched to English. The seaman, he remembered, could understand French perfectly but spoke it in a way that was painful to the ear, like most of his countrymen.

'Only once. Like your explorers, I didn't stay.'

'*Ah, oui,*' said the Frenchman enthusiastically. 'Du Fresne, Bruni d'Entrecasteaux and Huon de Kermadec, they made explorations 'ere. Nicolas Baudin also — it was his visit that made you English settle 'ere in case Napoleon decided to

248

come, *non?*' He stared along the jetty. 'But what is this?' He pointed. 'Men chained, guarded by soldiers with guns. *Des assassins fameux,* per'aps?'

'Convicts. Poor bastards brought to unload a ship, most like.' The Englishman turned away. 'I'm going below.'

'Wait.' The mate grabbed his arm. 'You know this place, maybe we go ashore together, eh? You can show me where to drink, where — '

'Go ashore?' The Englishman looked at him oddly. 'I'd as soon go into a pest-house as go ashore here.'

'Orright!' The mate shrugged. 'You don' want to be friendly, I go alone.' Piqued, he stumped down the gangway and said to an old man sitting on a bollard in the sun, 'A surly one, that Englishman. As miserable as those convicts of yours there.'

'Miserable?' The elderly man looked up at him. 'Aye, you might say that, to be sure. Them's four of those what seized the *Frederick* five years ago. Sentenced to death and reprieved, they was, poor devils.'

The Englishman had gone very still, his pipe dying in his hand. Down on the wharf, the mate said, 'Per'aps I do not understan' so well. They are poor devils because they were saved from death, you say? But why is that?'

Shiers could have told him — Shiers, who was first in the line of convicts, his right leg shackled to Cheshire's. It had been just over a week ago, on a morning very like this one, when the constable had come for him and Porter and taken them to the turnkey's room where Cheshire and Lyon were already waiting. The two constables stood one on either side of the door; the gaoler in his dark uniform stood by the table with the clerk Harker.

Rejected. Shiers felt his stomach turn over as he looked at their faces. None of them would meet his eye; just as a jury will refuse to look at a prisoner in the dock when they find him guilty. He said, his voice rasping in the silence, 'It's no go, then?'

The gaoler opened his mouth to blast a convict who spoke out of turn but Harker spoke first, 'Oh, it's worked right enough, Will. The appeal's been upheld. You won't hang.'

They looked at one another, the four of them — not over-excited, because they'd hoped, and been encouraged to hope, that it would be like this. They grinned, nodding their thanks to Harker. But he didn't smile back.

Shiers said, 'Well, why so glum? If there's more news, it can't be worse than the gallows.'

Harker looked down at the paper in his hand and, some-how, his lack of agreement with what Shiers had just said was more frightening than the moment when Chief Justice Pedder had pronounced the sentence of death. His language, too, was oddly formal when he said, 'The indictment for piracy has been struck out. In effect, you have been found guilty of a felony.'

Well, thought Shiers, that's only to be expected. We stole an unnamed collection of timber, sails and other articles out of His Majesty's Penal Settlement at Macquarie Harbour. 'We didn't expect to get off scot-free,' he said uneasily. 'What's it to be?'

'Life.'

Shiers looked at the others, perplexed. They were already serving life sentences, all of them. They were no worse off now than on the evening five years ago when they'd watched MacFarlane and the soldiers a-fishing in the Harbour. 'Look,' he said roughly, 'happen I'm a bit stupid, like, but I don't see what's to be so grim-faced about. We're to be sent to Port Arthur, I suppose?' In the last five years, with Governor Arthur gone, conditions at Port Arthur had become very tolerable, he'd heard; easy-going, almost. So, really, they'd come out of it on the credit side of the ledger.

'Not Port Arthur.' Harker paused. 'It's to be Norfolk Island.'

In the silence, a blowfly buzzed loudly on a windowpane. Cheshire, his voice strangled in his throat, said, 'Oh, God.

250

No!' and the thoughts tore like barbed wire through Shiers' brain. Norfolk Island, a thousand miles out in the Pacific. Norfolk Island, that had been set up as a substitute for Macquarie Harbour, a penal settlement for the lowest and most degenerate of the convicts, a dumping ground for those who were considered irredeemable by any means.

Norfolk Island, of which Governor Darling wrote: 'My object was to hold out that Settlement as a place of the extremest punishment, short of Death.'

'Well, Harker.' They hardly recognized Charles Lyon's voice. 'My thanks for what you've done. But I wish to God you'd let us die in peace on the end of a rope.'

And now they dragged their feet, stumbling awkwardly in step, along the dock. First Shiers, then Cheshire, then Lyon, and Porter last in line. They didn't look up. What was there to see? Only the uniformed back of the man in front. A convict transport moored to the jetty. A warder marching ahead of them. And the sunlight — the hateful, free, bountiful sunlight, that shone as uncaringly on them as it shone on a town in South America where two wives and two children were still learning how to live without their men. And where an Indian girl could never learn how to live without hers.

Only Porter raised his eyes, one blind, one seeing, as he passed the French barque where an old man sat on a bollard and a man in a woollen cap stood by him at the foot of the gangway. There was another man on deck. Watching . . . free . . . a seaman with a pipe in his hand . . . Porter stiffened, stopped, and the others stumbled in a clash of leg-irons. The warder shouted, 'Damn you, prisoner! March, can't you?'

And, as the seaman's eyes met his in pity and in anguished recognition, Porter almost laughed at the joke of it, at the twist fate had given to something he'd said long ago on a cold, wet day in Valdivia. He heard his own voice saying: *Don't do it, John, lad. I don't want to think of you back in Hobart Town, shuffling along the quayside with the clank of leg-irons in your ears, and the warders a-shouting, and nothing*

251

in your mind but the thought of the liberty you've lost. That
would be a sad and bitter end to it, after enduring so much.

Aye, thought Porter. An end — but not as sad and bitter as
it might have been. At least I know we didn't all fail. One of
us is still a Liberty Man.

And, as the warder shouted again, furiously, James Porter
closed his cyclops eye in a wink at the man on the barque,
and moved on.

Epilogue

And so, as Lieutenant Governor Sir John Franklin reported on 31 May 1839 in his dispatch to the Prime Minister, they went to Norfolk Island for life.

Death at the end of a rope, as Charles Lyon had said, would have been infinitely preferable. For it was as if, at that time, there was a desperate urgency on the part of those in authority over the Penal Settlement at Norfolk Island to repress the new ideas of liberty and reform that were gaining ground elsewhere —a kind of last-ditch stand out in the Pacific by the eighteenth-century mind against the revolutionary ideas of Wilberforce, Ashley and the Chartists. Abandoned once already in 1813 as unworkable, the Settlement had been re-opened in 1825 to become, by the time the four convicts arrived, a place that matched all the horrors of the Burma-Siam Railway camps under the Japanese in World War II. It was at Norfolk Island that a group of men condemned to the gallows thanked God and received the congratulations of their friends, while a man who had been reprieved wept and was regarded as an object of pity. It was a place where, in the words of one of its gaolers, 'the clashing of irons, the dull echo of the lash, with execrations both loud and deep, make men's flesh creep and fill their minds with horror and despondency'.

It is here that Shiers, Lyon, Cheshire and Porter came to the end of their five-year odyssey. They were rough, uneducated men, convicted thieves who, one might say, had failed at every stage of their lives. They failed even in their search for liberty. But, sometimes, there is a point at which it is difficult to distinguish failure from success. Captain Robert Falcon Scott was not a failure when he did not arrive first at the South Pole. And Lady Jane Franklin would have bitterly resented any suggestion that her husband was a failure when it was discovered that he had perished in the Arctic in 1847 on an abortive Polar expedition.

At all events, William Shiers, Charles Lyon, William Cheshire and James Porter fade at this point into history with only a line in some long-lost prison register to mark their passing. Yet one small speculation remains. On 21 June 1842, the brig *Governor Phillip* was about to leave Norfolk Island for Sydney when she was boarded by a group of convicts from the Settlement boat who put her armed guard under hatches and seized the vessel. The Captain, however, shot the convict who took the helm and the mutiny failed. The ringleaders were hanged.

An attempt to seize a brig just before she sails, the overwhelming of an armed guard without loss of life, the use of a boat similar to the one James Porter and Charles Lyon had crewed in Macquarie Harbour . . .

One wonders.

254

Bibliography

Hobart Town Courier, 7 February 1834; 26 April 1837; 28 April 1837.
Launceston Independent, 8 February 1834.
Arancano of Santiago. Chile, 9 May 1834.
Convict Records of John Barker, William Cheshire, John Dady, John
    Fare, John Jones, James Lesley, Charles Lyon, James Porter, Ben-
    jamin Russen, William Shiers.
Report of the Court of Inquiry into the seizure of the *Frederick,*
    CSO 1/700/1533.
Executive Council Minutes, 4/4, pp. 561-62.
Governor's Dispatches, 33/16, pp. 246-59, 7 February 1834;
    2/10, pp. 1-2, 14 February 1835;
    1/24, pp. 333-36, 8 November 1836;
    1/32, pp. 34-7, 9 Ooctober 1838;
    33/32, pp. 683-735, 31 May 1839.
Return of Buildings at Macquarie Harbour, Van Diemen's Land, com-
    piled by Brevet-Major P. Baylee, 63rd Regiment of Foot.
Narrative of James Porter, *Hobart Town Almanack & Van Diemen's
    Land Annual,* 1838.
Information sworn by Captain Charles Taw, David Hoy, James Tait,
    William Nicholls, Joseph MacFarlane, Corporal Henry Dearman,
    Private Henry Gathersole, Private William Gillespie and Private Philip
    Kent.
Letter from Captain William Moriarty, RN, Port Officer, Hobart Town,
    to Mr I. N. Bateman, 3 February 1834.
'The Penal Settlements', *Hobart Town Almanack & Van Diemen's
    Land Annual,* 1831.
Wylly, Colonel H. C., *The History of the Manchester Regiment — Vol I,
    1758-1883.*
Bonwick, James, *The Bushrangers,* George Robertson, Melbourne, 1856.
West, J, *The History of Tasmania,* 2 Vols., Henry Dowling, Launceston,
    1852.
Lawson, Will, *Blue Gum Clippers and Whale Ships of Tasmania,*
    Georgian House, 1949.
Bateson, Charles, *The Convict Ships,* Brown, Son & Ferguson, Glasgow,
    1959.
Forsyth, W. D. *Governor Arthur's Convict System,* Sydney University
    Press, 1970.
May, Charles Paul, *Chile, Progress on Trial,* Thomas Nelson & Sons,
    1968.
Bryant, Arthur, *The Age of Elegance,* Wm. Collins, 1950.
Bigge, John Thomas, *On the Judicial Establishments of New South
    Wales and Van Diemen's Land,* 1823.

255